ANDREW AND TOBIAS

Andrew
AND
Tobias

J. I. M. STEWART

W · W · NORTON & COMPANY

NEW YORK · LONDON

First Edition

Library of Congress Cataloging in Publication Data
Stewart, John Innes Mackintosh, 1906–
  Andrew and Tobias.

  I. Title.
PZ3.S85166Ak   1980   [PR6037.T466]   823'.912   80–14910
            ISBN 0–393–01405–3
            1 2 3 4 5 6 7 8 9 0

CONTENTS

PART ONE

Toby

I

THE PRINCIPAL APPROACH TO FELTON HOUSE was through tall wrought-iron gates which turned, or had once turned, upon two heavily rusticated stone pillars. Perched on each of these was a rearing stone hippogriff ambiguously cavorting behind a bulbous and curly stone shield. When first ensconced, these composite monsters had witnessed to the respectability, indeed to the consequence, of the Feltons; now, lingering on in a markedly abraded state, they might be taken to testify to the antiquity of the family as well. This was fair enough. The property had descended from Felton to Felton over a long period of time. The first dwelling on the site had been built by a Thomas Felton who, at the close of the fourteenth century, was seneschal of Aquitaine.

On the west side of the entrance was a lodge lived in by two old women of whom it was dimly remembered that they had once formed part of the domestic establishment of the mansion. These faithful retainers, seldom seen, were in no condition to perform janitorial functions of any sort, and here may have been one of the reasons why the gates, although preserved beneath a decent lick of paint, had not been moved on their hinges for many years.

On the east side of the entrance, running on a curve some thirty yards long up the drive and then away from it, was a high and dense prunus hedge incongruously out of scale with the rest of the scene. It had been planted long ago by the present Mr Felton in order to mask an unsightly metallic contraption, almost as large as the lodge opposite, which the electricity people had asserted to be essential were Felton House to be provided with more electricity than it had consumed hitherto. Mr Felton suspected at the time that this was nonsense, and that it was the better servicing of the neighbouring hamlet of Felton Canonicorum that

9

was in question. But this had the more constrained him to grant the electricity people what his lawyer called an easement. So there the monstrous thing was, and there the hedge had been planted which now so inordinately flourished.

All this was set back from the public road behind a fan-shaped expanse of tarmac narrowing gently until it reached the gates. Long before tarmac was thought of, matters had been thus disposed in order that the sovereign, should he or she conceivably be prompted to honour the Feltons with a visit, could turn into the drive in a coach-and-six at an unimpeded trot. Nowadays it was possible for a skilful motorist to perform the same manoeuvre at fifty miles an hour. This was the habit, in particular, of Toby Felton, the son of the house. Toby owned an Aston Martin (almost his sole substantial possession so far, since the Feltons, though unembarrassed, were scarcely wealthy) which he could marvellously control, and in which he delighted to shave past one or other of the rusticated pillars in a manner alarming only to a passenger, should he chance to be carrying one. There had, indeed, been a single occasion upon which, being concerned deftly to avoid a cow-pat, he had allowed his bumper to clip the stone and detach a fragment of its artificially pitted surface. He had retrieved this and mounted it with a piece of plasticine on his dash-board—as a reminder, he said, not to get too frisky. It was a talisman witnessing to a lurking prudence in Toby Felton.

Nevertheless this particular evolution, performed every week-end to celebrate his return to a home to which he was deeply attached, was not without hazard to himself and others. Of course the Aston Martin had superb brakes. Another vehicle would have to be coming down the drive at a great lick (almost his own lick, in fact) if he failed to stop without a good yard to spare in front of its bonnet, and any stray pedestrian would be safer still, since a pedestrian moves at practically no lick at all. If this reasoning was a shade specious, so that Toby's driving could be objectively viewed only as a little on the risky side, he owned a particularly accurate measure of his own reaction times. The wheel would swing in the right direction at sudden need.

10

This evening, an August evening so warm that the stubble in the fields shimmered like still unreaped wheat, Toby approached the turn-in to the drive rather less rapidly than usual. The cautious side to him often operated in a spontaneous way, and he may not consciously have considered that, over the last couple of miles, his concentration had been flickering rather in the manner of the fields around him. This was because of Elma Loftus.

Elma was the doctor's daughter, and like Toby she worked in London during the week: Toby in an acceptance house in the City and Elma as receptionist to a consultant in Harley Street. Toby often drove Elma back from town on Friday afternoons, the occasion ending with his decorously carrying her small suit-case up the garden path between roses and hollyhocks to her parents' house. Usually Dr and Mrs Loftus would be around, and he would have a short palaver with them on local topics. But on the present occasion Elma had insisted on parting from him at the garden gate. In fact she must be said to have dismissed him, and it was something he wasn't unaware that she had lately been learning to do. There had been no question of any sort of concealment; Elma would of course have to mention to her parents that he had brought her home as usual. She just hadn't wanted him to have that small domestic (and faintly privileged) encounter with the old folks at home. Toby couldn't help feeling this to be perverse in Elma: part, indeed, of a certain unknown aspect of her which should have dissipated itself by now. Elma had been his girl-friend —his 'mistress' as his father would say if he knew about it—for several months.

Of course one mustn't get amorous at inconvenient moments. Perhaps, standing there by the door of his car, Elma had sensed that his head had been swimming; even that beneath the familiar scent of the roses there was creeping from concealed herb or shrub a queer warm muskiness which somehow took his mind at once to the thought of Elma in bed. And this was so exciting that he felt he really might go dotty before the surprised gaze of the senior Loftuses if given the chance.

Yes—perhaps, there at the garden gate, Elma had been acting

circumspectly in face of considerations such as these.

But Toby didn't really believe this. The small rebuff formed part of a pattern which he had seen emerging for some little time. And his awareness of it was part of his beginning to think about the whole thing. At first there had just been no thinking at all. The quite sudden establishing of his relationship with Elma had been an event too staggering for thought. Nothing remotely like it had ever happened to him before. Nobody had seduced him at school; as an undergraduate at Cambridge he hadn't been sexually enterprising; and after that there had been nothing to record except a few dismal and perfunctory experiences entirely shaming to look back upon. So Elma in her new character (for he had known her from childhood) had been tremendous, apocalyptic. When impressing her with robust talk he had declared their performances to be everything that is advertised. But as for *thinking,* he just hadn't done any. He had simply vaguely assumed that Elma and he would get married whenever it proved most convenient to fix matters that way. That seemed the regular thing, and he took it for granted that Elma saw the situation in the same light. In fact when his mind did begin to stir, it was in the direction of prosaically supposing that she would be more keen on the idea than he was. He believed—it was perhaps an old-fashioned belief —that a girl takes a risk unknown to a man when she gives herself to a lover in bed with nothing yet signed on the dotted line. And the prospect of Felton—he told himself in these reasoning moments—was quite something for a doctor's daughter. So it seemed odd that now, when his own impulse was for shifting the affair discreetly from the clandestine to the approved, Elma's inclination seemed to be moving the other way. Why otherwise should she cut down on those occasions of his being smiled upon by her dad and mum?

Very properly no doubt, he had begun to question his own fitness as a lover. Being a child of his age, and having absorbed several small manuals appropriate to his situation, he proceeded here on what was perhaps rather a narrow technical basis. But Elma really seemed very contented in bed; her expectations might

12

be described as keen but (in terms of the manuals) on the conventional side. Fleetingly, he even wondered whether this might be an index of a conformist disposition in other areas of life—or even of its all being not quite so new to her as to him. But on the whole it was himself that he tried to examine. Was he unattractive just to look at? By and large, he supposed not. He mightn't strip as pretty as Elma did, but supposed that he was reasonably up to male standards when his vest and pants came off. But how was it with him above the collar? He certainly wasn't handsome or even what is indulgently described as nice looking. He had no illusions here. 'Strongly marked' would be the tactful way of referring to his features. His chin stuck out too far, and his nose was too long, and his eyebrows met above it like he couldn't quite remember what animal in the zoo. Perhaps, just as a piece of domestic portraiture, he was beginning to get on Elma's nerves.

Struck afresh by this chastening speculation now, Toby edged himself sideways on his seat and briefly scrutinized himself in a driving-mirror. He was wearing sun-glasses of an exaggerated size fashionable at the time, so he was unable to come to any fresh judgement in the matter of the eyebrows. But nose and chin reassuringly announced themselves as at least falling far short of any Punch-like bizarre—and there was on view, too, a clear complexion and a shock of fair hair now agreeably riffled through by the wind of his own speed. So the whole department wasn't really all that bad.

But now the consciousness of having succumbed to this unmanly stock-taking suddenly displeased Toby Felton very much —with the result that he did, after all, a little press on the accelerator as he made the turn into his home territory. It was lucky—as it was also to prove momentous—that no serious accident ensued.

The Aston Martin was at a dead halt, and the brakes hadn't even squealed. The young man perched on the big step-ladder aslant the drive, intent on his job, seemed unconscious of what had threatened him. He just went on clipping away at the hedge: an operation which had already resulted in a small tossing sea of

13

greenery over a wide area beneath him. Toby, viewing this barring of his way with displeasure, touched the button of his horn. The Aston Martin obediently announced its presence in a manner more commanding than its owner had designed, so that the young man on the ladder gave a visible jump.

'Sorry!' Toby shouted—and was at once uncertain that this would carry as an apology and not as a further noise of an imperious character. This upset him, since politeness to servants had been instilled into him from an early age. So he threw open the door of the car and jumped out. The young man was already descending from his perch, briskly but without any impression of discomposure or subservient haste.

'Sorry mysel',' he said. (So that had been all right.) 'It'll no tak' a couple of minutes, sir, to shift some of this lot.'

'I'll lend a hand,' Toby said. 'Are you the new undergardener?' He remembered that such a recruit had been expected to arrive at Felton that week.

'I expect they ca' it that.' The young man's tone hinted the sardonic, but not to any disagreeable effect. He was of about Toby's age and stature, and was stripped to a pair of faded jeans hung low on his hips. His skin was burnt brown as if he had been working through the summer similarly unclad; it was glistening with sweat; his long fair hair, almost concealing his eyes, was damp as a swimmer's might have been. Toby took this in at a brief searching glance from behind the cover of his dark glasses. He grabbed a fork with which to begin clearing up the mass of clippings—being intent, after that peremptory hoot, upon civilized behaviour. Then his eye fell on the shears the young man had been using.

'Good God!' he said. 'You can't trim a bloody great hedge like this with those, man. Why haven't you got the electric ones? There's a power socket just outside the lodge there.'

'He said they were no' in order, and he gie'd me these.'

The young man offered this reply inexpressively, and got on with his own share of clearing the drive. Toby knew who 'he' was, and in consequence quite failed to believe the story about the

14

electric shears. Hawkstone, the gardener, had imposed on his new assistant the stiffest task he could think of by way of making it clear that at Felton his subordinates toed the line. He had looked at this young man—for he was that and not a mere un-licked garden boy—and resolved to break him in. Toby was instantly furious. He had acquired at school something he hadn't yet parted with: a large dislike of arbitrary authority, particularly as evinced by prefects and their ways. Hawkstone had been behaving in a similar authoritarian manner, and Toby would have liked to hunt him down and denounce him roundly. But that wouldn't do. Felton was his home—but after a fashion which, although he seldom thought about it, did make him a little careful of throwing his weight around. So he held his peace, and took another glance at Hawkstone's sweating thrall. It came to him, as indeed it had come to him at a first glimpse, that there was something faintly familiar about him. The explanation of this was probably the cricket field. Long ago he had played cricket often enough with the village boys, and later on there had been occasional rather grand affairs when he had been required to muster a team of his own friends to compete against an all-rustic eleven: this in the interest of what was regarded as a liberal view in the field of social relations. The new under-gardener might well have been among those rustics.

'What's your name?' Toby asked—impulsively, but on a careful note of cheerful informality.

'Andrew,' the young man said. 'Andy.'

Chaps like this, Toby remembered, are always curiously un-communicative about their surnames. They seem to think you have a right to know that they are Tom, but not that they are Jones. Toby felt snubbed, all the same. This prompted him to another question, although he knew perfectly well that a cate-chism wasn't at all the thing.

'Where do you come from, Andy?'

'Glesgy.' The young man made a pause. 'Sir,' he added.

Toby had never heard of Glesgy, and wondered where it was. Certainly it was nowhere local. And, of course, the cricket field

15

theory wouldn't do, since Andy's accent was far from local either. It was perhaps as he reflected on this that a first curious uneasiness invaded Toby Felton's consciousness. His sense of having seen Andy before sharpened itself into a feeling that this previous acquaintance had been almost no time ago at all; that there was about it something of the *déjà vu* conundrum one ran into from time to time. So as he paused in his forking now to take yet another look at the young man it was with an odd apprehensiveness which momentarily inhibited direct scrutiny. He found himself beginning, more or less, with Andy's toes. Then he was looking at his naked tummy—flat, bronzed, and with a delicate spire of dark hair running up from the low-slung jeans to the navel. Toby himself carried precisely that around with him—but otherwise there was a very imperfect correspondence between what he saw and what would be visible were he to strip to his own waist. He was far from thinking of himself as unathletic, but his muscles didn't ripple gently beneath taut skin to quite the effect achieved by Mr Hawkstone's toil-tempered Andy. Toby fleetingly wondered whether Andy had a girl, since it seemed wasteful that he should not. Seeing the sweat now trickling down Andy's chest, and smelling it too, he also wondered where the newcomer had found a lodging, and whether he could there command a shower or a tub at the end of the long chore wickedly imposed upon him.

But these were random and inconsequent thoughts, and Toby now became aware with a jerk that beneath them he was for some obscure reason threshing around in great confusion of mind. He had sorted this out only to the extent of realizing that some enormous new fact confronted him when Andy, standing directly in his path, put up a hand and brushed his abundant hair back from where it had been tumbling over his eyes and forehead. Toby's head swam. It swam precisely as certain actions performed by Elma Loftus could make it do.

'I can edge past now, thanks.' Toby heard himself call out this roughly, was aware of himself as wading almost knee-deep in prunus clippings back to his car, before Andy had time to do more

16

than turn and stare at him. He wrenched open the door, leapt inside, banged the door to behind him, much as if he had behaved venturesomely in a wild-life park and had suddenly felt the hot breath of a tiger on his neck. But as he turned the ignition switch this mindless panic broke like a soap bubble, and something at least with the character of a decision took its place. Andy, a pitch-fork still in his hand—and so looking, if not like a tiger, at least like a demon—had come up to the car, and now Toby flung open the near-side door. 'Come up to the house,' he said.

'What for should I do that?' Toby's perturbation had communicated itself to Hawkstone's assistant, and he spoke on a frankly insubordinate note.

'I tell you, I want you up at the house. Get in!' This came from Toby with a curtness that he scarcely heard and wouldn't have believed himself to command. Andy, who could be assumed to recognize an order when he received it, obeyed at once—but not without throwing himself back on the seat with a hint of defiance and to the diffusing of a further strong whiff of sweat. Then the Aston Martin hit them both in the back as it catapulted itself up the drive. The house was in view before either spoke.

'Are you Mr Felton's son?' Andy asked—without turning his head, and glowering darkly through the wind-screen.

'Wait!' Toby, confronting an undreamed-of possibility which had crashed down on him out of the blue, knew that for the moment little could usefully be said. He also knew that he never wanted his head to go swimming again as it had recently done. 'I've got something to show you,' he muttered, almost at random. 'And here we are.'

He had swerved off the drive and round to the courtyard at the back of the house. It was the side on which his own quarters lay, and the most direct access to them was by a door and staircase close to the kitchens. He regularly took this route on arriving home, but the momentary notion came to him that perhaps it wasn't quite right on the present occasion—or that it mightn't look quite right to anybody who was around. But there was nobody in view. He bundled Andy out of the car—actually with

17

a push on the bare shoulders—and through the doorway and upstairs. He flung open a door at the end of a corridor.

'This is me,' he said, and stood back to let Hawkstone's kidnapped underling (for it came virtually to that) enter first, as a guest should do. It was a small undistinguished room, untidy in defiance of an elderly housemaid's ministrations, in which Toby smoked his pipe and read his books and did a little fiddling with guns and fishing-rods. There was a revolting stuffed badger in a glass case, which he had been given in early life and become obstinately attached to. But now he glanced round this sanctum and was dissatisfied. 'No good,' he said impatiently and going over to an inner door. 'Come in here. My bedroom.' This time, he led the way.

Andy followed misdoubtingly—as was reasonable enough. This was a much larger room, and grander as well. The undergardener glanced at the unnecessarily large bed, the dim ancient tapestry along one wall, the bits and pieces of furniture that had begun life very long ago. It must have been as strange to him as would have been the interior of Buckingham Palace, or Noah's Ark. And the room's owner must have been striking him as stranger still.

'You know what you're going to do now?' Toby, who felt his wits in danger of clouding again, flung out this question almost wildly as he gazed fixedly at the man from Glesgy.

'That I do not.' But as Andy said this his frame tautened and his fists clenched, like one who suddenly sees that he may have to fight his way out of a trap.

'You're going to stand *there*.' Toby's hand had gone out and he was pointing—with an effect of drama he was quite unconscious of—to a spot midway between the room's two high windows. 'And damn well take a look at yourself.'

This was so extraordinary that Andy simply obeyed wonderingly. Between the windows hung a broad pier-glass set in a dull gilded frame.

'If you weren't so bloody thick,' Toby said—this time aware with dismay of senseless and panicky rudeness—'you'd have seen it straight away. Now, *look!*' Toby took a step forward as he reiterated this command, so that the two young men stood shoulder to shoulder before the glass: Toby in a rumpled but elegant linen suit and Andy still naked to the hips. And only now did it occur to Toby to whip off his sun-glasses. There was a long moment's silence.

'Aye, to be sure,' Andy then said—and the Doric syllables trembled—'I can see, a' richt.'

There was another silence. And then, quite simultaneously, the two young men turned and confronted one another. Quite simultaneously, also, on the face of each that eyebrow—for it was like a single eyebrow, thought up for a Cyclops—lowered, contracted, darkened yet further over the bridge of the long nose. Perhaps because Toby's period of complete confusion had exhausted him, it was again Andy who first spoke.

'I was for asking you,' he said, 'if you're this Mr Felton's son.'

'The proper short answer is Yes.' Toby had employed this formula before. 'I'm legally that, for what the law's worth in such a thing. Actually I'm an adoptive son.'

'Adoptive?' Andy had been listening intently, like a man requiring to make out something said in a foreign tongue. 'Wad you be a foondling, Mr Felton—sir?'

'My name's Toby.' It seemed necessary to say this at once. 'Yes, foundling's quite the name for it. Not found on a doorstep or under a gooseberry-bush, but at sea. Actually floating on the waters of the Atlantic, I've been told. Like in Shakespeare.' This last and not very well-informed joke was one Toby was not in the habit of hurrying forward with. He was quite off-balance still.

'Something aboot Hitler's war?'

'Yes, Andy, just that. Look—what about you?'

This was the million-dollar question. An answer unequivocally clear, and the whole thing became no more than a meaningless freak of nature followed by a freak of chance: something the embarrassment of which decent wits and decent feeling would suffice to cope with.

'They never tel't me ower much.'

19

'Who never told you—your parents?'

'Aye—them. They were close.'

'Then they'll have to stop being close now.'

'They're deid, the twa o' them. My faither a year syne, an' my mither no more than weeks ago. It's why I've come doon here to England.'

'I'm sorry.' Toby found that he was breathing with difficulty. 'But they must have told you *something.*'

'Aye—that I was a foondling. My father would ca' me his wee mite o' war-work. There was a bit paper about me yince, but I was never let see it. It'll be lost by noo.'

'I see.' What Toby saw—and it was literally nothing but a sheerly visual experience yet—was a twin brother of whom he had never heard suddenly standing before him. The fact, although staggering, was beyond human doubt, and he wondered why, before speaking again, he had to take thought to what he'd say, and even more thought to the tone in which he'd say it. It seemed almost an occasion for an embrace, or at least for some expression of strong feeling. But for the moment, like a man numbed by a thunder-clap, he was capable of singularly little: nothing more, in fact, than a sense of irritation. He was shocked by this discovery, and even more by tracing it to what, in the circumstances, appeared an appallingly trivial source. It was simply Andy's Scottish speech—doubtless his thoroughly plebeian Scottish speech. There ought to be nothing wrong with that. What he really sensed and resented—Toby told himself—was something defensive about it. Andy was laying on the Doric thicker than came naturally to him; it was as if he had hastily grabbed a shirt to slip over his naked body; he was saying that he remained a Glaswegian (for Toby now knew where Glesgy was) whether he had suddenly tripped up over a boss-class brother or not. If there was to be an embrace, in fact, it wouldn't be Andy who'd initiate it.

'Well,' Toby said cheerfully, 'It's pretty clear, wouldn't you say, Andy?'

'Aye.'

'Toby.'

'Aye, Toby—unco clear.'

Toby Felton put out a hand, and very diffidently touched his brother's arm.

'Nearly six o'clock,' he said. 'I'll have to take you downstairs and introduce you.'

This drew a blank from Andy, but Toby was quick enough to see it wasn't now a hostile blank. Andy simply hadn't caught on to the conception which had been proposed. It was another trivial matter: this time, of vocabulary.

'But we'll have a drink first,' Toby said. 'Fair enough, when it's a bit of a jolt to both parties. There's some sherry in the other room.'

'I've niver been a short drinker. An' after perspiring o' sweit on yon hedge I'd be for beer—Toby.'

'I expect there's beer as well. But I suppose it should really be champagne.'

'It should be salt water frae the Atlantic Ocean, mebby.'

Toby had no reply to this remark. So they left his bedroom —scene of so stiffly Aristotelian a transition from ignorance to knowledge—and sat for a time with glasses in their hands. Both young men were numb. It was all inescapably baffling, and the beer was without sacramental effect.

II

A FEW DAYS AFTER THIS SURPRISING EVENT Howard Felton, young Tobias Felton's father by adoption and the present proprietor of Felton House, drove the thirty miles into Oxford to lunch with his younger brother, Hugh Felton.

It was a family tradition that in every generation there was a 'clever' Felton, and that just occasionally there were two 'clever' Feltons or even three. This sort of Felton would become a bishop or judge or minister of the crown. It must have happened from time to time that it was to an eldest son that the extra measure of brains was meted out. But little record had been kept of anything of the sort, perhaps because the family as a whole would feel such a state of affairs to be anomalous and awkward. Howard Felton himself stood in no danger of being thus unfavourably regarded as an intellectual born to the wrong destiny. His vigour was more of the body than the mind, and he put in much time marching energetically around his estate without quite knowing whether it was in the interest of this project or that. His decisions when he came to them were sometimes surprising, but seldom other than benevolent in their intent.

His brother, although he had not become a prelate or a prime minister, was undoubtedly the 'clever' Felton of his day. Being attracted by academic life, Hugh had entered it as a historian, and had then very soon discarded what he came to regard as a lethargic discipline in favour of a more taxing career as a philosopher. In this he quickly won a high if perhaps still local reputation, with the odd result that his college—a small old-fashioned place—had judged him the right person to preside over its affairs. He was elected into the Wardenship in his forty-second year, and at once fell to performing his duties of governance conscientiously and well. Yet a number of his colleagues suspected him of being, intellectually, a little at a loose end. Those inclined to indulge a touch of malice—and no collegiate society is likely to be without a few men of the sort—would from time to time solicitously express some such hope as that he was 'managing to keep going at the logical chopping-block like the rest of the old gang'. The Warden received pleasantries of this sort with perfect good humour. He knew that his lot was cast in agreeable places. And he was an uncomplaining man.

He had never been known, for instance, to complain even to an intimate of his elder brother's having adopted an infant son and thus introduced a problematical factor into the succession to a considerable estate not entailed or settled in any way. It had certainly been an unusual thing to do. But it had been done— Hugh would say briefly, if he talked about the matter at all—in unusual times and upon a generous impulse in face of an appalling spectacle of the helpless wickedness of men. In his private mind he may have reflected that a sporadic impulsiveness could be seen through several centuries as a constitutional liability in the family, and one which had occasionally produced calamitous results. Indeed, it might have been possible to argue that the cleverness of the 'clever' Feltons inhered chiefly in their being exceptional in this regard and disposed to think and not merely look before leaping.

But at least Howard had been lucky in the little pig that eventually emerged from that war-time poke. Toby, whether his unknown antecedents were gentle or simple, had developed as a very decent lad. Moreover Toby wasn't going to be an anomaly within his adoptive family even if it did turn out that he were to inherit Felton and settle on the land. He was very far from being a fool, but he wouldn't be wasting any large measure of genius upon its turnips and Charollais.

As frequently happened on those occasions, Hugh had to begin by apologizing for the absence of his wife. This time Mercia was at Heathrow, putting her younger daughter on one plane and waiting to receive from another plane, by way of holiday exchange, the daughter of a professor of philosophy at Rennes. This

23

means of furthering the comity of nations and the education of the young was one in which, it seemed to Howard, his brother's household was almost unceasingly engaged. The juvenile guests were expected to put in much time listening to English conversation upon topics somewhat advanced for their years, and this under the hideous knowledge that they might at any moment be courteously invited to offer their own thoughts on the matter in hand. If in this strait they fell back upon their native tongue Hugh would make a few kindly responses in French, German or Italian before, as it were, gently returning them to the front line.

Howard was relieved that nothing of this kind was in train at the moment. Silence obtained in the Warden's Lodging—as indeed, at this time of year, so deep in the Long Vacation, it did for the most part in the college's three modest quadrangles as a whole. And the brothers, it transpired, were to lunch in solitude on cold ham, pickles, and what was still called audit ale.

'I can't think of the thing,' Howard said as they sat down, 'without being astounded.' He had already written to Hugh with a brief account of what had happened at Felton.

'The originating occasion, you mean? I rather agree. It's disconcerting that rational beings should plan to drown one another either piecemeal or wholesale. It's uncomfortable.'

'Don't be a fool, Hugh. What has just happened, of course. It's an almost astronomical improbability.'

'My dear chap, when we say that something is enormously improbable we commonly mean no more than that we have decided beforehand to be enormously surprised by it. Perhaps we ought to husband our surprise in order to loose it off when what happens is what we've been expecting to happen. Expectation was created by the treacherous gods for the fun of seeing us agape and at a loss when, yet once more, they bowl us out with the ball we weren't thinking of.'

'One can accept the identical twins separated at infancy.' Howard had long since learnt to ignore routine academic badinage in Hugh as no more than a ritual prelude to serious discussion. 'It's like the start of some old folk-tale, no doubt. But it was

24

a perfectly sober possibility in the circumstances under which the
Cornucopia went down.'

'I agree with that. Has it ever occurred to you what an uncommonly ironical name that old tub of a liner bore? Nearly everyone
on board must have been more or less stripped—rich and poor
alike—of almost everything they possessed.'

'In a general way, yes. I suppose there may have been excep-
tions. It was the complete loss of all documentation that was the
most staggering thing. You'll remember how it was, Hugh. Almost in the hour that the torpedoes struck, the entire duplicate
dossier went up in flames in London. But all that's not the point.
It's this unbelievable coming together again, utterly by chance—'

'Howard, are you quite sure it has really been a coming together again?' The Warden was now entirely serious. 'That there
truly is, I mean, this relationship between the two young men? I
doubt whether there can be any establishing the thing scientifi-
cally. Other than in a negative way, that is. It might be possible
to say conclusively that they are not identical twins—"monozy-
gotic" is the word, I think—but the alternative conclusion could
only be that they may be or may not. One would be thrown back
upon any other sort of evidence that there is. And isn't the only
assured evidence at the moment the fact that Toby and this Andrew are astonishingly like one another?'

'No, not quite. You see, Hugh—'

'Just pause a moment, Howard. You'd agree that as far as any
conclusion based upon this extreme likeness goes, we are at least
well within the area of what may be called mere innocent misconception and suggestibility?'

'Whereas outside that area there is the possibility of fraud?'
There was dismay in Howard Felton's voice. 'I thought of fraud,
Hugh, very early on. But it made me ashamed of myself—simply
because it isn't my sense of the thing. And that brings me to the
other piece of evidence there is. I have to agree that it could be
attacked. You see, it was like this; I've questioned Toby very
closely, and he says it was like this. It was after Toby told this
Andrew something of his own story that Andrew came out with

25

the statement that he was the same sort of refugee war-orphan himself. So if you suppose a cunning and quick-witted young man inventing a complete lie on the spot—'

'I don't think I do.' The Warden had raised his carving-knife in air in order to halt the conversation while he replenished his brother's plate. 'In fact I'm quite certain I don't. The sudden framing by such a lad, at a glimpse of this physical resemblance, of a complete plan of imposture bang out of the blue is wholly implausible. But has there been an element of milder deception, all the same? Did this Andrew . . . by the way, Andrew who?'

'Andrew Auld. He calls himself Andy.'

'Very well. Did this Andy Auld—whom we'll regard for the moment as Toby's authentic brother—really turn up as your under-gardener by sheer chance? I was talking rot about that, you know, and I apologize. It *is* uncommonly odd, although it would be extravagant to call it inconceivable. What I'm wondering is whether there was somewhere a thread of knowledge connecting the two adoptions, and whether this young man came by it when his parents died—I think you wrote they'd both died recently—and then set off to spy out the land.' The Warden paused to pour ale from a large silver jug, and then for some moments brooded darkly. 'No,' he said. 'That doesn't make sense either. Getting a job in your gardens! All nonsense. Of course there are investigations that can be made—if it's proper to make them.'

'My dear Hugh, of course we must get to the bottom of the thing.'

'I suppose so. Yes, I suppose it must be done. Inquiries wherever this young Auld was brought up.'

'It seems that latterly he was living in Glasgow—because of some family misfortune or slight come-down in the world.'

'Not a big come-down?'

'He himself says quite definitely not. His adoptive parents were very simple people. But countryfolk all through his boyhood. Somewhere in Galloway, I think he said. Howard finished his ham. He was a hearty eater, with an appetite not to be blunted even by this perplexing affair upon which he had come to seek his clever brother's advice. 'But—you know, Hugh—there simply *can't* have been any such thread of knowledge as you speak of. The entire circumstances of the *Cornucopia* disaster are against it. Among the score of survivors as many as a dozen children of whom nothing was known at all. Not a thing! Not a single fact of interrelationship established between any of them—and all back in England and, as you might say, on the market. Of course a record was compiled of how they were all severally adopted or otherwise decently provided for. I went into that, as a matter of fact, and everything was as it should be. Scores of people, needless to say, had had the same idea as myself. Humble folk, some of them. It was an uncommonly moving thing.'

'Certainly it was.' Howard, the Warden thought, had these starts of sentiment, and there was something self-indulgent about them. Hence, indeed, the existence of Toby—and now, it seemed, of Toby's ticklish twin. The Warden had long ago accepted Toby, but he wasn't sure that he wanted to accept Andy, or that there was any imperative obligation upon anybody else to do so. But this was ground upon which it would be necessary to go carefully.

'Tell me,' he said. 'Just what is your impression, to date, of young Andy? I take it you've had a certain amount of talk with him—and not just about aphis on the roses?'

'Yes, of course.'

'Over the port, Howard?'

'In effect, yes.' Howard had received a serious—if flippantly framed—question seriously. 'I have accepted the thing, you know. You and I have been discussing the issue as an open one over that excellent ham, but I must make it clear that I accept Andy as Toby's brother. That being so, I can only treat him as an equal.'

'As a gentleman? He isn't one.' The Warden picked up the

silver jug again, and shook his head over what he failed to find in it. 'You always expect one bloody awful speech from me, Howard my boy. So there it is.'

'It's well below your usual form, Hugh. Of course he's not a gentleman. And you want me to say something high-minded about an honest cow-man being anybody's equal. I'd rather tell you that my first impression of Andy Auld was of a young man of aggressively demotic speech. It's ordinary plebeian lowland Scots, of course. But it's difficult to resist the feeling that he's laying it on.'

'It sounds better than trying to talk nice to his grand new acquaintances.'

'You do quite right to laugh at me, Hugh. It's a very petty reaction, indeed. And it's small comfort to me that Toby admits to it, too.'

'Ah! Now we come to the heart of the matter. Toby, having rashly dragged this strange relationship to the light—'

'Don't talk rubbish, Hugh. Toby may have been impulsive about the thing—and in a way that does him decent credit. But there could have been no question of keeping anything dark. All Felton would have been goggling at the two of them in just no time. Stand them side by side, and the thing's quite comical. I can sometimes feel there's nothing to do but laugh at it. They're like Tenniel's Tweedledum and Tweedledee in *Alice.*'

'I could imagine the fissiparous effect to be disconcerting rather than ludicrous. But what I am asking is how Toby, having taken that bold initiative in acquiring a brother, now in his more reflective moments regards the matter. And how Andy regards it. Any action—if any be to be taken—must turn on what seems likely to establish itself between them. It's their problem rather than yours, Howard. Attempt to move actively in the affair yourself and you may be astonished to have them both turn on you and tell you to mind your own business.'

'That may well be so.' Experience had taught Howard Felton to heed his brother when he came out with decided remarks like this. 'And if there's one thing I'm clear about it is that *they* are

28

clear about nothing. They don't know how they feel, or how they ought to be feeling, or even whether any particular feeling is called for.'

'That sounds to me at a wholesome remove from premature commitment. Nature produced them at a birth, but nurture has set a formidable chasm between them. Are you publicizing all this, by the way?'

'Publicizing it?' Howard was horrified.

'Divulging it, then, more than need be. I can see inordinate interest at two levels. It's a marvellous story for the most vulgar public prints. But that would soon fade out. The interest of the learned would be more tenacious. The nature-and-nurture business again. There are beady-eyed biologists and geneticists, my dear Howard, who ransack the continents for identical twins parted at birth and reared in radically differing environments.'

'Good heavens—that must certainly be so!' Here was a view of the matter that had not occurred to the retiring proprietor of Felton House. 'And what can I do about it?'

'For a start, acknowledge the more obvious difficulties. Local interest is inevitable. Take your village and the other villages within gossiping range. They must contain a reasonable number of clear-headed people who are accurately informed about Toby's origins. But there will be plenty who simply have a muzzy sense that he isn't quite your son. And now another Toby—or say a replica of him—suddenly turns up. It provides marvellous material for scandal. You're not likely to be affected much by that, Howard, but it might trouble the young men themselves. That's one thing. And now, more immediately, there's another. Does Andy regard himself as still in your employment?'

'I think he does. He's certainly not making any claim to a transformed status. I'd say he has a good deal of pride.'

'I'd expect so. And, of course, he is a little more than moderately intelligent.'

'Fair enough. Although I don't know about the "of course".'

'Good Lord, Howard! If there is such a thing as innate intellectual ability, and any sense at all in the foggy talk about intelligence quotients, Andrew Auld will be in such regards precisely as Tobias Felton is.'

'I suppose that must be true.' Howard was perhaps not too gratified at hearing that Toby possessed a little more than moderate intelligence.

'I'm afraid you won't find many surprises in Andy, any way on. Were Toby homosexual, which of course he is not, Andy would almost certainly prove to be homosexual too. If Toby prefers a violin to a piano so, infallibly, does Andy. And if Toby —say at the age of sixty-three—develops a particular sort of pain in his tummy when working in New York, so simultaneously will Andy do while on holiday in Kamchatka. These are of course cheap exaggerations, such as an old college tutor has got in the habit of pitching at the sluggish noddles of his pupils. But the general proposition is valid. From either of these two it will be reasonably possible to predict the reaction of the other in any nearly identical situation.'

'I doubt whether I shall have occasion to do anything of that sort.' Howard said this mildly, although with a hint that his brother was proving a little slow in coming forward with practical counsel. 'But aren't you shoving the nurture side of the thing rather out of the picture?'

'A valid point.' The Warden exhibited mild pleasure—much as if Howard were a pupil whose noddle had indeed been successfully jolted into action. 'And of course it's here that what may be called the intellectual interest of the affair lies. It's clear that your two young men would react a little differently in, for example, superficial social situations—such as confronting a battery of knives and forks. But when it comes—'

'Confound your knives and forks, Hugh! I want your advice on how to regard this situation in its general bearings.'

'I don't know enough—not by a long way—to say much that can possibly be useful. I haven't met your new-comer, and that leaves me particularly in the dark as to how the relationship between the two brothers is likely to develop.'

'Which is the whole thing. I realize, Hugh, that I'm pretty well

'Not quite the whole thing. What about your womenfolk? How do they feel? Grace, for a start.'

Grace Warlow was another Felton. A little younger than either of her brothers, she had been married and divorced, and now kept house for Howard, a widower of several years' standing. Grace's husband had been a sculptor, economically not a promising occupation, and although variously talented he had proved without flair for married life. Grace was an artist too, specializing in portraits in water-colour or pastel. At Felton she had provided herself with a studio and persevered with her professional labours: partly because she liked them, and partly with the prudent aim of maintaining for herself an independent status both in her brother's household and in the world at large. Howard, after all, was in no more than a robust middle age, and it was not unreasonable to suppose that he might marry again. His brother, indeed, had for years been expecting him to do so. A vigorous man doesn't go on being celibate indefinitely just because by nature slow to make up his mind about anything.

'Grace accepted Andy at a glance,' Howard said. 'As to the fact of kinship, I mean. And if I'd had doubts myself, I think I'd have felt her instant conclusion as carrying what you might call a technical authority. Because she puts in such a lot of time staring at people's faces, you know.'

'Ah, yes.' The Warden accompanied this concurrence with an indulgent nod. It indicated that he didn't very strongly feel the cogency of the consideration. 'We'll go and have coffee in the library, shall we? They'll have put it there by now.'

The move involved a walk to the other end of the Lodging, and it was made in silence. The carpets, the furniture in the broad corridors, the portraits of former academic worthies on the walls, the seemingly ageless and always slightly dusty curtains and hangings: these invariably produced an uneasy feeling in Howard Felton. They had all been precisely as they now were when, as an undergraduate member of the college long ago, he had been accustomed to enjoy certain heavy and ritual hospitalities from a

31

Warden now three Wardens back. At Felton, Feltons lived for generations amid the same daubs and sticks, and even the rugs looked good for another hundred years. That was as it should be. But here, where everything went with the job and successive Wardens moved in, you might say, on a suitcase, the effect must be almost of living in a hotel. And all round about you, too, people were perpetually moving in and out: the young men on their three-year or four-year conveyor belt; the dons always with half an eye to a better job across the road. Howard sometimes remembered how he had once attended a gaudy dinner at the college, and had heard in a witty speech about a professor who had come from a great continental university to work in Oxford and had so been baffled by the organization of the place as to cry out finally in despair that it appeared to be no more than a collection of damned boarding-houses. The story had been thought very funny, but was true enough when you thought of it. Poor old Hugh ran a boarding house. There was a little more money in it, presumably, than there had been in all that holding forth in lecture-rooms about Existentialism and heaven knew what.

It would have much surprised the Warden to learn that his brother was sorry for him in this way, even felt guilty about the lengths to which the English took the principle of primogeniture, and was, in particular, at least intermittently troubled by the quandary in which he'd landed himself in such matters through action long ago. Hugh was only aware that his brother admired him as one who awesomely commanded the life of the mind. Or so Howard might have put it in an expansive moment. But intellectual eminence was really rather a vague conception with Howard, and what he really respected in Hugh was his unfailing power of confident decision.

'We were speaking of Grace,' Hugh said, when he had provided his brother with coffee and a cigar. 'She accepts, you say. But does she approve?'

'She agrees that we owe—that in particular I owe—some sort of duty to the lad.'

32

'Agrees? You mean, Howard, that it is a view you have put to her, and that she concurs in?'

'Well, yes.' Howard paused on this. 'But, yes—certainly,' he reiterated with unusual firmness. 'Not that she doesn't see the inconveniences, as they may be called. She has put them to me pretty firmly.'

'We are back with this Andy's lack of breeding and education of any sort and so on?'

'It can be expressed that way. I'd call it the lack of much to catch hold of.'

'Why not just acknowledge him freely as a relation—as a relation of Toby's, that is—in a humble walk of life, and leave it at that?'

'Plus a hamper at Christmas?' The sharpness of this question appeared to surprise Howard as he uttered it.

'An alternative possibility would be a crash course. Linguistic at the start, I gather it would have to be. Professor Higgins and Eliza Doolittle.' The Warden frowned. 'But, yes,' he said. 'Let's pause seriously on that. Steady support to establish him at something more promising than weeding paths and clipping hedges. Tuition of some sort, and then a polytechnic. Training for some decent trade, and always an opportunity for other things, if his ambition and abilities call him to them.'

'My mind has been moving that way, I confess.' Howard had brightened a little. 'And, of course, the freedom of his kinsfolk's house as well.'

'I'd say there's a question there, Howard.' The Warden glanced at his brother a shade warily. 'The whole plan would hang upon how the lad feels himself. And as for kin, it's really only Toby who comes in there. One has to come back to that. You didn't adopt Andy too, you know, and then mislay him for twenty years.'

'If we treat him fully as Toby's brother, as I think we ought to do since it's what he is, it's really a distinction without a difference, isn't it?'

33

'And so quite my sort of philosophical thing?' The Warden was amused. 'Perhaps you're right.'

'It would have to be made quite clear from the start that he could have no financial expectations except of the most modest sort.' Howard Felton moved to this ground as if under the impulsion of much practical sagacity. 'I don't say we've no money. But we've the next thing to no money. Particularly after getting Toby into the City as we have. But with that once established, you know, I can't see any mischief in—well—letting the thing develop.'

'I suppose Andy is quite an attractive lad?'

'Certainly he is.'

'In some basic ways he's bound to be—being Toby's other self. Attractive, by the way, in spite of his proletarian cut—or partly on the strength of it?'

'My dear Hugh, what an odd question!'

'It is not an odd question.' This came with that sudden air of intellectual authority which was always apt a little to intimidate Howard. But in a moment his brother was relaxed again. 'You've told me what Grace thinks,' he said. 'But what about Ianthe?'

Ianthe was yet another Felton. She was more securely a Felton than Toby was. The orphan of the *Cornucopia* might never have seen Felton House had Howard Felton's marriage not been a barren one for several years before that ship went down. But then the arrival of the baby within its walls had produced the consequence which frequently ensues with a childless couple who have thus provided themselves with an adopted infant. Within two years of Toby's arrival Felton's wife gave birth to a daughter. Ianthe Felton then remained the only child of Howard Felton's body. For years he hoped that a brother would be born to her. But it didn't happen. And Toby, perhaps for the very reason that during this period of expectation he grew up a little in the shade, was then all the more cherished by his adoptive parents. The Feltons were unable to think of Toby and Ianthe as other than quite simply brother and sister. And the children themselves

'Ianthe is visiting one of her Girton friends in Yorkshire,' Howard said. 'Good people, I gather, although I don't recall their name at the moment. It would have been extravagant to call Ianthe home for a family council, don't you think?'

'I certainly do.'

'Of course I've written and told her the facts of the case. No doubt she'll be astounded like the rest of us. But I don't know that she'll be all that interested. Cambridge and fresh associations have been drawing Ianthe away from us a little. It's probably no more than a temporary thing. But there it is, for the present. What I've most noticed is that she doesn't even go around with Toby as much as she used to.'

'I see.' The Warden looked curiously at his brother, but made no further comment. 'Toby himself is coming and going at Felton all through the summer?'

'Yes. His office is giving him only three weeks' holiday, it seems, and he doesn't yet appear to know what to do with it.'

'No young woman around?'

'Absolutely not. He used occasionally to be stalking one girl or another—but notably ineffectively, it seemed to me.' There was a tinge of disapproval in Howard's voice, as if he took a surprisingly poor view of any lack of pertinacity in sexual enterprises among the young. 'But he appears to have dropped even that for the present. We suppose that he finds his new work pretty absorbing.'

'What—in that discount house?'

'Acceptance house.'

'Another distinction without a difference, I expect. Am I right in thinking you're a shade disappointed, Howard, by Toby's having taken to that bowler hat and those striped pants?'

'I don't think he wears anything like that. Yes—a little, perhaps. But it's a real opening, and Toby has been thoroughly prudent to go after it. I went into the money quite carefully. Not a doubt of that.'

'I'm delighted to hear it.' The Warden watched his brother

35

put down the butt of his cigar. 'Must you be off? Well, I'll be anxious to meet this young man. If he's staying on for a time at Felton, that is. And Mercia will be most interested, too. You must have Grace ask us down as soon as may be. Nothing doing here in Oxford. The last of the Class Lists up a week ago, and this college as usual just avoiding the dusty rear. Tutors a damned sight too learned to deign to tute. I tell them I'd gladly sack the lot.'

With these more or less routine remarks, the Warden saw his brother to his car.

III

TOBY'S SUMMER HOLIDAY—the three weeks allowed him by those employers and destined partners whom Howard Felton called 'your acceptance people'—was beginning, and he had declared that he was going to spend the entire time at home. He let it be assumed that the coming of Andy—the coming of Andy viewed as a problem and a responsibility—was the reason for this decision. He couldn't well explain that he wanted to be near Elma Loftus, who would be on holiday too; still less that he was coming to suspect Elma as having to be kept an eye on; and still less again that it was under cover of companionable walks with her on the downs that the most essential part of their relationship could least inconveniently be maintained.

He had to admit to himself that the mere motive of possessing his mistress with facility at need had something threadbare and even demeaning about it when faced up to. But he did want just that: to keep Elma in the picture without the expenditure, as it were, of more than defined physical energies. And this was because it was in fact true that Andy was now so much the centre of his thoughts as to diminish almost every other sort of energy that he possessed. But Elma still had her pull. When Howard tentatively suggested that the brothers might most easily and quickly get on terms with one another by going off together on a walking tour or a short trip abroad Toby turned down the idea with few words. He was chiefly conscious of having a lot to work out, and of his having to do it on his own. Moreover, Andy was the big problem, and if Elma was becoming increasingly a problem too it was something he felt to be happening at a middle distance and within a contracted perspective such as he wouldn't have dreamed possible when she had appeared to fill to the brim any cup he was able to hold out to her.

From the first it had been necessary to take the initiative with Andy. Toby didn't suppose that this proceeded from his possessing a stronger character than his brother, or any superior purposiveness in a general way. Having hastily provided himself with a certain amount of text-book learning on identical twinship, he accepted it as axiomatic that they would hang in poised scales when such matters were in question. It was simply that Andy was in the more pervasively bewildering situation of the two: the situation he himself would have been in had he wandered unwittingly to 'Glesgy' and there discovered unsuspected kin amid a social order of a totally alien sort—where it would be taken for granted (Toby reflected with a robust flight of fancy) that he would cool his tea by blowing on it in his saucer and move around the house unshaven and in carpet slippers. Andy, abruptly invited or almost ordered into an unknown scheme of things, was understandably kittle. He wasn't nervous; he wasn't, quite blessedly he wasn't, uneasy on trivial accounts; but he had the air, although he didn't grossly obtrude the fact, of suspending judgement on the whole situation. He wasn't defensive any longer. If it is possible to be frank and open in a guarded way Andy Auld was exactly that. But one had to admit that at any moment he might make up his mind it wouldn't do, ask for his cards (from Hawkstone, presumably), and vanish for good from the Felton scene.

Toby knew that he would regard this as a great defeat. Of course it would be irrational, he thought, to imagine that at present he felt anything to be termed affection for Andy. Love could spring into being almost at a glance and was the more formidable on that account, but affection requires a long procession of days in which to build its house. So what he felt about Andy Auld—and he *did* feel something—was hard to define. If he fished about among the paperbacks on his bookshelves, or remembered that silly admiring of himself in the driving-mirror, or called up—rather hazily—the myth of Narcissus and his pool: if he did any of these things he could fancy a pathological self-love to be operative in him, and Andy absorbing only because Andy was in a dotty way himself over again. Yet he wasn't greatly troubled by such notions, since he wasn't at all a viewy young man. And what he had to do, he saw, was to bring to bear on the situation whatever power of practical and down-to-earth judgement he possessed.

The big immediate conundrum was clear enough. It could be called simply the class thing. (Like most public-school boys of his time, Toby had thought about the class thing a good deal.) He knew that if he and Andy went off on that suggested trip together they'd be deferring rather than solving this problem. Between themselves they'd ignore it, for the most part, without much difficulty, and even derive amusement, it might be, from the bewilderment of casually encountered persons before the spectacle of two young men so obviously brothers and so oddly disparate in speech and superficial comportment. That in itself would confirm something, would gain quite a lot. But Toby believed, whether rightly or not, that he and Andy were well on that road already, and that what had to be worked out was a relationship which took account of everybody who lived, or even just visited, at Felton. This was because, if the revealed relationship was going to produce any shift in the material circumstances of the two parties principally concerned, that shift must consist in a modifying of Andy's future rather than of Toby's own. Such a conclusion seemed simply among the facts of life. Andy, to put it crudely, could be given a hand up, whereas there would be no point in his brother being booted down. But what Andy felt about a hand up was as yet unknown, although it was already evident—to scramble the metaphor—that his tongue wasn't hanging out for anything of the kind. He might turn down flat the entire notion of any assimilation within Toby's world. But until he did so it was clear to Toby that something of the sort should be seen as the natural, indeed the minimally brotherly, thing. His father (from the first Toby had been taught to address Howard Felton as that) seemed to be of a similar mind about Andy, although he was characteristically hesitant over just how to begin. Toby was attempting a beginning in various concrete ways. But these all had to preserve a due regard for Andy's evident disinclination to be

39

made a spectacle of before Felton at large.

It was something that Andy could scarcely escape, all the same, and this he seemed to accept. Even if he bolted at once he would be more than a nine days' wonder. That Mr Hawkstone's new assistant was the split image of the young squire (which was how the better-affected of the tenantry and their labourers referred to Toby) had been widely evident at a glance. So there had been nothing for it but to face the situation full on. Howard Felton himself explained it to Hawkstone, the most closely concerned of his employees. With what he felt to be considerable address—even guile—Howard had treated it as no more than a mildly surprising thing. Long-lost brothers, he seemed to be saying, were regularly turning up here and there, and quite often it was under odd and surprising circumstances. Hawkstone, a grim character who had grown fond of his employer during a long course of years, received the story with respect, and even refrained from intimating that, since the long-lost brother in question showed no disposition to cease being an under-gardener as well, he, Hawkstone, looked likely to be in a position of some difficulty. If young Auld had become Mr Andrew—which seemed to be the only proper way of regarding him—was Hawkstone to continue giving Mr Andrew orders, or was Mr Andrew entitled to give him orders by legitimate proxy, as was perfectly proper within bounds on the part of a son of the house? Hawkstone in fact uttered not a word of this, but every word of it was implicit in his mere glance. Howard, perhaps weakly, left him to work out an answer for himself. With the indoor servants it was easier. He no longer kept a butler—with whom, if of any seniority, a certain man-to-man communicativeness would have been requisite—and the women with whom his sister ran the place would scarcely expect to be formally addressed on what could be treated as a peripheral, if perplexing, change in the family circumstances.

It might have been different here had Andy at once moved into the house—a rash proposal which Toby had persuaded Howard to advance under the first shock of the affair's unfolding. It had been rash as nearly precipitating a crisis, Andy having been telling Toby he 'mon ken he'd no be made a monkey o' '. It was evident that Andy regarded the situation into which he had tumbled as sufficiently bizarre without the hanging out, as it were, of further wholly outlandish flags. Fortunately he was for the time being comfortably and respectably quartered—with those superannuated domestics, as it happened, before whose portal Toby and he had first encountered one another. The Misses Kinch (as they were always called) had never before been known to receive a boarder in their lodge, and one might indeed have judged them too decrepit to do so. They must both have been elderly women before the brothers were born. It was soon being asserted in the village—and in particular in the public bar of the Felton Arms— that these ancient persons were privy to some sensational hinterland to the late phenomenal appearance of an unknown Felton (as Andy was judged to be) at the big house. That twin brothers were in question was a view held only in very hazy focus at the Felton Arms, majority opinion being inclined to see a succession of obscure illegitimacies as accounting for what was self-evidently a pleasingly scandalous state of affairs.

It was Toby's rational notion that he and Andy would most readily get to know one another better by doing things together. His first thought was that he'd teach his brother to drive the Aston Martin (which was almost the next best thing to offering to share Elma with him). But it turned out that Andy could already drive a car perfectly well, and that he saw no particular attraction in being promoted to the wheel of Toby's vehicle. 'For sure it's no' withoot class,' he said. 'But you mon mind it's just that, Toby, that ye canna' gie me alang wi' a plate o' porridge.' This was the Doric coming over more than commonly thick, but it was accompanied, as Andy's remarks now just occasionally were, by a quick smile that Toby once or twice found himself hoping he commanded himself.

'What games do you play?' Toby demanded.

'Football.' (It was as if Andy had simply forgotten to say 'futba' '.) 'There's more sense in playing it badly than in bawling your heid off in a gomeril crowd o' what they ca' fans at a match.'

Toby agreed, but didn't feel that football, thus regarded, offered much scope for what he had in mind. Had he and Andy come together at half their present age, they could have kicked a ball about the stable-yard or a near-by paddock with entire satisfaction. But it would be widely supposed that a yet greater madness had descended upon Felton if they did that now.

'What about tennis, Andy?'

'I never played tennis, and no' golf, either. Nothing with wee ba's, Toby, not even billiards.'

'All right! I'll teach you tennis.'

'I'll learn you to use a sickle, Toby. And a scythe foreby— that's harder by a lang way. Work first, then play.'

'Agreed.' Toby was encouraged by being thus relegated to a pupil's rôle. He had been sustaining too much of the burden of jockeying things along. So he was emboldened to risk a question he hadn't hitherto ventured on. 'Andy,' he asked, 'do you think there's something artificial in our trying to muck in together—I mean, in quite a close way? Strangers and brothers: it's queer.'

'It's queer, all right.' Andy was looking straight at Toby, and speaking almost in a new voice. 'But there's nothing artificial about being brothers, let alone twins.' Andy's quick smile came again, and along with it his accustomed dialect. 'We monna jink it, Toby. Not if there's the Deil to pay.'

So Andy wasn't going to quit—or not yet, anyway. Toby comforted himself with this persuasion when, later that day, his muscles began first to ache and then (if muscles can crack) to crack under the unaccustomed use to which they were being put. For the hand-up to Andy was in abeyance, and he himself—at least in a symbolical way—was being booted down after all. He had become a gardener's boy. He was so completely this that if Hawkstone in passing by had barked out a harsh order to him he'd scarcely have been surprised.

They'd begun, Andy and himself, not with sickle or scythe but with a couple of pairs of hand shears, on that still largely un-

42

It was blazing hot, and this time Toby was even further stripped than Andy, since he had thought to show willing by turning out in nothing except old running shorts and a pair of gym-shoes. A prunus hedge in a dry August is an abominably dusty thing, particularly when close to a country road, and it was soon in muddy trickles that the sweat was running down Toby's chest and back. Whenever a tough twig or two resisted the snap of his shears and jarred his wrists he had recourse to one or another of the four most improper expletives he knew. Andy, more accustomed to the brute obstructiveness of material things, worked in silence and was amused by this. The Misses Kinch, apprized of what was going on and of the company their lodger was keeping, came in an unheard-of way to their little parlour window and peered through its lace curtains.

In the course of the afternoon another spectator arrived in the person of Mrs Warlow. She came down the drive wearing a broad-brimmed hat with a fluttering green ribbon, and lightly burdened with a camp-stool and a sketching block. Toby got down from his ladder in order to help her dispose of these objects as she wished—an automatism which Andy, still clipping, marked with that hint of the sardonic occasionally to be detected in him. Mrs Warlow, when not, in her brother's words, staring at people's faces, was willing to put in time staring at the face of nature instead—transferring to paper small rural scenes judiciously animated by people's figures here and there. It at once appeared that this was her object now. She was going to commemorate the not wholly unremarkable occasion of the two brothers labouring together.

'That's just right,' she said briskly as she glanced from one to the other. 'Both of you in shorts or both of you in trousers wouldn't be nearly so good. But it would improve matters if the step-ladders were nearer together.'

'They're where they are,' Andy said from his perch, 'for a guid reason, the wark regairded.'

This was not a remark that Andy, if at all considered as Mr

43

Hawkstone's assistant merely, might have been expected to offer. Toby felt that it showed Andy as coming on. But Andy, who must find the idea of being made to serve as an artist's model while he worked strange and disconcerting, was getting down from his ladder as he spoke, and seemed disposed to arrange matters in the way Mrs Warlow required. Toby found this absurd; he didn't think that his Aunt Grace (as he was accustomed to speak of her) had been serious in proposing actually to squash them together in the service of art; it was simply one of the rather tiresome jokes she went in for. But now here was Andy picking up the idea of trivial polite attentions to a woman and actually shifting the ladder as he was told. Toby didn't feel that Andy had taken any particular liking to Mrs Warlow. He couldn't have seen much of her; and her conversation, although not more astringent when directed to him than to other people, must come to him as unfamiliar and off-putting. Yet Toby had once or twice been aware of his brother as turning upon Grace a certain intentness of regard, almost as if she were the most puzzling of all the puzzles—all the unknowns and unaccountabilities—to have gathered around him at Felton. And this was in turn a puzzle to Toby. He had never thought there was anything very special about Aunt Grace, unless it was her being rather challengingly 'well-preserved'. She must be past forty (which spelt for Toby later middle age) but seemed not at all resigned to change and decay. Indeed, he had a notion—although it wasn't really terribly nice—that Aunt Grace retained an interest in the sexual life, and was disposed to direct it upon Colonel Motley, a neighbouring widower even older than herself and with a similar tendency to defy the years. Toby knew perfectly well that if Aunt Grace were to marry Colonel Motley it would be a commonplace and quite suitable match. But he did at the same time feel it embarrassing that persons a whole long generation older than himself should still be involved with the sex thing.

Work was resumed. The two young men clipped away industriously, and Mrs Warlow made various preliminary gestures with a pencil poised above her paper. Presently she began to draw, and for a time the snip-snap of the shears and the gentle swish of severed twigs falling to the ground were the only sounds heard. Then Mrs Warlow spoke.

'I came down here partly,' she said, 'because I have news for you. But go on with the job.'

The young men had both turned to look at her as she spoke. It was to find her holding out a vertical pencil at arm's length for the purpose of measuring her scene. Her own job was certainly going to continue.

'My brother has had the answer to his inquiries,' she said—and by this form of words indicated that she was chiefly addressing Andy. 'It adds only a little to his own recollection. Three male infants were rescued from the *Cornucopia*. One was in a bad way and died before being brought to land. The second we know as Toby Felton. The third was adopted by a Mr and Mrs Auld of Newton Stewart in Galloway. So if the two of you have felt that your relationship was in need of any confirming you can now reach out from your perches and shake hands on it.'

Neither Toby nor Andy felt this symbolic act to be seemly or called for, and for some moments there was an uncertain pause. Then Toby spoke.

'Well, that's that,' he said. 'And we can go on with the job, as you say.' He found himself resenting the fact of his aunt's having taken it upon herself to give this information, even although it conveyed nothing momentous or new. It ought to have come from his father, and no doubt his father had meant to communicate it in the course of the afternoon. Toby was inclined to be sensitive about Mrs Warlow's position in the household, and understood very well it was because she was a Felton and he was not. He also knew that she was an honest woman. She took no enchanted view of Andy—or so he believed—but had been absolutely straight in supporting her brother's view that he was to be at once accepted as belonging to the family. This didn't perhaps include the thought that he should join it. But it was the essential thing. And now Mrs Warlow addressed Andy directly, emphasizing the fact by pointing her pencil at him as she spoke.

45

'Toby declares that that's that,' she said. 'What about you, Andy? Have you anything more expansive to say?'

There was a pause, presumably because 'expansive' was a word that Andy had to decode in some fashion.

'Och, aye,' he then said. 'If I mon hae a brither—a thing I never thocht on—Toby will suit me fine.'

This definitely *was* expansive. In fact it revealed in Andy, less uncertainly than had that dark remark about the Devil to pay, a drift of feeling so masked hitherto that Toby now found himself on the verge of being startled into tears. And perhaps it deserved better than the rejoinder it drew from Mrs Warlow.

'And Felton,' she asked, '—does that suit you fine too?'

'I canna' say that. I dinna' ken.'

'So I'd suppose.' Grace Warlow, who was at least a woman concerned to arrive at the truth of a situation, gave a briskly approbatory nod over her still raised pencil. 'But you'll find it to be something you must make up your mind about.'

'Ithers can do that—tell whether I've anything to gie or tak frae sic a place. It's only simple folk that hae come my way afore.'

Mrs Warlow received this with a reflective pause, the result of which appeared to be the drawing of a single strong diagonal line on the paper before her. Over this she again indulged a considering impulse before speaking.

'I've changed my mind,' she said. 'Your shoulders are very nice, Toby, but much too pink. Quite horribly pink, even although I haven't got my paint box. What's more, you irritate the composition. Andy, very appropriately, makes a big St Andrew's Cross on his ladder, and his shears make another little one. That's quite enough. So would you mind going away? Get Hawkstone to find you your next job.'

Mrs Warlow's sense of agreeable whimsy was frequently disconcerting. But Toby was used to it, and didn't resent being thus dismissed by her in the way he did resent Elma's recent permitting herself similar cavalier conduct. He simply jumped to the ground, achieved with his brother the satisfactory intimacy of an exchanged glance of amusement and alarm, tried to put his hands

in his pockets only to find that he hadn't any, and strolled off up
the drive. Aunt Grace might annoy Andy in this tête à tête she
had so badly brought about. But it wouldn't be other than in a
forthright way. And Toby was coming to feel that his brother,
although (for the second time in his life) so very much cast upon
wide waters, would prove a strong swimmer at need.

Mrs Warlow remained seated on her stool as Andy got down
from his ladder, planted himself squarely before her, and lightly
hitched up his jeans. He then remained with his knuckles resting
on his hips. It would have been easier to say that the attitude
hinted challenge than to identify the nature of the challenge
involved.

'It may still no' be legal,' Andy said.

Here again an observer could have felt in doubt. Andy Auld
might have been attempting a canny probing of his situation with
an eye to some dimly discerned advantage. Or he might, equally
gropingly, be seeking what could crudely be called a way out. At
least the remark occasioned in Mrs Warlow one of her considering moments. In these an observer familiar with the family might
have noted that she took on much the look of her Oxford brother.

'My dear lad,' she said, 'I can hardly imagine circumstances in
which the point would become material.'

'Material?'

'Important. Of practical significance in any way.'

'I see. But ye canna' tell.' Being addressed by Mrs Warlow as
'my dear lad' had been not without effect on Andy. He had
stiffened, and if he looked at her rather wonderingly as he had
done once or twice before, he also for the first time—and very
briefly—looked her up and down. 'Would the doctors ken?' he
asked.

'I don't think so, Andy. And I don't know what a lawyer
would say. It's my guess that, if a judge had to decide, he'd take
a single look at the two of you and accept the presumptive evidence as overwhelming. But there's a much simpler question. Do
you *want* to be treated as what you are—as Toby's brother?'

47

'It's still atween the twa o' us, that, Mistress Warlow.'

If Andy had never been addressed by a handsome woman as 'my dear lad' before, neither had Grace Warlow ever been called 'Mistress' by a young man whose glance was at once combative and sexually appraising. It made her feel like an elderly female character in a novel by Walter Scott.

'I do beg your pardon,' she said, without coldness. 'It is indeed entirely between the two of you. Only don't be so reticent, Andy, as to make us feel you believe yourself to have any enemies at Felton. You have not.'

'Yon Hawkstone's an enemy. Times I'd like to gie him a clout on the heid, only he's ower stricken in years for it. Hawkstone's a regular auld Nickie Ben.'

'Don't talk nonsense, Andy.' Mrs Warlow had in fact perceived that this odd speech was in no correspondence with anything Andy actually felt; it represented mere evasive action while he took the measure of what was going on.

'A' richt.' Andy, who had remained standing with his weight poised evenly on either foot, now slightly flexed one knee and dropped the corresponding hip. This *débanchement,* although his figure was such as to lend it quite as much elegance as Praxiteles and others have achieved with it, had chiefly the effect of enhancing the hint of challenge in him. 'A' the same, ye'd hae me gang awa'?' This question had come a little swiftly for Mrs Warlow, and it seemed almost from a considerate wish to cover up her hesitation that Andy immediately added, 'And perhaps hae a wee postal order sent me frae time to time?'

Despite the humorous intonation which Andy had lent this question, Mrs Warlow didn't at all care for it. But she told herself that she was not entitled to be displeased, since Andy had expressed, if in a reductive fashion, a perfectly conceivable way of dealing with the situation. Indeed, Howard had told her that their brother (over excellent cold ham) had suggested the feasibility of establishing Andy Auld as an honourable family pensioner at some remove.

48

'Don't be difficult, Andy. The thing is difficult enough in itself, without you turning pernickety about it as well.'

Andy looked thoughtful. He may merely have been wondering whether 'pernickety' had been used to make fun of him, or was a word in common use south of the border. But his next action suggested that his mind was more seriously engaged. There was a wheelbarrow at the side of the drive; he went over to it, trundled it across to where Mrs Warlow sat, and deposited himself in it much as if he were a sack of potatoes, although at the same time with a practised ease such as a gentleman might display when sinking into an arm-chair in a club.

'Then I'll be listening,' he said. 'And you'll run ower the difficulties.'

'We'd better say the possibilities. But there are impossibilities as well, and they ought to be cleared out of the way. There's the plain fact, for instance, that you can't stay on at Felton as an under-gardener. I suppose you'll agree to that.'

'Mr Felton could gie Auld Clootie the sack, and hae me to be his heid gardener instead. I could dae it fine. And I'd tak' on Toby to get the weeds oot.'

Mrs Warlow, assured by this last remark that Andy's intention was still humorous and merely marked a continued disposition to bide his time, gave a few moments to the study of her interrupted sketch. She even took up her pencil and with a dozen strokes evoked a creditable impression of Mr Hawkstone's assistant asleep in his wheel-barrow. She handed this to him, observed with satisfaction his eyes widen over such an accomplishment, and then tried again.

'What I feel is this, Andy. Although it is indeed you and Toby who are alone closely involved, what you are going to work out isn't going to be worked out in isolation. Other relationships will be affected.'

Andy made no response to this. What he did do was to put a hand to his mouth and bite his thumb. This startled Mrs Warlow. She went in for hands. And it wasn't merely that Andy's left

49

hand was indistinguishable from Toby's—and was a very nice hand as a consequence. It was also that the gesture was Toby's as well. When some extra degree of concentration was required of him, Toby would bite his thumb and go on biting it. His nursery days lay sufficiently in a past age for thumb-sucking to have been regarded as a monstrous evil in them. But of this slightly less infantile habit neither nanny nor governess had ever been able to break Toby Felton. And now Mrs Warlow could tell that Andy had been reduced to thinking hard. Andy was almost certainly no less bright than his brother. But any generality, any proposition involving even a slight degree of abstraction, he'd take longer than Toby to absorb and cope with.

'Weel,' Andy said a little roughly, 'I've got twa lugs, and am listening wi' them. Sae have on with ye.'

'Consider this. For a long time now Toby has been, quite simply, my brother's son. And again never mind the law, Andy. It's the accepted thing—what we all take for granted in this household. You understand that?'

'I understand it fine. And I'd think poorly o' any folk that thocht it otherwise.'

'Very well. My brother is Toby's father, and Toby is your brother, but you are not my brother's son.'

'It's to talk like a conundrum out of a cracker, that.'

'No, it isn't—and you understand it perfectly well.'

'Aren't you meaning it's going to be confusing? That's what a conundrum's for—to muddle ye.'

'We just mustn't get muddled.' Mrs Warlow paused for longer than usual, since she found great difficulty in expressing herself at this point. 'I've already suggested what I mean. Your arrival among us may bring about a shift in a good many relationships, and so it has to be considered with care. First this may slip, and then that. I know I'm putting it badly. But do you at all get what I mean?'

For a moment Andy was silent in his turn—perhaps aware that this confident lady's sudden diffidence before her own power of expression had to be received with respect. But his colour had risen, all the same, as if in a moment he might flare up in a very unexpected way. And there was something of this in his next speech.

'Is it a gowk in the nest you'd be taking me for, Mistress Warlow?'

'Certainly not!' It was with a new severity that Toby's aunt made this reply, and as she did so she rose from her stool and faced the young man. Then she relaxed. 'Anything less like a cuckoo than you, Andy Auld, I'd find it hard to imagine.'

'Aye.' Andy failed to respond to this more amiable note. 'But, a' the same, you're for seeing me gang awa', are ye no'? I can tell that fine.'

'Absolutely not.'

'Havers, woman! Ye say a' this o' slipping and slithering if I bide amang ye—'

'*I* want you to stay at Felton.'

Andy stared at Grace Warlow—on the verge, it may have been, of some enormous misunderstanding. But an innate prudence saved him.

'What for should you want sic' a thing?' he asked. 'If trouble is all I can bring to this hoose.'

'I think that a shake-up may do us good, Andy. We make all sorts of assumptions in a family like this, and some of them are no more than illusions, likely enough. I dislike illusions. I like to see this and that put to the test from time to time.'

'You're a wise yin, too,' Andy said, still staring—and perhaps without much reflecting what the final word in this judgement betokened. 'But just how I can bide here, kicking my heels like a keelie in a sweetie-shop, I canna' tell.' Andy picked up his shears as he arrived at this obscurely bizarre image. 'But you'd better be sending Toby back to me. I'll drive him so that we finish this side by tea.'

IV

ANDY KNEW ABOUT TEA, since it was the family occasion to which he had now been persuaded more or less regularly to turn up. At this time of year it happened outside a small incongruously Gothic pavilion on the west terrace. You went into the pavilion itself for what you wanted—it was supposed to be impenetrable to flies—and then returned to the open air. Here you could be as sociable or unsociable as you pleased, since there was a scattering of chairs along the terrace and in the small Dutch garden on one side of the house. Andy found this informality reassuring, and on the whole he was more conversable than not. Of Felton House itself, which although not opulent was rather splendid in various ways, he still fought shy. Toby had to exercise his imagination to estimate in advance how one or another of its strangenesses would strike his brother. It had never occurred to Andy, for instance, that one might find a billiard-room other than attached to a pub; and he had appeared worried rather than amused when it was explained to him that the gate half-way up the main staircase, which dated from the seventeenth century, was designed to prevent dogs from going up and not children from coming down. Toby's own quarters, with their separate approach, alone became familiar ground to him.

The inner face of the hedge had been finished by four o'clock, and Toby managed what would have been a quick shower had it not required a surprising amount of soap and water to get the dust off him. He wondered, as he had done once before, about the ablutions available to his brother. The Misses Kinch, he decided, must certainly run to a bath. But Andy's wardrobe was restricted, and Toby had not yet ventured to suggest that borrowing from his would be a reasonable fraternal arrangement. This bothered him now, since it suggested that in the mucking-in process there was still much to be achieved. He scrambled into an older Viyella shirt and pair of trousers than he might otherwise have chosen at this hour. When he got downstairs, and had made his way through what was called the new dining-room (which had been designed by Robert Mylne in 1770) into the open air, it was to find that Elma had come to tea. She had brought with her her younger brother, Vivian Loftus, whom Toby was no more than vaguely aware of as a sixth-former at some appalling North-of-England public school.

'Oh, hullo,' Toby said to Elma. 'Oh, hullo, Vivian.' He felt these noises, even as he uttered them, to be particularly lame. That the Loftuses should drop in at Felton like this was of course entirely in order, but Tony sensed an awkwardness in it, all the same. He was also rather surprised. Elma made no secret of being fond of the house, and in fact knew more of its history than Toby did. But lately she had seemed to be keeping away from it, in much the same way as she had been keeping him away from her own home. It was, he hoped, a matter of delicacy, and he was aware of something of the same sort in himself. He had ceased to see the secret he shared with Elma as conspiratorial fun, and had begun to tell himself that he was deceiving Howard—and for that matter Aunt Grace and Ianthe as well—to no good purpose at all. In fact he ought to speed up the marriage thing straight away. Once he and Elma declared themselves as headed in that direction Howard, he believed, would prove sufficiently aware of the present way of the world to take no exception to the fact that they were already going to bed together.

'Hullo, Felton,' Vivian Loftus said. Vivian was standing on the terrace with his legs straddled, his hands in his trouser-pockets, and his chin dropped on his chest. Toby judged him to be thoroughly oafish—and moreover didn't care to be addressed by his surname, as if he were somebody in an old-fashioned school-story. 'Where's this brother?' Vivian added.

'He'll be coming along,' Toby said curtly. He hadn't liked this either. 'We've been doing rather a mucky job together.'

'I'm so thrilled,' Elma exclaimed—chiefly addressing Howard, who was handing her a tea-cup. 'It's such a wonderful thing to have happened.'

'Yes, indeed.' Whenever Howard Felton's attention was particularly attracted by Elma he conveyed an impression of being pleasantly surprised. As he had known her since infancy it was perhaps as a consequence of having regularly forgotten that she had grown up. 'Andrew is a great accession,' he added with some formality. 'Do have one of these little sandwich affairs.'

Although Elma had of course heard about Andy from the first, they had not yet met—Toby having been for some reason prompted to defer the occasion. It was curiosity, he supposed, that had brought her to Felton today—and her brother too, for that matter. Toby felt faintly jealous about this—almost as if he and Andy might become rivals—and the feeling was not wholly abated by Elma's disposition, as she drank her first cup of tea, to offer him from several yards' distance what could only be called a speaking look. He had himself done the same thing in not wholly different situations. But he didn't, somehow, at all care for speaking looks on his home ground.

Andy did now arrive, unconscious that by thus appearing last for tea he had occasioned a certain build-up of expectation. His route, moreover, chanced to lie through a vista of a peculiar character. First he rounded in the distance a lily pond where the formal garden began, and then advanced up a long path leading directly to the terrace. It was a path bisecting a series of parallel clipped hedges—very much older than the hedge at the bottom of the drive—the maintenance of which was Hawkstone's particular pride. But as these hedges were successively higher as one moved between them towards the house, a small optical trick (borrowed, Howard would explain to guests, from Palladio) was played upon any watcher from the terrace. Andy, in fact, had the appearance of diminishing in stature as he advanced. Toby wondered whether this piece of nonsense had been explained to him. It was of course familiar to everybody else, and no more to be commented upon than that dog gate on the main staircase. But it did serve to concentrate the regard of the small company assembled on the terrace upon the young man who now—~~if in so odd~~ and exiguous a fashion—belonged with them.

There had been a momentary check in Andy's progress as he passed the last of the hedges on either hand. There were no more than two unfamiliar figures before him at this tea-taking affair, but it could be felt that even this was something he had to think about —even brace himself in the face of. Then he climbed some steps, and both Howard and Toby advanced a pace or two by way of judiciously casual welcome. But Andy was unnoticing—or at least appeared to be so—and walked straight up to Grace Warlow.

'Would I be late for your tea?' he asked. 'Toby an' me hae had a richt mucky time, as ye saw. But we tholed it, and the wark's half done.'

Toby had also spoken of a mucky job, but not with quite the satisfaction carried by his brother's tone. Andy was feeling that he had deserved his tea—a thought that wouldn't have occurred to Toby. Andy might also have been feeling that Mrs Warlow's personal regard had been earned by his exertions. Not that he had come up to her in the least, as it were, wagging his tail. Mrs Warlow herself, making some suitable rejoinder about the continued availability of tea, on this occasion directed upon Toby's brother a brief intentness of regard such as her profession no doubt licensed her to exercise at will. There seemed nothing particularly new to observe in Andy—and certainly not in his clothes. His jeans were a replica of those he had worn at work, and he had added to them a faded blue cotton shirt which had already appeared on several occasions. It would have been apparent to any woman that this last garment had been laundered and ironed by careful hands, and from this there might have been drawn the inference that its owner was now in good standing with the Misses Kinch.

'Come and meet our guests,' Mrs Warlow said, not without a touch of brisk command, and led Andy across the terrace. 'Elma, this is Toby's brother, Andrew. You will have heard that he comes from Scotland and has never been at Felton before.' This reticent formula had probably been prepared for use on more frequented occasions than the present, but nevertheless Mrs Warlow was prompted to it now. 'Andrew, this is Elma Loftus, a neighbour of ours, and her brother, Vivian.'

Elma, although she had learnt already that Toby's twin resembled him virtually to the point of a freckle here and a pucker there, was wide-eyed as she now absorbed the fact at first hand. Vivian glanced rapidly from one brother to the other—they were separated by the breadth of the terrace—and was prompted to sharp laughter singularly graceless in effect.

'Oh, I have been *so* glad!' Elma said, and took Andy by the hand. It was a gesture rendered slightly awkward from Andy's having momentarily misinterpreted it as signalling a desire to be provided with a slice of cake or a bun. Elma—Toby thought—was rapidly developing a social manner, but was still prone a little to lose her bearings on the job. There was really no reason why she should be quite so glad as she suggested, unless Toby had been murmuring in her ear in bed that he had found a long-lost brother who was proving to be a pearl beyond price. This he had certainly not done. Indeed, he hadn't got around to saying a great deal to Elma about Andy—and to Andy he had said nothing about Elma at all. So here was something more to bother him—and another immediate spectacle to dislike. He didn't care to see Andy even briefly confronted by a girl he wasn't aware of as being his brother's mistress, and he again felt that any relation of confidence established between Andy and himself couldn't yet come to much if it had involved no exchange of information on sexual matters in general. But he quickly told himself that he was probably wrong about this; that he didn't, after all, know the first thing about brothers; and that even between brothers who were pretty thick together a certain reticence in this sphere might obtain. He wished he'd told Andy about Elma, all the same. It would be very horrid, somehow, if Elma straightway took Andy off into a corner of the garden and told him herself. It was at least probable that in the course of this small tea-party she would want to have his brother for a spell on her own. There really was a good deal of curiosity in Elma's make-up, although it wasn't exactly of the intellectual order that Toby's Cambridge supervisor had been fond of commending to him.

These thoughts somehow lent urgency to Toby's new sense that the sooner he got on with the marriage thing the better, and he decided to begin by rather obtrusively claiming Elma's society for himself during the rest of her visit. He might even put an arm round her shoulders or—better still—give her *coram populo* an affectionate pat on the bottom. That would settle the matter in everybody's mind at once. A chap was certainly going to marry a girl to whom he did that.

This plan was frustrated, however, by Elma's brother—who had, it turned out, now left school, and who was anxious to impress the fact upon Toby, together with various other circumstances of interest and importance to himself. Vivian was 'going up' in October—a phrase which he supposed should be used without further particularization by a university man. Toby asked, 'Up what?' and then, feeling penitent about this joke, resigned himself to listening to whatever else Vivian had to say. At least Vivian had quit being a prefect. Perhaps because his mind had been running on bottoms, it came into Toby's head that Vivian's was surely the school at which the biggest boys were awarded little dog whips as badges of office, and with these encouraged the smallest boys to develop their limbs and lungs on gargantuan marathons over the appalling moorland wastes in the midst of which the school was located. Toby wondered whether he might with adequate propriety seek confirmation of this piece of public-school mythology from the boring Vivian, but decided that the question might be a little offensive as coming from a host. In any case, Vivian was busy asking questions of his own.

'Isn't it a bit dull, this office place they've put you in?' he demanded.

'Yes, frightfully dull. No romance in it at all. And not even a pool of typists laid on. It's a nice idea—don't you think?—a typists' pool. Down in a basement, I suppose. There they are—diving and swimming around in the most marvellous scraps of this and that.'

'Jolly good.' Vivian was in fact a little at sea before this. 'I don't want to do anything dull myself. I'm thinking of going into the army. It's an adventurous life.'

'So the adverts say.'

'That's right. I've been reading them, and it seems just the thing.'

'But what about the exams?'

'Oh, they don't say much about exams. You just have to have those things they shove you through at school.'

'The exams come later, Vivian. Once they've got you in. You have to keep on taking them until you're about forty, and as soon as you fail one you're out on your ear. The idea is that senior officers have to be rather intelligent.'

'I never heard that. I wonder if you can be right?' For a moment Elma's brother was quite dashed. 'What about this brother?' he then asked. 'What are you going to do with him?'

'*Do* with him?'

'Will he just live here and potter around?'

'I'd hardly think so. There's not all that much scope at Felton.'

'Couldn't you put *him* in the army?' Vivian offered this as one stung by the splendour of a sudden thought. 'Of course I don't suppose they'd see him as officer material—not with that awful prole's accent. But he seems a terribly nice chap.' Vivian paused as if to emphasize the correctness of this ritual remark. 'He'd probably end up as a rattling good NCO.'

'By which time you'd be an ex-captain in the dole queue.' Toby was instantly shocked at having produced an angry and discourteous remark, and at the same time reflected with dismay that this great sod was Elma's brother. But Vivian Loftus had merely laughed loudly, which must be his standard treatment of anything he judged to be jolly good. Moreover his eye had strayed in the direction of his senior host, whom it was evident that he designed to favour with his conversation in turn.

So Toby slipped away. He slipped away and looked round for Elma, whom he had last glimpsed being nice to Mrs Warlow. But Elma had vanished, and Andy had vanished too.

Elma's interest in Andy was no less lively than Toby had supposed, and she had secured that spell of sole companionship with him for a while by simply announcing that she was going to show him over the house. Andy may not have been particularly taken with the proposal, but his notion of who this pretty girl was had remained entirely vague, and he was quite without the sort of social sense that might have suggested to him anything odd in the proceeding. And he decidedly saw nothing unattractive in Elma as revealed by that quick up and down (and indeed round and about) glance which his own code of the fitness of things sanctioned. He contented himself with saying warily that Toby had shown him a guid bittock o' the place and that it was gran' eneuch. Toby, had he been present, would at once have said that Andy was laying it on. Andy, after all, was having to keep his end up in a long series of difficult situations, and a firm adherence to his native tongue had been proving a considerable moral support to him.

Leading him back through the new dining-room, Elma offered explanations which were not at all required. Her family, she said, although not of the immemorial antiquity of the Feltons, had lived in this part of the world for a good many generations, and there had even been some intermarriages a long time back. Since she was a quite small girl she had always been interested in Felton House and its history, and during her growing up Mr Felton's daughter, Ianthe, had become her best friend. It was a joke among them all that if it ever became necessary to throw Felton 'open to the public' at five bob a head it would certainly be she who would have to become chief cicerone to the enterprise. So she got into training by showing friends around from time to time. They must really begin in the hall, because Grinling Gib-

59

bons had been sent to Felton by John Evelyn in 1681, and had done a marvellous job with the new panelling which was installed during the following couple of years. But the best portraits, of course, were in the saloon.

Andy found this patter, and a good deal more that Elma said or implied, more confusing than anything that had yet come to him. He had a sense of this young woman as belonging to a world somehow more remote from him than the world of the Feltons themselves. Of course all sorts of things were odd about the Feltons: for example, that they should own a saloon—an amenity which he thought of together with billiard-tables as being a cut above the public bar. He wondered whether this girl's greater strangeness meant that the Loftuses were really grander than the Feltons, and more remote-seeming on this account. Yet Andy was learning all the time—at very much the pace, it may be supposed, that Toby would have learnt in an answering situation. So he knew that this couldn't be right. Elma Loftus, he saw, was an admirer of, rather than a full participant in, what in the Aulds' world would have been known as high life. It was a situation that he didn't want to find becoming his own.

They began in the hall. Andy, who had determined to meet all these people half-way (and Toby a good deal further, if need be) and give them a fair go, did his best to exercise his historical imagination. He started with great big dogs—dogs probably had to be very big when there were bears and dinosaurs around—and set them pawing and slavering at the dog gate on the staircase. The floor of the hall would be littered with straw instead of being carpeted; it would also be littered with the bones chucked away by lords and ladies after they had finished a good gnaw at them. Knives, perhaps; certainly no forks—but what about spoons? He might ask this girl about that. Mostly they ate peacocks and boar's heads—so another doubtful point was what they did with the rest of the boars. They might be boiled up, he supposed, as broth or brose for the servants. There would be any number of servants —who would be just like himself. Some of them might be bastards of the laird—the lord—and as a consequence uncommonly like the son of the house.

'. . . Reginald de Felton recovered his lands from the King and drove out the monks.' This information from Elma came dimly to Andy as his unaccustomed effort of fancy faded out on him. If she detected him as inattentive she probably thought that he was engaged, as Toby might have been, in working out the exact lines of her figure beneath her light summer dress. It was not perhaps in Elma's nature to be displeased by this speculation as she continued her talk. 'But the barony was declared to be extinct, and the Feltons have remained commoners ever since. I suppose it must be said that they have *chosen* to remain commoners. They are in consequence among the very few commoners whose ancestors are known to have held land before the Conquest. They were allowed to retain it, of course, because of their Angevin connection.'

'Aye.' Andy had no idea what a commoner was, let alone an Angevin, and didn't believe it would prove to be important if he found out. Moreover, although a good-natured young man, he resented being—as he felt it to be—shoved back into school. At the same time he did now clearly see that this girl possessed points that he didn't recall in his schoolmistresses. So he signalized the realization by giving Elma a new sort of look. It was perfectly inoffensive, quite brief, and with no urgency about it at all. It was a look, nevertheless, frankly inviting acknowledgement of one of the simpler facts of life. Elma, being by nature one who took that sort of thing in her stride, felt no impulse to be snubby, and contrived a nicely calculated modest glance in return. But Andy seemed merely to feel that something proper to be done in regard to a girl like Elma had now been done, and he showed no disposition to advance further. 'We'd better be getting alang round,' he said. 'You'll be wanting to be for hame soon, Miss Loftus.'

'You must please call me Elma,' Elma said—and added as a quick afterthought, 'Ianthe always does.'

'Elma, then.' Andy didn't think much of Elma as a girl's name;

61

he felt it was a name you might give to a female elephant in a zoo. As for Ianthe—that struck him as a name outlandish beyond imagining.

'And I may call you Andy? I heard Mr Felton call you Andrew once or twice. But Andy sounds friendlier.'

'I'd say there's no muckle in it.'

This was not particularly encouraging, and Elma led the way into the saloon. It was a very large room, elaborate beyond the general character of the house, and was almost unused except when a dance had to be got up for Ianthe. A couple of generations back somebody had injudiciously concentrated in it an excessive number of family portraits of very varying historical interest and artistic merit, and the general effect of these was costive rather than imposing.

'Are all they folk Feltons?' Andy asked. 'Yin's much like anither—but mebby that's just how the painters had their way at it.'

'It's partly that, I suppose. Artists do have their conventions. But one comes to see a real strain of family likeness too, I think. Over quite a number of centuries, as you can see.' Elma pointed from one canvas to another. 'I find that rather fascinating, I must confess.'

'Aye, mebby.' Andy didn't sound impressed. In fact he seemed definitely to be taking against Feltons viewed *en masse*. 'They're a' gowking at ye sideways under thon helmets and wig-things an' whatever. They're no thinking to know ye at a', I'd say.' Andy was silent for some moments. 'An' they a' hang thegither. That's it.'

These were comments of little aesthetic interest. It was plain that Andy was not among those who would exclaim with sudden interest, 'That must be a Bartholomew Dandridge!' or indicate awareness that Romney is as inferior to Lawrence as Lawrence is to Reynolds. But Elma was quite clever enough to know that at a simple human level he had made a not imperceptive remark. The likeness running through the Feltons for many generations was not of the kind manifested in Andy and his brother. It was a matter less of features than of regard. They were different people, you would have said, and although they didn't look at you with arrogance they did look at you as from a certain distance. An observer more sophisticated than either of the young people now surveying them might have judged that there was something clannish and provincial about them, such as may show itself in the hereditary nobility of some out-of-the-way continental state. Although many of the men were exhibited in gowns and robes and uniforms of one sort or another, and the women were sometimes attired as if for court, there was an over-riding impression that as a crowd they hadn't perhaps got around a great deal, and that they judged it—or rather quite unconsciously accounted it—of more importance simply to be Feltons than to be Feltons achieving this or that.

'You mean that they're rather stand-offish?' Elma asked.

'I'd no' ca' it that.' Andy had been obliged to take a guess at this expression. 'They'd gie ye a beck in the street as soon as if ye were a laird yoursel'. An' they'd dae mair for ye than that— just as if they really believed that we're a' Jock Tamson's bairns. But in their hairts it's no' quite like that—an' no shame to them either. For there's aye the bluid, ye ken. An' they folk can think o' bluid when we hae' to think o' siller.'

Elma in her turn had to grope for the sense of this, and she was startled when she found it: partly by Andy's embarking upon philosophic generalities at all, and rather more by what, in terms of enlarging social awareness and judgement, was implied by his use of the word 'we'.

'I don't think you're being fair,' she said—not very coherently. 'Think of how they've all welcomed you—Mr Felton, Mrs Warlow, Toby himself. Absolutely genuinely. And Ianthe will be like that too.'

'Aye, it's as kind as kind—and dinna' think, Elma lass, but that I ken it weel. But we're no' connected, them an' me, but by a freak o' fortune. There canna' be ony hurt done, either way on. It's Toby I'm thinking o'. It's Toby and me that are thegither in our ain bluid, whatever that bluid may hae been. Tak' a look at the twa o' us, and then at they folk gowking from the wa's, and that's as clear as clear. Toby has grown up amang them, but his distance is written on his face. And it maun be the clearer still wi' me beside him, like we were twa china dugs on a mantelpiece. If there's any may be hurtit, it's him.'

Elma was silent. In fact she said little more until they were out on the terrace again. She might have been taken for one who had been given food for thought—or even whose own thoughts had been lent unexpected definition by this strange Scottish plough-boy (Toby even down to those strange eyebrows) who had turned up at her cherished Felton House.

V

'WHERE,' HOWARD FELTON ASKED soon after dinner that evening, 'has Toby cut off to in such a hurry?'

'He said he was driving off with Andy to a pub.'

The elder Feltons, brother and sister, were sitting together in a deep window-embrasure in the drawing-room—Howard with the glass of port he had brought from table and Grace with her embroidery frame. In the garden outside the summer dusk was deepening, and against a clear sky house-martins were darting high—behaviour approved by Howard as presaging another fine day.

'That's pleasantly companionable,' he said. 'I wonder where they've gone?'

'I can tell you where Toby meant to go, and I'm glad he mentioned it to me. He was proposing that they'd walk up to the Arms.'

'Well, it would be a nice evening for that. This fine spell is quite a relief, I must say. Holden's people ought to have another good day in the corn. And they've gained a great deal already. I walked round there this morning, you know. It was all quite dry by eight o'clock.'

'Was it, indeed?' Mrs Warlow was seldom interested in agricultural intelligence, and would sometimes murmur 'How a good yoke of bullocks at Stamford fair?' when her brother embarked upon it. 'I told Toby the Felton Arms would never do.'

'You mean they've had to go somewhere they're not known?' This came from Howard on his note of dismay. 'Like people who get in a mess and find themselves in the newspapers?'

'Approximately like that.' Mrs Warlow gave some moments to matching threads in the basket beside her. 'Nobody would venture to be openly impertinent, but I can imagine some of the younger men sniggering over their dartboard. And Toby firing up at it.'

'I should damned well hope so!' Howard exclaimed—and then chuckled suddenly. 'But I'd say our two could take on any four of them.' The squire of Felton, like many mild men, was attracted by vicarious violence.

'I scarcely think, Howard, that a brawl would be agreeable to us.'

'No, of course not.' Howard was dashed. 'You think, Grace, that we should get Andy away? It's Hugh's view, as you know.'

'I less regularly approve of Hugh's views than you do.'

'Yes—but what *do* you think?'

'I don't think he should go away, or not at present. I told him so earlier today. I said that—' Mrs Warlow checked herself. 'It's my feeling that nothing would be gained by the boy's leaving us —or not until we have a clearer view of the whole problem he presents.'

'I wouldn't be at all sure you're not right, Grace.' Howard said this like a man carefully studying an issue that hangs before him in balanced scales. In fact he was much relieved by his sister's attitude—or by what his sister had judged it prudent to say. And Grace, after giving close attention to several stitches, glanced up at him with a certain dry affection. Howard, she perfectly well knew, had taken to Andrew Auld. In his heart of hearts he saw Andy's rising up, as it were, from the ocean as romantic beyond anything he had experienced; as renewing in him, indeed, the spirit in which, long ago, he had brought home a fatherless child to be reared in love and to splendid chances. It was touching. It was even charming. But Mrs Warlow believed that—whether unfortunately or not—it by no means certainly reflected what was likely to be a stable condition. 'Our two', Howard had said. With two sons—or dream-sons—where one had been a week ago, her brother almost certainly had some stiff bewilderments before him. But now wasn't the time to conjure them up. Mrs Warlow, drawing her needle gently to its repose, pursued the subject on an immediately practical level.

with Toby's brother. More, in a way, than Toby has. And what authority you have, I think you should now exert. It would of course be absurd to speak of the boy as presentable in any conventional sense, or of his possessing innate refinement, or anything of that kind. He is a Scottish peasant lad. But I think he is intelligent, and sensitive as well.'

'And good-hearted. I feel Andy is a good-hearted lad.'

'Of course I hope he is that too. But my point is this. Despite the difficulties, he must be persuaded that while at Felton—which is where we want him to be—he can only live as Toby's equal and therefore ours. The Misses Kinch must give him up, although I suspect they'll be sorry to do so. Hawkstone must give him up, and will be uncommonly glad to be rid of him.'

'My dear Grace, you are absolutely right.' Howard was once more the sagacious and level-headed elder brother. 'But, you know, he must have something to do. In two or three weeks Toby will be going back to his acceptance people. And Andy can't simply be left taking tea and sandwiches with us. He wouldn't stand for it, for one thing.'

'Perfectly true. But if you were to guarantee young Purbrick the continuance of his uncle's lease he'd take over running that farm for the old man like a shot. And that would leave Mr Tarling without an assistant in the estate office. Andy could start in like that. Even if he were fully a member of the family that sort of job and training on the estate would be perfectly unexceptionable. It's a gentleman's position as often as not nowadays.'

'Absolutely true. That really is an idea. I suppose Andy can read and write—and even manage sums after a fashion?'

'At least he'd come to command these accomplishments rapidly.' Mrs Warlow in fact had no doubts about Andrew Auld's elementary literacy and even numeracy. 'And Mr Tarling is a most understanding man, and would see that the key to the thing would be working Andy very hard right from the start.'

'So it would.' Howard was impressed by his sister's grasp of this point. 'The boy would respond to challenge, and to a sense

67

that he must pull his weight. I'll talk to Tarling in the morning. And to the Purbricks after that. By Jove, yes!' As he said this, Howard actually sprang to his feet, much as if under the persuasion that it was morning already. A sudden small impatience of this sort was familiar to Grace Warlow in her brother. It was quite harmless: a kind of ritual counterpoise to that tendency in himself —of which he was perfectly aware—to drag his heels a little as the necessity for some decision drew on. But it faintly reflected, too, that deeper impulsiveness, running in the family, which could occasionally produce what Mrs Warlow thought of as irreversible surprises.

'But ought you not perhaps to begin with Andy himself?' Mrs Warlow now asked. 'You give those other people—the Purbricks and even Mr Tarling—orders, in the last resort. But Andy you will have to persuade.'

'Yes, of course. And I don't find him difficult to talk to. It was pleasant that he came up to tea again today. Elma Loftus apparently showed him some of the pictures, which was kind of her.'

'I think myself that it was slightly out of turn.'

'Oh, surely not, Grace. Elma is almost one of us in a way, and a very nice girl. Or woman, rather, since she is now entirely grown up. Her brother, though, remains rather the unlicked cub, wouldn't you say? Almost what might be called a little underbred.'

'Which would not be said of Andrew Auld.'

'No more it would.' Howard gave this assent with satisfaction, but at the same time looked slightly puzzled. 'Of course with Andy there are expectations one doesn't have. Yet it's not quite that. Do you know? I think he's learning from Toby rather rapidly.'

'Howard, dear, you didn't bring the decanter with you. Shall I fetch it?'

'No, no—although thank you very much. The single glass is just right.' Howard had been pleased by this sisterly attention. 'Now, what was I saying?'

'We were talking about the Loftuses.'

'Ah, yes! I hadn't quite realized that Ianthe and that charming girl were such close friends. Elma and her brother walked across, it seems, because they thought Ianthe was home again.'

'Are they such friends? I feel we have chiefly Elma's word for it. Has it occurred to you, Howard, that Elma's friend at Felton may be Toby?'

'Oh, I should think they're very good friends too.' Howard said this easily and not particularly attentively. Although a single glass of port had contented him it had come in the wake of half a bottle of claret, and his mood was benign. 'They've known each other since they were children, after all. So you see—' Howard broke off, and stared at his sister in surprise. 'You're not suggest-ing—?'

'I was wondering about Ianthe. I'm not sure that she really cares greatly for Elma Loftus. Of course they play tennis together, and so on. But the point is quite unimportant.'

'Well, yes.' Howard didn't quite look as if he judged the point to be this. But he was always disappointed when he heard of anybody as not greatly caring for somebody else—his vision of society being coloured by the theory of universal benevolence. Then he took heart again. 'Anyway,' he declared, 'Toby and Andy at least are getting on uncommonly well.'

This was true of the two young men as they drove through Felton Canonicorum in the search for anonymity in the next county. Toby, having concurred in his aunt's view that the Felton Arms wouldn't do, had declared that it was just the evening for a decent spin, and that of course even without getting on the motorway they could do thirty miles in thirty minutes flat. Once or twice since his first and fateful trip in the Aston Martin Andy had agreed to be conveyed short distances in it. But he had yet, Toby said, to see it put through its paces.

Toby was wearing the jacket and tie without which he could hardly have sat down at Mrs Warlow's dinner-table, and Andy, on observing this, had said doubtfully that perhaps he'd better get back to the lodge and put on his suit. Toby didn't much fancy the idea of Andy in his suit, which he thought it likely would be of the sabbath order and more suited to hearing a sermon in than to drinking several pints of beer. So he persuaded his brother to get into a jacket of his own. It was an old jacket, but very much of the sort that looks all the better for that. It inevitably fitted Andy exactly, and it had the effect, for what the point was worth, of making the pair of them as socially indistinguishable as when they were working on the prunus hedge in practically nothing at all. This was a first step towards realizing Toby's short-term plan for a common wardrobe upon necessary occasions until matters (as they must do) happily sorted themselves out. He was put in good humour by this; his spirits rose; he drove accordingly.

On his driving it might have been felt that Andy reserved judgement for five or ten miles. Then his spirits rose too, as those of any young man would have done in the circumstances unless he were too wet for words. 'Wet' was a favourite dyslogistic term of Toby's, and Andy had been puzzled when introduced to it. He had concluded—and it wasn't a bad guess—that it meant 'dreich'. And Andy particularly didn't care for people 'dreich i' the draw', having as fair a share of his brother's active temperament as he had of his underlying prudence. So whenever on this breakneck drive Toby shouted to the winds for no reason at all Andy shouted too. It particularly delighted Andy that his new-found brother owned and commanded the splendid projectile in which they sat. Its very smell of leather amazed him. As for Toby, he rejoiced that he was coping with the strange relationship that had come into his life; that he was bringing off an adequate and successful response to its challenge. These were thirty minutes of unflawed happiness. Even the Aston Martin purred contentedly when touching ninety on a straight stretch.

'Wha was Tobias?' Andy suddenly shouted. The oddity of his brother's name had been troubling him for some time.

'He had a dog.' This was a riposte that had been available to Toby since his prep school days. 'It's the only dog to be mentioned at all politely in the Bible.'

'Did they ca' ye that because Mr Felton liket dugs? There's nae dugs to go slavering at that dug gate now.'

'No more there are.' Toby had never much considered why he had been christened (for he had been promptly christened in Felton parish church) with his not very common name. He had vaguely supposed it to be a Felton family name, but he had never inquired about this. If it had been chosen merely as a fancy name any assumption to the contrary might be tactless. But he had read the Apocrypha. 'It was Tobias they dug a grave for on his wedding-night,' he said, 'because they were sure it would be too much for him. But he got away with it, and lived to be a hundred and seventeen.'

'It's a daft tale, that yin,' Andy said, apparently on an impulse of disapproval. But suddenly—and for the first time since his arrival at Felton—he gave a shout of laughter. 'We're no' like to live to e'en a hunner, you an' me, Toby. But it wad be a richt randy lass should moil us deid on our bride-nicht.'

This was a satisfactory exchange, and on the fringe of fresh territory. Toby would have liked to tell his brother about Elma at once, but felt it wouldn't be very nice to do so hard upon his ribald perversion of an episode in Tobit. So when they had both stopped laughing it was Andy who spoke again.

'There's no' ony story like that aboot Andrew,' he said. 'But when they'd crucified him and a' that, there was a chiel ca'd Acca that brought his banes as relics tae Scotland an' some say it was to Galloway. They learnt me that at school—an' that it was why there's more Andrews in Kirkcudbright than there are bristles on the back o' a pig.'

'And I expect the relics were pigs' bones,' Toby said irreverently. He was in fact rather impressed by this evidence of his brother's religious education. 'But here's a fairly decent-looking pub—and high time too. I could down my first pint at a gulp.'

This wasn't quite true, Toby not being in any notable manner a gulper down of beer. But he was remembering that first glass of the stuff with his newly-discovered brother in his room at

71

home, and how the occasion had somehow fallen quite flat. It would be different this time. For as two young men in a genuine fraternal relationship Andy and he were now well on their way.

It was rather a large pub with rather a large car park, at the entrance of which there was the usual notice saying 'Patrons Only' and the almost equally usual one saying 'No Coaches'. But there were several coaches ranked on it, and facing them was a large number of cars of which the majority were quite of the Aston Martin class: Lotuses and Bentleys, a Rolls or two and a whole leash of Jaguars. Toby drew up between a Mercedes and an Aston Martin a good deal younger than his own, and viewed the whole scene with some misgiving. The coaches all bore labels announcing themselves as conveying the 'supporters' of a soccer team whose 'supporters' were notorious, and the cars looked as if they belonged to what some poet or other had called the loitering heirs of city directors. The scene in fact reeked of the class war. Toby, who had the establishing and consolidating of what might be called a class peace on his hands, didn't like it at all. As for Andy, he seemed not to make much of what he saw, and he certainly wasn't discomposed. He must still be at the stage of finding a lot in England very odd indeed. And, of course, similar spectacles were perhaps on view outside large Scottish pubs generally.

'Saloon or public?' Toby asked.

Andy hesitated for a moment, which wasn't a common thing with him. He may have been reflecting on that grand room with the portraits and feeling that a saloon was his brother's customary home ground.

'It's a bawbee or twa less in the public,' he said non-committally.

So they went into the public bar. It didn't look as if anybody was there because bawbees were scarce in their pockets. Among a large crowd of people a large amount of lavish drinking was going on. There was also a great deal of noise, a great deal of tobacco smoke, and a heavy alcoholic miasma permeating the

72

whole area. Toby, although quite fond of a drink in a pub, didn't much care for the place, but Andy seemed to respond to its atmosphere almost at once.

'They're back frae a match a' richt,' he said, 'and this has no' been their first pub. And a guid mony o' your gentry hae come in here too.'

Toby resented 'your gentry', supposing—probably wrongly—that his brother was intending to include him in that category. It was certainly true that a good many of the chaps with the big cars had come into the public bar. They were drinking in two or three small groups by themselves. Toby eyed them with disfavour, and was further irritated by the term Andy had just used. Having taken over—quite unconsciously with the years—a good many old-fashioned conceptions and perceptions from his foster-father, he was at once aware that there wasn't a gentleman among them. But he was without those old-fashioned resources of vocabulary which Howard Felton could have called up at need, and had never in his life described anybody as a bounder or a cad.

'Awful men,' Toby said gloomily.

'They think they own ony place they care to mak' a big mouth in—an' could own me an' my kind tae, did they care aboot it.' This was a surprisingly resentful speech from Andy. Toby, foreseeing some danger of these loud and opulent-seeming persons getting under his brother's skin, steered him away from the nearest bunch of them. Together they squeezed up to the bar and got their pints, for which Andy managed to pay. Toby felt that the 'supporters' were some of them jostling a bit more than they had to, but when Andy got jostled by one of them to the extent of slopping some of his beer he seemed at once to regard the chap who had jostled him as a personal friend, and even exchanged several remarks with him in the loud tones required by the general clamour in the place. Then he turned back to his brother, glanced at him bright-eyed, raised his tankard in salutation, and took a handsome swig at it.

'Their side lost, if you ask me,' he said, 'and they're drooning their sorrows on the lang road hame.'

'They look proper hooligans, some of them.' Using this per-mitted term, Toby spoke injudiciously loudly himself. Aware that a couple of men were staring at him, he hastily got down quite a lot of his own beer.

'Och, aye—but ye canna' blame them if they put in a few hours in the week that way. Their wark's awfu' monotonous, mair like than not. So they like a bit o' argie-bargie wi' t'ither side o' a Saturday. They'll have left yin or twa o' theirsel's in the cells, I dinna' doot.'

Andy's dialect was becoming harder to penetrate, and Andy himself somehow seemed to be drawing a little further off. He had finished his first pint already. So Toby finished his own, grabbed his brother's tankard, and struggled back to the bar for fresh supplies. Andy shouted some cheerful instruction after him, and shouted again as soon as he had begun his return journey with the foaming stuff in either hand. Toby was aware that the two of them were now attracting a certain amount of attention from the company at large, and his mind went forward rather anxiously to the third pint. He was somehow sure that Andy would insist on that.

'Safe back and awa' through the hooligans,' Andy said—again cheerfully and again loudly. 'It's true their crack wadna' much please the meenister, an' they'd cut a puir figure gin they had to tak' tea with the Queen at Balmoral. But we're a' Jock Tamson's bairns. I was saying something to that wee dunty came to tea at Felton aboot Jock Tamson's bairns.'

Toby was puzzled by this, and he had no idea (fortunately, as it was to turn out) what a 'dunty' was. But he did suddenly realize that Andy had a light head for drink. He might have known as much, since he had a light head himself. Earlier in the evening, and perhaps influenced by literary sources, he had envisaged a short progress from pub to pub as advancing his relationship with his brother in an agreeable way. Now he was only anxious to bring the misconceived expedition to a close and to drive home in tolerable sobriety. It was vaguely in his head that recently the police had been permitted to lurk outside pubs and pick up heavy-

beastly to have to appear before the beaks about a thing like that, and a calamity if he were denied the Aston Martin for a year as a result.

Nevertheless they had their third pint. Something in Toby—a muzzy sense that he wasn't going to be beaten—made him down his at one go—much as if he were an Oxford undergraduate being 'sconced' according to the disgusting usage still said to persist in that university. Andy, although without these academic associations, did the same, and then fetched the fourth pint. This time they drank more slowly, eyeing one another with a certain animosity. Toby wondered if it would improve matters if he made a dash for the Gents and managed among other activities to vomit. But he and Andy were now mysteriously penned in. He didn't quite know how this could be, but when he pulled himself together sufficiently to look round in a collected manner he saw a circle of curious hooligans—with here and there a patch of those loitering heirs of city directors. Probably they weren't that at all. They were bloody car salesmen, which was even worse. A diffused belligerency invaded Toby. Why were all those people staring at him—and some of them even (for he felt sure of this) making jeering and taunting remarks? It suddenly came to him that Andy and he would never be able to be in a public place together without occasioning at least some slight curiosity and remark. When one saw grown up identical twins together—which was very rarely—they were usually for some reason female. Perhaps brothers so circumstanced had an impulse not to hang together but to keep clear of one another. He'd rather like to be clear of Andy now. For they might be getting by more or less unnoticed if only Andy wasn't being so loud-mouthed and argumentative. He hadn't a clue what Andy was hectoring him about, and he was astounded when he suddenly caught the sound of his own voice raised in the same way. The two of them, in fact, stood confronted in the most unaccountable fashion—and inside this circle of what could be detected as pleasurably expectant toughs. One little rat of a man, with his own pint pot in his hand, was

75

grinning round as if inviting covert attention to his own cleverness. It was all most disagreeable and perplexing.

Toby tried to reason it out. Andy, pitched into a totally alien environment, had been too much on his best behaviour for too long. He was now letting go a bit. Toby wasn't sure he didn't admire and envy this, but at the same time his feeling of animosity towards his brother grew. He realized—it was very horrid—that what Andy was loudly doing was boasting about girls. He said something about a dunty again. And then Toby heard Elma's name.

'And that's my thocht aboot *her!*' Andy said triumphantly.

'What? What do you think about Elma?' It was in amazement that Toby heard himself press this utterly injudicious question. But there was Andy, grinning in front of him, and with his pint pot circling hazily in air. And Andy seemed surprised that this particular lady should much arrest his brother's attention.

'Och,' he said, 'I could hae that yin for the speering. She'd dae fine for a quick touzle, or a bit o' sprunting amang the stooks o' a dark nicht.'

There was no mistaking at least the general sense of this. Toby made a swift movement—he had no notion to what end—and in the same instant was blinded by the better part of a pint of beer dashed into his face. He hit out wildly, and his fist crashed against Andy's jaw. He heard a roar of laughter, and then Andy caught him just below the eye. They were taking breath for less random blows when, amid further raucous laughter, officious hands were laid upon them and they were hauled apart, panting. In this operation the revolting motor salesmen were prominent in an organizing way—proving to themselves (Toby weirdly thought) that they were genuine executive types, accustomed to giving orders.

'This is a respectable house,' a voice said from behind the bar, 'and you'll both please leave it at once.' But this wasn't good enough for some of the hooligans, who had the pleasant sensation of an unexpected return to the terraces. Hands were laid on Toby and Andy anew, and for some further minutes there was a real rough-house. When this ended they found that they had been pitched out of the pub and into the semi-darkness of its car park.

Moralists and novelists alike have been known to choose as the very type and acme of human ignominy being chucked out of a pub as a quarrelsome drunk. The simultaneous suffering of this disgrace—quite as scarifying as the gritty surface from which they had to pick themselves up—had at once the effect of rendering Andrew and Tobias a little less at odds with one another. The pub's windows shed enough light for a brief mutual inspection— although each was more aware for the moment of a kind of sheepishness in himself than of any figure the other cut. Then they walked in silence to the Aston Martin, and in silence climbed into it. Toby switched on the headlights and started the engine. Andy spoke first.

'I'm fair fashed,' he said.

'For Christ's sake! Can't you speak a word of English?' There was fury in Toby's voice, but he wasn't at all clear whom he was furious with.

'I'm vexed, and want tae beg your pardon. But did ye think it was me, Toby?'

'That what was you?' The car was on the high road again, and Toby already felt a little better.

'That threw that beer, of course. It's an auld trick enough, but maist times it's done wi' a kick up the doup.'

'What on earth do you mean, Andy?'

'Ye hae twa men, no weel-pleased yin wi' anither, an' at a right fliting-match. An' when yin turns his back on t'ither, in nips a third jokie gomeril an' lands him this kick on the backside. An' if he then jinks awa' quick enough, him that got the kick thinks the first loon gie'd it him. An' see they fa' to by the lugs. An' it was no' me, it was a wee weasel o' a man wasted that guid beer on you.'

'Then I'm very sorry.' It seemed to Toby that adequate formal apologies had now been exchanged. 'We were both pretty tight. It's queer that we don't seem to be now.'

This was more or less true. There are shocks which do have, at least for a space, a sobering effect. And both young men were really very shocked indeed—much as Cain and Abel might have been had they both survived their disagreement. Behind them they had no common nursery in which every now and then they had cheerfully sought to maim one another. So it was going to be days before they quite recovered from this ludicrous incident.

'Was it jist,' Andy asked with some perceptiveness, 'that your sort dinna' like talking in publics aboot the lasses they've had?'

'I don't know what you mean by people of my sort.' Toby realized that this was a stupid and dishonest remark. 'But, no— it wasn't. It was what you said about Elma Loftus.'

'Oh, her!' There was simple surprise in Andy's voice. 'It was naethin but a bit stite an' boasting, that. I expect she's a decent lassie enough.'

'We're in love with one another, as it happens.' Toby didn't know why this sounded so awkward as he said it. 'We've been making love.'

It took Andy a moment to be certain of the meaning of this expression, which wouldn't have been his for the activity indicated.

'It wasna' fair!' he said with sudden vehemence. 'Ye should hae tellt me, Toby.'

'One doesn't tell.' Toby said this sulkily, knowing it to be another dishonesty, again with the class thing behind it. But then Andy's boasting in the pub had been similarly prompted; to Andy those vulgarly confident business types had been the rich, the bosses; and they were jostling with the football crowd, who were Andy's own people in a way, but clearly far from attractive to him. It was all this that had started the edginess.

'Would you ca' it serious?' Andy asked. 'This ganging wi' Elma, I mean.'

'I suppose we'll be getting married.' Toby had to resist putting his foot hard down on the accelerator. It seemed to him that he could say nothing just right. However, he continued to drive cautiously, and the headlights of the Aston Martin moved in an almost stately way down the empty, gently winding road before them. Although he felt so sober, a police surgeon might take a different view of him—if only because he must stink of beer, and would continue to do so until he had got out of his clothes and into a bath.

'At least I got yon wee weasel cratur yin in the ba's,' Andy suddenly said with retrospective satisfaction. 'But they were ower mony for us, Toby, and it canna' be said we came off weel. We'll hae sair ribs morie-morning, and nae look tae guid, either.'

'We can go straight to bed tonight. And nobody need know if we feel a little stiff and bruised tomorrow.'

'Aye, mebby.'

Toby further slowed the car. He was by now familiar with this locution as an expression of sardonic scepticism on his brother's part.

'I do feel a bit uncomfortable,' he said, 'round about my right eye.' He paused on this, for it was a new aspect of their situation that had come to him, and then took his gaze from the road for a moment to peer uncertainly at his brother's face in the dark. 'Shall we stop and take a proper look?'

'Here's yin o' they park-places just aheid.'

So Toby pulled in, switched off the headlights, switched on a spot-light angled on the windscreen, and swung it round so that his brother was garishly displayed to him.

'Jesus!' he said. 'You're a gory mess, Andy. I must have done you a cut lip.' He spun the spotlight round. 'What about me?'

'It'll be a richt black e'e the mornin'.' Andy didn't say this without a hint of the satisfaction that had attended his recalling having got the weasel where it would hurt him most. 'We'll just hae to say we got in a rough hoose in yon public.'

'We can't say that.'

'And what for no'?'

'It wouldn't be true. Not about our bashed faces. That was us.'

'Wee Geordie Washington! Faither, I canna' tell a lee.' Andy accompanied this outrageous taunt with honest laughter. 'Toby, ye daft wean, can't ye see it wadna' do at a'? Mr Felton wad hae no onnerstanding o' sic a thing as you an' me belting the yin the ither. He's a dacent man ye owe mickle to, and there's nae cause tae perplex him. But if he thinks we did no' badly when a bunch o' keelies were jeering us, he'll be as pleased as Punch on his wee platform.'

'I don't like it.' Toby said this half-heartedly; he had been a good deal impressed by the acuteness of his brother's perceptions.

'Verra weel! I'll tell him I lost my temper with ye ower naething at a', an' that then ye had to hit back at me.'

'I like that even less.' Toby let in the clutch again. 'So you win. Let's get on.'

They drove for a time in silence. The car started a hare, which then behaved as hares in such circumstances do. Persuading it to abandon the fairway became for some minutes an absorbing pursuit, and the brothers were now as happy on their homeward journey as they had been on their outward one. Then Andy turned to a new theme.

'But I dinna' ken,' he said, 'that we'll tak' in Mrs Warlow. She's a canny yin, your auntie.'

'Aunt Grace is?' It had never occurred to Andy to consider his foster-father's housekeeping relative particularly in this light. 'She's very capable, I suppose. And outspoken at times.'

'Sin when has she been a weedow?'

'She isn't one. She's divorced. Or at least I suppose so. She'd tell you her marriage had been dissolved.'

'I dinna' see mysel' asking her.'

There was something so odd in Andy's manner of saying this that Toby glanced at him curiously in the dull glow that came from the instruments on the dash-board.

'You sound quite scared of her,' he said. 'Just as if she might take that strap to you.' Andy had provided his brother with various reminiscences of his upbringing in the Auld household. 'Of course she's old enough to be your mother.'

'Aye, that's it! I never kenned the like, Toby. It's a'most no' in nature.'

This was odder still, and Toby made very little of it. But he

did see that Andy was for some reason disposed to accord Mrs
Warlow a surprisingly prominent position in his Felton scene.

'I sometimes wonder,' he said, 'how it's going to be with Aunt
Grace and Ianthe a little later on. They get on quite well at
present, but there might come a time when it was natural for Aunt
Grace to pack up and leave Ianthe to preside, as they say, over
her father's household.'

Andy received this in a silence perhaps betokening incompre-
hension. No doubt he was unfamiliar with people to whom it
would occur to 'say' anything of the sort. But after a minute or
two he asked a question.

'Will Ianthe be coming hame soon, do ye ken?'

'In a few days' time, I think. She's been inclined to flit around
a little lately. And after a first year at Cambridge Felton can seem
a bit dull. I remember that myself.'

'We're doing our best, you and me, Toby. We hanna' had a
dull nicht o' it the day.'

'True enough.' This amused Toby. 'And Ianthe may find it
more exciting with you on the scene.'

'Aye, mebby.' Andy was again silent, and his brother wondered whether his delicacy had somehow been offended by this
joke. But when Andy did again speak it seemed to be in an
equally light vein. 'It'll be a sair and awkward thing atween us
twa,' he said, 'if there's any like excitement stirring in your Elma.
But our wee dander thegither roond Felton was no' like that at
a'. I could scarce get her to take a gowk at me, she was that fu'
o' bits o' history and a' they pictures.'

Toby had to suppose that this reassuring speech was designed
to wipe out any ill impression occasioned by those unseemly
words uttered in fatal ignorance in the pub. If they rather naïvely
divulged the fact that getting a 'gowk' out of Elma had at least
been in his brother's mind there was no harm in that. Any normal
chap would want to kindle at least some small spark in such a girl.

81

PART TWO

Ianthe

VI

Almost from its inception, Ianthe Felton had observed her foster-brother's affair with Elma Loftus. Toby hadn't told her of it, and it was because of this that she thought of it as an 'affair' and not as a courtship. (The word, in the sense in which she was using it, was a rather old-fashioned one out of books: less specific than 'intrigue', she felt, but meaning the same thing.) Ianthe was of an age at which engagements and weddings are beginning to happen among a girl's contemporaries, and so to reveal themselves as in the order of nature. But nature runs to other arrangements as well, and Ianthe also numbered among her acquaintances, at least of the more casual sort, people who were 'living together', and others who hadn't got around to that, but who made love as occasion offered.

Ianthe soon understood that Toby and Elma were in this last category, although she couldn't have told how she was convinced of the fact. It certainly wasn't the result of operations of a detective character, nor were there any hints from a gratified Elma. She did somehow always know a lot about Toby: more than he (she knew) ever thought to know about her. So Toby's present state of mind in the matter was far from closed to her. He had it in his head—although not perhaps with full conviction—that this was the common sort of run-up to marriage nowadays, and that sooner or later the 'engagement' would be shoved in *The Times,* with various normal consequences until the wedding bells were ringing. Ianthe wasn't at all puzzled about Toby. But she was a little puzzled about Elma Loftus.

It was true that she and Elma counted as old friends. They had been at school together, and in various areas of practical enterprise Elma had proved a satisfactory companion. Even in the middle of the dullest term she was never without some clear

85

objective and the necessary 'go' to arrive at it. What she had arrived at now was Toby, and there was nothing surprising about that. What was perplexing was a sense that had come to Ianthe of the small commonplace drama as now somehow hanging fire. She had ended by becoming really uneasy about this—even to the extent of cutting down on messing around with Toby, and eventually taking herself off for a fairly long stay with friends in the West Riding. (It was still, in the later 1960s, called that.) She had in fact found it difficult to be much with Toby without betraying some wish that he should confide in her. As long as the 'affair' was running smoothly—towards either its legitimization in Felton parish church or an uncomplicated and not too painful petering out —she felt Toby to be entitled to keep his own counsel. But if he was in real trouble with it, if there had emerged some aspect of the situation baffling to him, she would have expected to hear about it. Toby's problems had regularly been made hers from an early age. It had happened that way partly because Ianthe was rather clever (she was almost one of the 'clever' Feltons) but rather more because she was so often ahead of Toby himself in knowing what was happening to Toby and what his problem demanded.

Between them there had never seemed to be any problem at all—or none springing from the fact that they shared no common blood. Having been treated as brother and sister since long before any explanation of their parentage could be conveyed to them, they had grown as that. Toby said 'my father' when speaking about Howard Felton as naturally as Ianthe did. What might have come to stand between the two young people as they grew older was, very obviously, the Felton property. The time was far past at which Howard's intentions here should have been made explicit to the whole family. As they hadn't been, it had to be presumed that they were not yet formulated; that Howard, in fact, had quite failed to make up his mind. This didn't come hard on Ianthe, since Ianthe's mother, perhaps conscious of her husband's infirmity of purpose, had left their daughter her own substantial, though scarcely magnificent, fortune. It did, however, come hard on Toby, much of whose pride was bound up with being as silent on the matter as the grave. The acceptance house had, of course, cost Howard a good deal of money, since Toby was in process of being bought into it (and the assurance of a fair income one day) in the discreet and devious manner in which such things are arranged in the City of London. But the very magnitude of the sum involved was felt by Toby (Ianthe knew) as sinister. He had to envisage the possibility of a time when, although he could hunt or shoot here or there if he wanted to, at Felton he would still be the guest of a Felton.

During her stay in Yorkshire all this had been much on Ianthe's mind. She saw how, as soon as any serious thought of marriage confronted Toby, he was bound to be more sharply aware of what was anomalous in his position. He could offer Elma Loftus or any other girl the prospect of a comfortable sort of upper-middle-class life. (And young men still did 'offer' girls 'lives', archaic as the language seemed.) But Felton was another matter. And very much another matter to Elma Loftus.

This last perception recurred to Ianthe when her Yorkshire visit had ended and she was on the train south. Elma wasn't exactly mercenary. Under a modish, rather 'hard' exterior there was something romantic in her—or soft-centred, if one preferred to put it that way. She was the doctor's daughter—but firmly persuaded of the existence of previous Loftuses not constrained to peddle pills and potions. No doubt she wanted Toby in bed. Today and tomorrow she wanted Toby in bed—or, failing that, just between clumps of furze on the down. But what she wanted for keeps was Felton House. Ianthe contemplated this as she made her way through an unambitious meal purveyed by British Rail. So far as the bare fact went she didn't blame Elma a bit. Tobias Felton with Felton House thrown in (but one could express it the other way round) would be a wholly rational object of desire on any young woman's part. If, to begin with, one considered just Toby himself—But here Ianthe broke off with a request to a hurrying attendant for, after all, a glass of wine. It was Toby's position, not Toby himself as eleven-and-a-half stone of vigorous young manhood, that constituted the problem.

But now there was another problem as well. There was the astonishing news that had come to her in a letter from her father to the effect that Toby had discovered a brother. Her father had been—although without deliberation—rather vague about it all, but the brother appeared to have turned up, as in a fairy-tale, in the character of a cowherd, or at least a garden-boy, about the place. He was a twin brother, and of the identical sort. If Tobias and Andrew (her father had written) chose to dress themself in identical clothing and comb their hair the same way it would be impossible to distinguish between them. Until, that was to say, they opened their respective mouths. Ianthe's father appeared to have been, at the time of writing his letter, so possessed by the fantasy, the weird improbability, of such a thing that he had quite failed to go on to any useful assessment of the situation. But he was running over to Oxford, he had written, to discuss it with Ianthe's Uncle Hugh.

Ianthe tried to decide what, disregarding its mere oddity, was to be made of such a discovery. It was, for a start, something for Toby to cope with. So far, so good. Toby—she told herself dispassionately—had been as he grew up a little short of things to cope with. Apart from the Felton issue everything had come his way. He had been a success at school: the kind of boy who, with decent abilities, successfully conceals the slog he has had to put into things, and who is duly admired as a result. At Cambridge he hadn't notably 'developed'; he had simply continued the same highly agreeable existence he had enjoyed as a senior boy at school. At home he was variously admired. And then, after a few oafish episodes of which Ianthe wasn't wholly unaware, he had fallen—if the image wasn't too gross—neatly into Elma Loftus's lap. Ianthe finished her wine while looking steadily at this last picture. One ought not to dodge things simply because there is something disturbing about them.

Yes, Andrew was a problem for Toby to cope with. But might he not be a problem for her father to cope with too? In an immediate practical sense this was obvious, since something was clearly due to a brother of Toby's discovered in a humble situation. But there might be more hazard to it than that. The sudden bobbing up of this young man—a second Toby with a background totally remote from Toby's own—might well suggest to Howard Felton that there had been something a little arbitrary, socially regarded, in an action of his own more than twenty years ago.

Aunt Grace was waiting for Ianthe at Didcot in Ianthe's own car, a diminutive Fiat known to Toby as the sewing-machine.

'I might have brought his nibs's grand conveyance,' Mrs Warlow said, 'and got you home in style.' This was a reference to the Aston Martin. 'He suggested it, most magnanimously, himself. As it is, you'd better drive.'

'He didn't go to the length of suggesting that he'd fetch me himself?'

'Toby is extremely busy, my dear. Clipping hedges and cleaning out ditches and ha-has, and heaven knows what. All in company, of course, with Andy. Don't forget there are now traffic-lights up there at the top.'

'Andy? Is that this Andrew—and is he still at Felton?'

'Certainly he is. He may be described as in process of assimilation.'

'You mean, Aunt Grace, becoming a member of the family?'

'A compromise is adumbrated. Andy will work in the estate office, and eventually become agent. I am assuring your father that it is entirely suitable.'

'It would only be suitable—in the long run—if Toby had Felton.' Ianthe had said this like a flash, and in the instant of changing gear. 'Don't you agree?'

'Certainly I agree, Ianthe. There are a good many things at Felton that are overdue for a tidy round.'

'You think Andy might help? Tell me about him. Is he nice?'

'He is Toby's brother.'

'But quite different in how he has been brought up—and that sort of thing?'

'He cleans his nails and washes his hair, and smells only when

89

he has been working like mad, which he does nearly all day, or drinking beer, which I gather to be his intermittent weakness. These things apart, he could scarcely be more uncouth than he is.'

'Oh, dear!' Ianthe appeared more amused than dismayed by this intelligence. 'How does it show? By the way he blows his nose?'

'I have remarked nothing peculiar about that. But he has been reared in the hyperborean unknown, and various mysteries surround him. The couple who adopted him are dead. But he has an auntie—a foster-auntie, if there be such a thing—whom he refers to respectfully as having been well-left. I rather gather that she owns a sweet-shop. But Andrew's speech is virtually unintelligible. Or he insists on making it so. I suspect that he could talk like his schoolteachers if he chose to.'

'And he and Toby are really getting on well as companions?'

'They had what appears to have been a vicious set-to together three or four days ago.' Mrs Warlow gave this information entirely composedly. 'They came home one night, that is to say, decidedly the worse for wear, and the next morning Toby told your father a cock-and-bull story about how they had been assaulted by football fans in a pub, but had given as good as they got. Your father was rather pleased. It was quite comical, really, because Toby was so evidently telling fibs and hating it. Then Andy came to me privately, and said that in the first place it had really been a fight between them and entirely his fault. That was quite comical too: this simple lad, I mean, turning himself into the best type of English public-school boy for the nonce. It was a matter of my having made a conquest of Andy—I can't think how.'

Ianthe produced no direct response to this. Her aunt being very little given to silly ideas, or even to merely idle remarks, she noted the information as something to reflect on. If Andy had quickly become rather impressed by Mrs Warlow it suggested at least that he wasn't thick. Of course Toby's twin wouldn't be that —wouldn't be exactly that. But Toby's inclination to take his aunt

90

lightly had never struck Ianthe as one of his strong points, intellectually considered.

'Has Andy's arrival,' she asked, 'taken Toby's mind a little off Elma Loftus?'

As Ianthe asked this question she had the satisfaction of knowing that it had sprung a surprise on Aunt Grace. Aunt Grace must certainly believe that she alone had penetrated to the fact that Toby and the doctor's daughter were in the enjoyment of a special relationship.

'Ah, that!' Mrs Warlow glanced sharply at her niece, whose conversation had never before touched at all freely upon matters of this sort. 'They represent different fields of interest, wouldn't you say, Andy and Elma? Of course Toby may be feeling he has less time for Elma now, and may therefore be employing it in a brisker and more immediately purposeful manner.'

'Yes, of course.' Ianthe was still young enough, was still sufficiently the nicely brought up girl, to receive as promotion from the nursery this frankness of implication. 'I suppose my father hasn't noticed anything. Do you think he would approve if he did?'

'He has, as a matter of fact, expressed a vague momentary alarm.' There was frequently a note of indulgence in Grace Warlow's references to her elder brother. 'But it will probably have passed from his mind. As for his approving of Elma, I don't at all know. He refers to her very pleasantly—but would certainly be disconcerted if she became engaged to Toby. I don't think he quite sees the Loftuses as the Loftuses do.'

'I suppose he is rather old-fashioned at heart.' Ianthe had arrived at a cross-roads, and drew to a halt with care. 'I wonder whether he looks around, as they say, for Toby among eligible girls in general? It wouldn't be very like him, really.'

'He has never mentioned anything of the kind. Why is there so much traffic this afternoon? But now's your chance—before the lorry.'

Mrs Warlow was inclined to give this sort of assistance to any driver she happened to be sitting beside. Nevertheless she appeared to have felt that these interesting speculations had been carried far enough for the present, and Ianthe accordingly turned back to a previous topic.

'Tell me one more thing about Andy,' she said. 'Is he now living in the house with us?'

'No, he is not. He is lodging with the Misses Kinch at the bottom of the drive—which is where Hawkstone found him digs in the first place.'

'It seems very odd, that. Doesn't it illegitimatize him, in a sense?' Ianthe paused as if to consider this seemingly outlandish question more carefully. 'You know what I mean? It sounds like an eighteenth-century compromise over something that has happened on the wrong side of the blanket.'

'My dear child!' By thus affecting to be shocked, Mrs Warlow indicated that she was amused. 'A by-blow—a term yet more picturesque—is one thing that we do *not* have to make do with.'

'It is possible for twins to have different fathers, you know.' Ianthe wasn't quite sure if this was in fact true, but it pleased her to seem to command so recondite a subject.

'Not our sort of twins, my dear. But the point about where Andy puts his head at night is certainly important. If your father's plan comes off, it will of course be natural that in time he should have a place of his own. But for the present he must certainly live with us. Anything short of that would be impossibly awkward.'

'But won't it be impossibly awkward too if he starts blowing his nose on the tablecloth?'

'Don't be silly, Ianthe.' Very justly (as Ianthe felt it to be) Mrs Warlow was displeased. 'The trouble is that Andy himself is not very keen on the idea. It is a feeling one must respect. He must see it as a point of positive commitment to a new way of life, and one which he is entitled to have misgivings about. There is no reason to suppose that the simpler classes feel unqualified admiration for the life of the lesser landed gentry.'

'Are we "lesser", Aunt Grace? It had never occurred to me.'

'We shall be, if your father has to sell much more of the

which had presented themselves at the time of fixing up Toby in
his acceptance house. (Toby had rather wanted to enter Lloyd's,
as one of his Cambridge friends had done, but hastily concealed
the fact on discovering it would cost a good deal more.) 'But the
difficulty is that becoming, so to speak, a parlour-boarder, and
moving in on us, is proving, for one reason or another, a sticking-
point with Andy. Toby can't get him past it.'

'Was it what they had their fight about?'

'I haven't asked—but I think probably not. Toby is banking
on you heavily.'

'I don't see why he should do that. It's his business much more
than mine.'

'I suppose he sees his brother as one likely to be fondly over-
come with female charm. The mirror-image effect again.'

Ianthe marked her disapproval of this haling-in of the poet
Milton by silence and a slight quickening of the Fiat's pace. She
was full of curiosity about Andrew Auld. But it was with the last
odd remark of her aunt's that the strangeness of the situation came
to her fully for the first time. There was nothing all that strange,
she supposed, in a man's discovering a long lost—or even a never
suspected—brother. The strangeness was going to consist—at
least for her—in what her father's letter had made clear from the
start: the visual near-identity of the two young men. She had
grown up with Toby from infancy: a constantly changing Toby,
transforming himself from boyhood to man. And all through this
long process of development a second Toby (for in imagination
it could only be that) had been going through the same transfor-
mations in some distant strange place. And now there had been
a coming together. It struck Ianthe that if her aunt could think of
Milton she herself could think of Hardy; could think of that very
rum poem in which while the *Titanic* is being wrought into being
on the Clyde the iceberg is similarly being wrought into being
somewhere within the Arctic Circle.

The comparison that had come into Ianthe's head was much
lacking in imaginative propriety, and her Uncle Hugh would

certainly have viewed it as indicating an imperfect literary cultivation. It was of her Uncle Hugh, as it happened, that Ianthe thought now.

'When are Hugh and Mercia coming over?' she asked. She and Toby always referred to the Oxford Feltons in this modern way, but for some reason called Mrs Warlow 'Aunt Grace'. 'Couldn't Hugh cope with this domesticating of Andy? It must be part of his job to sort out young men.'

'They will be coming some time next week—and no doubt with several extremely bored French children in tow. I doubt whether Hugh has much experience of sorting out Andrew Auld's sort of young man.'

'Oxford colleges have a very broad intake nowadays, class-wise regarded. Or they do if they are at all like Cambridge ones.'

'Both universities only run to Andys who have been processed by much prior education. You will find that the chief difficulty about being civilized with Andy is that it is so easy to take him out of his depth on all sorts of subjects. It seems lazy swimming in a quiet sea—chiefly because he is an easy person, rather in Toby's manner. But it is as if there were treacherous currents around and you have been carried into some tactless assumption of knowledge he doesn't have.'

'I'd expect Toby to be rather good with him, without bothering terribly about tact.'

'You'd be quite right.' Mrs Warlow had an air of having expected the promptitude of her niece's last comment. 'But I rather fear Hugh may be another matter. We all know that the brains of the family are concentrated in Hugh—or at least that such is your father's conviction—'

'Hugh has always been very nice about Toby—very nice indeed.'

'It is not the point to which I am addressing myself. I was going to say that Hugh's reputation as an extremely clever man gives him at times a little too much confidence in the justness of his own perceptions.'

'What a shocking thing to say!' Ianthe wasn't really at all

shocked—but, for the second time during this drive, she felt that she was being promoted to a fully adult level of family talk. 'Isn't he going to be perceptive about Andy?'

'We were speaking of tact. I am afraid Hugh may arrive with a little too much of it; that he will have laid in a supply before leaving Oxford, and even bought a brand-new extra large brush to lay it on with.'

'I see.' What Ianthe was in fact seeing was the existence of an area of sibling-trouble between Hugh and Aunt Grace which she had never thought to remark before. 'And aren't you really thinking less of a paint-brush than of a broom? Don't you mean that it will be Hugh's impulse to sweep Andy deftly under the mat? That, surely, would be quite horrid.'

'The image is certainly disagreeable. And if Andy makes up his mind to stick by Toby—'

'It could be like that?' For the first time, Ianthe was startled by her aunt's vision of the new posture of things at Felton.

'Say simply that if Andy decides very positively to be Toby's brother, he might prove not at all sweepable under anything. But I don't underestimate my brother Hugh's abilities—and really in this matter there is common ground between us. We both see difficulties in the situation perhaps more clearly than your father does—or Toby, for that matter. But I have an additional feeling, which perhaps you have too. And as you've asked me so many questions I'll now ask you one—and about just that. Would you say we are in rather a muddle at Felton?'

'Not exactly. Or at least I don't see us as all grouped round one big muddle.' Ianthe paused on this, and with a sudden sense of the need for guarded utterance. She was glad, in fact, to see the grey roof of Felton House over the stubby bonnet of her car. 'Perhaps a few private muddles here and there. But I don't know that Andrew Auld much impinges on them.'

'If he impinges on any,' Mrs Warlow said, 'he'll impinge on the lot.'

VII

ALTHOUGH HOWARD FELTON had made a pilgrimage to Oxford to consult the better wisdom of his brother on the curious situation confronting him, and although he had come home feeling the trip to have answered reasonably to expectation, he found that the prospect of Hugh's return visit was something he looked forward to with misgiving. Mercia, his sister-in-law, would be coming too; she was a woman for whom he didn't greatly care; and as they would almost certainly bring with them any guests staying in the Lodging the effect would approximate to that of a commission of inquiry. Moreover he no longer judged that further light must succeed upon Hugh's inspecting or vetting Andrew Auld. In what was really a very short space of time this plebeian but by no means unpleasing Scot had made considerable headway in Howard's regard, and although Howard had not yet succeeded in coming to any firm conclusion about what action was required, he was indulging the sanguine expectation that he would quite soon do so. He almost regretted having made his visit to Hugh so much a matter of seeking advice rather than of imparting information. Hugh was extremely clever—but there was, after all, plenty of sound practical sense in his own household. Grace had already made judicious suggestions; Toby was clear that he wasn't going to lose Andy if he could help it; best of all, Ianthe would pronounce like a shot on the rights or wrongs of any proposal as she saw them.

Of course anything further that Hugh found to say would be extremely cogent. But even this fact made Howard uneasy. He was dimly aware in himself of areas of feeling upon which the arrival of Andrew Auld was at play in a manner at present eluding definition. But whatever the process was, and however vulnerable it might be to logical assault by his brother, it was at least part of

himself, and for a time he ought to be left alone with it. But along
with this right to independent judgement went the duty of doing
his best to exercise it. Convinced of this, Howard took long
striding walks—much as if he had an urgent letter to despatch
which could be posted only in the next parish—and did his best
to think things out.

He had made rather a stupid joke to Hugh to the effect that
Tobias and Andrew were so much alike as to be comical, like
Tweedledum and Tweedledee. Hugh hadn't thought the indistin-
guishableness of the twins at all likely to be laughable, and had
said something rather pedantic about a fissiparous phenomenon.
It was certainly true that Howard, although believing himself
deeply attached to Toby and becoming rather fond of Andy, took
more pleasure in seeing either the one or the other of them solus
than he did in seeing them standing side by side. This was puzzling, and indeed seemed quite wrong. Twins, unless deformed
or otherwise visually disagreeable, constitute a spectacle commonly regarded as pleasing in itself.

Perhaps what was troubling was not the similarity of the twins
—which was a sheerly biological affair—but their dissimilarity,
socially regarded. Or rather it was the clash of these two facts.
Arriving at this during one of his walks, Howard quickened his
pace on the footpath he was traversing. His mind, he felt, was
now coming to grips with his problem. If Andrew Auld had
turned up not as Hawkstone's new assistant but as the adoptive
son of a landowner in, say, Shropshire; if he had talked public-
school and been public-school; if his assumptions and knowledge-
ableness as well as his nose, chin and eyebrows had been Toby's;
if he too was making his way among acceptance people or their
like: if all these postulates had been true the situation would have
been quite different. So the core of the problem lay in the disparity between Toby's world and Andy's, and in the perplexing
system of claims and obligations which this seemed to set up. It
came down to what was due to Andy on the straight count of
kinship with Toby, and what was tactful and feasible in the light
of Andy's upbringing and outlook.

Howard, climbing towards the downs, realized that he had been over the problem in these terms before, and that his sister had placed squarely on the carpet a practicable plan for dealing with it. In fact there *wasn't* a problem—or not an intractable one —and he ought not therefore to be feeling in any confusion of mind. Being an elderly widower comfortably circumstanced and set in his ways, it was natural that he should sometimes simply wish that Andy had never turned up, even if at other times he was conscious of a positive affection for the lad as a sort of spill-over —he supposed—from his affection for Toby. The two didn't just have the same features and complexion; they continued like one another—he felt sure—quite deep down. So if Andy was a complication whom one could in weak moments wish away, he was also, in a sense, an enrichment of the Felton scene. It was like opening the nursery door in a dream, Howard reflected, and discovering oneself to have been under a misapprehension about the number of one's progeny—since there, playing on the carpet, are two little boys in place of one.

But individuals can fade into one another in a dream—or dispart in what Hugh would call a fissiparous way. And Howard was aware that, if he did have dreams about Toby and Andy (as hadn't happened yet), the two young men would be likely to play hide-and-seek with one another. Awake, he did rather more thinking about Andy than Toby at present—which wasn't unreasonable, Andy being the new-comer and unknown quantity that he was. Andy in fact was more interesting than Toby. Howard had to pause on this startling thought—and even to ask himself whether, for the moment, Andy didn't make the running in terms of simple attractiveness as well. Something almost atavistic in Howard Felton responded to Andy, stripped and helping to thatch a rick, more readily than to Toby sitting in an office and shuffling papers among his acceptance people. But this was only a flicker of feeling. The real point was that the image of Toby which Howard had for long carried around unchallenged in the recesses of his mind was in some way being modified by Andy's turning up. Something unsettling was happening. Howard didn't quite know what. But the subliminal process, whatever it was, had a disturbing quality.

Howard now found that, absorbed in these thoughts, he had reached without knowing it the goal of one of his favourite walks. He was high up on the down, still on Felton land, and with Felton House just visible far below. Immediately before him was a monument of what appeared to be the most awesome antiquity: a circle of gigantic sarsen stones set within a grove of venerable oaks. It dated, however, only from the mid-eighteenth century and had been devised by a certain Torquil Felton, whose antiquarian interests had been stimulated when, as an undergraduate at Benet College, Cambridge, he had formed a friendship with William Stukeley. Stukeley, who was a very learned youth, was already mad about Druids; Torquil—who was already a landowner in his own right—was, correspondingly, becoming a keen arboriculturist. Megalithic circles, oak trees, and a Druid priesthood were closely associated in the thought of that time, and Torquil had decided to embellish his estate accordingly. The result, although named on Ordnance Survey maps as Felton Temple, was known in the family—most unfairly—as Stukeley's Folly. It always amused Howard to enter this shameless fake and find that, despite his knowledge of its origin, a certain sense of the numinous assailed him. He was experiencing this now when he suddenly became aware that he was not alone.

Sunning himself in the middle of Stukeley's Folly was Andrew Auld. He had taken his shirt off (as he was rather fond of doing) and was lying supine and spread-eagled on the turf, staring at a kestrel high above him.

For some moments Howard studied this unexpected appearance unobserved. Andy's features—being also Toby's features—were rather too strongly accentuated here and there to make for any regular sort of beauty. But when viewed chiefly as a torso lying on grass Andy was attractive enough, just as Toby would be. Howard took spontaneous pleasure in what he saw—a fact reflected in the cordiality of his tone when he now broke silence.

'My dear Andy, what a surprise to find you up here!'

Andy, thus alerted, sat up. More precisely, with his arms still stretched above his head, he swung himself effortlessly upright from the hips. Howard found himself wondering whether Toby could do just that.

'It's the Bank Holiday,' Andy said.

Howard was perplexed. For one thing, Bank Holidays didn't much register with him (although they probably meant something in that acceptance place); and, for another, Andy's tone had been swiftly defensive—almost as if he had heard a rebuke for not being down at Felton, working furiously and much to Mr Hawkstone's annoyance as garden-boy still.

'And I'm delighted to tumble in on you,' Howard said hastily, and with equal promptness sat down on the grass. 'What do you think of this odd affair?' He made a gesture round Stukeley's Folly. 'At least there's a splendid view. I suppose I particularly like it because it has all sorts of associations with my family.'

'Wad it be what they ca' Stonehenge?' Andy asked. 'I've heard tell o' that.'

'Stonehenge?' For a moment Howard supposed that this was a joke. 'Well, no. This place was put together by one of my ancestors, as a matter of fact.'

'In the Stone Age?' Not unnaturally, Andy asked this question with a certain awe—although awe touched, perhaps, with suspicion as well.

'Not quite as far back as that. Not even in the Bronze Age, either.' In an entirely genial way, Howard showed himself entertained by this misconception. 'A good deal less than three hundred years ago.'

'That's a lang time, too.'

'It was the period when people went in for that kind of thing: classical cow houses, you know, and Chinese gardens, and horses and so forth cut out of the chalk.' Howard, not himself particularly strong in the scholarship of this subject, became conscious that Andy was of course even less so. Here in fact would be a main

100

difficulty with Toby's brother for a long time ahead; you never knew when he was going to be so at sea over matters of common knowledge that it became hard to talk on without talking down as well. It was notable, therefore, that conversation with him remained so pleasurable on the whole. If he had in a sense a discouragingly empty mind, it was in consequence an unusually open mind as well. 'Ianthe can tell you a lot about such things,' Howard went on. 'She's training, you know, to be an archaeologist.'

'Has Miss Ianthe aye been your sole bairn?' Andy always said 'Toby' but otherwise still remained uncertain about how to refer to other members of the family.

'Yes. My wife never had another child.'

'More ancestors than bairns,' Andy said—and appeared to judge the fact worthy of meditation.

'Why, yes. But that, you know, is true of everybody.' Howard glanced whimsically at the young man, and saw with satisfaction that he was again supine and relaxed upon the turf. It looked as if this was going to be as good a time for serious discussion with him as was likely to turn up in the near future. So Howard produced a pipe and a tobacco pouch by way of indicating a certain leisure ahead. As he manipulated these ritual objects Andy spoke again.

'Will Miss Ianthe be hame soon?'

'Andy, you must say just "Ianthe", please. You can't say what Toby doesn't say.' Howard felt that he had gained ground by venturing on this firm instruction. 'Do you mind my mentioning things like that? It's just a matter of small habits we happen to have.'

'Aye. But it's no' a' thegither a sma' question.' Andy glanced up at Toby's adoptive father with a whimsical look of his own. 'A' richt,' he then said. 'So just when will Ianthe be back at Felton?'

'By now, probably. My sister went to meet her train after luncheon.'

Andy made no immediate reply to this. But he rolled over on

his side, plucked after due inspection a promising blade of grass, transferred this between his teeth apparently as an aid to thought, and then rolled yet further over and came to rest on his stomach. Howard thus found himself invited to converse with the nape of Andy's neck, the gentle contours of Andy's shoulder-blades, and the long furrow of Andy's spine. This remained entirely agreeable. Supine or prone, female or male, the exposed human body always gave Howard pleasure when it came his way. Even his sister's studies from the nude, although he suspected them of being artistically undistinguished, afforded him this mild satisfaction. So now for some minutes he puffed in silence, sometimes glancing at Andy, and sometimes at Felton and its surroundings, stretched out like an estate map in the vale below. Andy, who presumably saw nothing of interest in the decorously clad figure of his elderly companion, contented himself with the view, which he commanded by raising his head and cupping his prominent chin in his hands. When he spoke it was without stirring from this posture.

'Will a' yon be going to Ianthe?'

'I beg your pardon?' Howard took refuge in this phrase because he was extremely startled. 'All what, Andy?'

'Felton an' a' they acres. They'll be hers, sin she's your sole ain kin?'

'It's a very difficult question, I'm afraid.' Howard told himself that Andrew Auld must not be considered as having wantonly perpetrated any impertinence. It would be very unfair to expect from a lad so simply bred an unfailing sense of his p's and q's. And his sudden question certainly had no background in expectations of his own, since nothing was clearer about him than his determination to decline anything approaching a pensioner's status. Andy was thinking about Toby. There could be no doubt about that. But this didn't make things any easier for Howard, thus suddenly confronted with so candid an onslaught. Not even his brother Hugh had ever tackled him in this direct way about his intentions with regard to the family property. Hugh probably guessed that he simply didn't *have* intentions, and even that a kind of mental block mysteriously befell him when he tried to get the matter clear. But it wouldn't do to let this young man glimpse so humiliating a fact. He must simply intimate to Andy at once that here was a subject not properly to be discussed between them.

But when it came to the point Howard found himself unable to do quite this. Somehow, he couldn't bear the idea of snubbing or rebuking Andy, whose only assumption was that a relationship of candour had established itself between them. Fortunately there was something perfectly definite about Ianthe that he could pronounce upon at once.

'Nowadays,' he began, 'the transmission of landed property can be a very ticklish business, Andy. With death duties as they are, a new proprietor may find himself burdened with more problems than he can cope with. I don't think my daughter would be daunted by that, but the plain fact is that she is quite clear she doesn't want to inherit Felton anyway. She has an independent fortune, as it happens, and she says it is as much as it is sensible for anyone to have. I'm not sure that there aren't factors which she is leaving out of account—but I needn't enter into that.' Howard paused on this hint of quasi-dynastic sentiment, and felt that he had said enough, and could now without unkindness shut Andy up. 'So much for that, then,' he said, 'and we won't take it further now. But there is something else I want to discuss, Andy, and this seems a good opportunity. It's the question of your own future—in which I am keenly interested, I need hardly say.'

The effect of this upon Andy was to make him do another roll, sit up, and clasp his knees within his arms—thereby assuming as formal and attentive a posture as the circumstances permitted.

'Mr Felton,' he said soberly, 'ye monna' think I feel there's any ca' on you that way. I'm Toby's brither, but I hanna' like him lived at Felton sin I was a wean.'

'Well, you're living there now.' Howard produced this with

103

a determined lightness of air. 'And we can begin at just that point. I must ask you, my dear Andy, to stop being so determinedly a junior employee about the place.'

'But I had my wages frae Mr Hawkstone but yesterday.' Andy accompanied this information with his rare quick smile, as if himself humorously disposed. 'And I signed a wee bit card for the insurance.'

Howard was about to say, 'Confound your wages!' when he reflected that Andy probably depended on them entirely both for paying the Misses Kinch and for defraying all the miscellaneous expenses of life. So here—in the area that might be called that of pocket-money—was one small vexatious problem rising up at once.

'Hawkstone,' he said, 'is in a difficult position, and we mustn't make fun of him. But, Andy, what you have to understand is that you are at present my guest. And as Toby's brother you must allow me to treat you as something more than that as well. Small sums of money, for instance. I shall take it very hardly if you don't allow me to provide you with anything of the sort that you may require. And we can forget about the insurance card.'

'You're verra kind.'

'You can see what we are like. We're not enormously wealthy' —Howard had recalled sagely assuring Hugh that he would make this point to Toby's brother on an early occasion—'but we have no call to bother about moderate outlays of one sort or another.'

'Like on Toby's car.'

Howard was disconcerted for a moment, this appearing to him to be the first occasion upon which Andy had offered a stroke of sarcasm to the world. Then he realized that nothing of the sort had happened. Andy understood a weekly pay-packet; in money matters beyond that sphere his orders of magnitude were hazy. Howard could remember his own misgiving—and Grace's decided disapproval—when the bill for the Aston Martin had to be met, and Andy would no doubt get this sort of thing right if he stopped to think about it. Now, he had just been expressing unreflecting pleasure in what could come his brother's way as matter of course in such a family as the Feltons.

'But it's some longer-term plan we must get settled,' Howard went on. 'What I am going to say to you I have thought over very carefully. And I have discussed it with my sister. Indeed, I think it fair to say that she originated it.'

'Mrs Warlow?' So far, Andy's attention might have been called respectful rather than intense, but now he straightened up further, and looked more sharply at Howard. 'She's been thinking o' me?'

'Indeed she has.' Howard was conscious that this news was of importance to Andy, and he recalled an earlier impression that his sister had somehow come to occupy a prominent place in the young man's regard. 'But first I must give you some idea of how the estate is run. We have brought things together a good deal in recent years, and everything passes through the office of my agent, Mr Tarling. Perhaps you've heard of Mr Tarling?'

Andy hadn't heard of Mr Tarling. But he asked a question that showed him to be not entirely at sea.

'Mr Tarling would be your factor-like?'

'Exactly! In Scotland Mr Tarling would be called a factor, I don't doubt.' Howard was about to add his sister's observation that nowadays the job could be a gentleman's, but checked himself from a feeling that this would be inapposite. Instead, he embarked upon Grace's plan. Andy listened with a promising intentness, rather as a well-disposed schoolboy might do to a fairly stiff lesson in geometry. It was always necessary to remember— Howard told himself—that the lad must be totally unused to sustained exposition of any sort. Yet such difficulties as Andy had, both in this regard and in almost everything else at present surrounding him, had no effect of shattering a native self-confidence which could be felt to be his. He was as well-endowed here as Toby was. For some moments, indeed, Howard was led away by this consideration to ponder the mysteries of heredity. Of what sort of parents had these two boys come? Peasants from some

105

steppe? Polish aristocrats? Hungarian intellectuals? So strangely assorted had been the *Cornucopia*'s freight that it was anybody's guess. But one thing that they were almost certainly not was the progeny of an English landowner of ancient lineage. Children of the Felton kind had of course been hustled across the Atlantic and away from Hitler's Europe. But not, it was almost assured, on that particular vessel.

'Gie me time, an' I could dae it,' Andy said suddenly. 'But would there be wark frae the start, as weel as learning?'

'Oh, certainly! Plenty of work.' Howard was astonished by the smoothness with which this seemed to be going. 'A practical training, you know, with plenty of physical labour to face.' Howard felt this to be deeply cunning. 'But at the same time, you see, a position that any young man of our sort could properly be in. If you happened, say, to be my brother Hugh's boy. Or my sister's. Absolutely in order, I assure you.'

'You might ca' it an apprenticeship—but o' the kind wi' a bit wage frae the start.' Andy remained firmly down-to-earth. 'So what siller there was I'd be earning.'

'Oh, most certainly.'

'There'd be this Mr Tarling—but a' the same it would be for yoursel' I'd be warking, Mr Felton?'

'Yes, indeed, Andy.' Howard felt things were now going forward quite famously. 'It can be expressed precisely like that.'

'So that yin day awa' aheed I'd be Toby's man?' It was with simple amusement that Andy seemed to advance this. 'I'd be Toby's Mr Tarling, wad I no'?'

'Just that.' Having got in the way of confident affirmations, Howard Felton had said this before quite realizing where it had taken him, or noticing the steadiness of gaze with which Toby's brother had accompanied these last questions.

'It's to be thocht on,' Andy said with decision, and reached for his shirt. In a second his head had disappeared into it and emerged again, and while thrusting its tails deftly with both hands inside his trousers he contrived simultaneously to rise to his feet as if his body incorporated some spring-like mechanism in the manner of

a jack-in-the-box. 'An' I can bide still wi' the Miss Kinches?' he
said.

'If you wish to, certainly. It's entirely for you to say. But we'd
all much prefer that, for the time being at least, you lived with
us in the house. It's what your brother would like, Andy. And I'd
say he's entitled to consider it the natural thing.'

'I could be up there in that back wing wi' him?'

'That would be the best arrangement, and there's plenty of
space. Although I think the two of you would have to share a
bathroom.'

'I think that's the daftest thing I've heard yet!' Andy followed
up this frank and not unjust remark with a shout of laughter which
at first perplexed and then rather pleased Howard. But then he
became serious again; became, indeed, almost grave. 'But that's
to be thocht on, too,' he said. 'What does Mrs Warlow think o'
it?'

'Of course she agrees. In fact, Andy, to be quite honest, I think
she'd stand on it pretty stiffly.'

'Insist, you mean?'

'She wouldn't treat you as other than your own master, my
dear boy. But, yes—something like that.'

'It's the hairt o' the matter, is it no'?' For the first time
in Howard's experience of him, Andrew Auld was a deeply
troubled youth. 'An' I dinna' ken, Mr Felton—I just dinna'
ken!'

'Do you mean that we're asking too much, Andy?' Also on his
feet now, Howard laid for a moment on Toby's brother's shoulder an almost fatherly arm. This time, he was not at all at a loss
as to what was going on in the young man's mind.

'Or gie'ing too much—I dinna' ken!'

'Then give it a trial, Andy. Think of yourself as an explorer,
content to rub noses for a time with a strange tribe. At least we're
not cannibals, and shan't eat you. And you needn't pick up our
songs and dances if you don't want to.'

Howard Felton—standing in the middle of Felton Temple or
Stukeley's Folly, and with the Felton lands at his feet—rather

107

surprised himself by his command of these bizarre images. But Andy at least didn't take them amiss, nor did their sense elude him.

'It wad be lang,' he said, 'afore I'd hear you speaking ither than a strange tongue an' a'. So it mun be thocht on. Just let me bide on it a wee.'

VIII

Mrs WARLOW, having on her afternoon's programme the necessary weekly patronizing of the village shop in Felton Canonicorum, dropped Ianthe at the bottom of the drive and took the wheel. For her niece it meant a walk of well over half a mile, since the blessed seclusion of Felton House from a jarring world was one of its more notable features. Ianthe, who as a traveller had been sitting down for most of the day, welcomed this modicum of exercise. She also felt that she wanted time to arrange her thoughts.

It would scarcely have been easy to say why. Her aunt had given her a certain amount of fresh information about Toby's miraculously recovered brother, but it wasn't of a sort appearing to demand any particular initiative from herself. She saw that the strangeness of the event called for the exercise of a certain circumspection, and that it was probably necessary to bear Andrew Auld's educational deficiencies constantly in mind while dissimulating the fact that one was doing so. These things were so obvious that they hardly needed thought, and there was nobody on the immediate Felton scene inadequately equipped for the job in point either of good manners or good will.

Why then did she feel that Andy's arrival sounded for her an obscure alert? She asked herself this question as she paused for a moment to glance at the humbly snug dwelling of the Misses Kinch. Since she visited these ladies regularly for the purpose of inquiring about their health and augmenting their wardrobes or larder, she knew the inside of the lodge very well. She could quite clearly visualize the room that must have been let to Hawkstone's new assistant, and by planting the figure of Toby in the middle of it call up almost precisely the spectacle enjoyed by one or another of the Misses Kinch when she stuck her ancient head through the doorway to call the young man to his tea. Possessing (like her Aunt Grace) a vigorous pictorial imagination, Ianthe went on to clothe this deutero-Toby in her mind's eye in garments appropriate to horticultural activities, and thus completed an almost certainly accurate conjuration of Andrew Auld in his habit as he lived. But she found that this innocent and almost involuntary play of fancy somehow enhanced her sense of elusive crisis round the corner.

Ever since her two years' juniority had ceased to count, and on through their later teens when her maturity had begun to outdistance his, Ianthe had been Toby's sentinel and guard. There were other facets to their relationship, some of them perhaps not much available to the view of either, but this one was as important as any. It had perhaps come into being as early as those years during which Howard Felton and his wife (but chiefly Howard himself) had been hoping still for the birth of a boy; now it had achieved very conscious focus in Ianthe's mind. Toby's rights at Felton would be violated were he to be treated other than precisely as an only son. And something atavic, tribal, deep in her father (too deep, indeed, for Howard's own ready comprehension) threatened the integrity of his purpose in this regard. Ianthe's business—it was thus she saw it—was to see Toby established beyond equivocation as the acknowledged heir to Felton. For several years now she had been vigilant over this. She had developed, indeed, a kind of early warning system round the activities of her foster-brother. It was a fact of which Howard Felton himself was totally unconscious. His sister Grace was not.

There had been a certain hazard when the project of the acceptance house hove up. It had been prudent in Toby—himself not quite confident that matters would go as he expected and hoped—to inquire around concerning the sort of business opportunities, the avenues to unquestionable independence and financial ease, which his contemporaries at school and university were so many of them heading for. Howard had been brought round to applaud Toby's sagacity, and indeed to claim a measure of it for himself. He had been disappointed, all the same. There wasn't much spunk to finding oneself a niche in Lombard Street. Ianthe had been briefly furious. But for her father's dilatory instinct the acceptance house wouldn't have happened.

And now there was Elma Loftus—about whose relationship with (and designs upon) Toby Aunt Grace had admitted to being as well posted as Ianthe herself. Ianthe was less clear about this, feeling the possible emergence of something latent in the affair which eluded her. Despite her father's seeming approval of Elma she found it hard to believe that he would much care for Toby's liaison with her, let alone for any notion of a marriage. Dr Loftus kept a whacking great family tree in a wash-place, but the Loftuses weren't Howard Felton's sort of people, all the same. Her father —Ianthe told herself—although scarcely a complex character, did harbour a sufficient number of paradoxes to save him from insipidity. His adopting a male child of whose parentage nothing whatever was known had been the product of an impulse liberal in the most admirable sense, and it now looked as if Andrew Auld's reception was exhibiting her father in the same light. At the same time there lurked in him prejudices (or loyalties, if one cared to put it that way) that might have come straight out of Victorian fiction. In Trollope there was that duke (a variously admirable man) who was outraged that the hand of his daughter should be aspired to by a mere private gentleman. Howard Felton might be described as a mere private gentleman himself. But at least a tinge of that sort of feeling harboured in him.

And now in turn there was a possible hazard in Andy. It was very much her persuasion that Toby and Andy had taken to one another: even the mysterious fight reported by her aunt seemed somehow to support that view of the matter. Andy must be finding his situation bewildering and in many ways disagreeable. But there was no hint that he felt, as counterbalancing this, that there was, in the vulgar phrase, 'something in it for him'. On the contrary, there was even a suggestion that he was fighting for his independence—or at least submitting only by cautious degrees to what Mrs Warlow had called a 'process of assimilation'. Perhaps, despite its strangeness, he found the general spectacle of Felton

111

attractive, but it looked as if it was decidedly just the discovering of a brother that pleased him in the main. Andy wasn't, in other words, the sort of person by whom her father would be radically upset, with any consequent undesirable rubbing off of irritation upon Toby. He was a new and imponderable element in the family situation, all the same. She would know more about him when she had heard what Toby had to say.

By the time that Ianthe had developed her thinking thus far she was nearly half-way up the drive. The house was still invisible since the drive, in the interest of a level progress, here swept in a gentle curve round a coomb dropping steeply from the down. This added considerably to its length, and also to the effectiveness of the avenue of beech trees through which it moved as through a leafy rotunda. Some of the beeches had a yellow tinge which Ianthe knew to be causing her father anxiety as less likely to be autumnal than a sinister consequence of exceptional drought a couple of summers ago. Ianthe had paused to assess this phenomenon when she became aware that somebody had emerged from the coomb and was advancing towards her down the drive. Recognizing the figure as Toby's, she gave a wave. The wave was returned, but only after a moment's perplexing hesitation. It was the hesitation, and not anything else visible to the eye, that told her this wasn't Toby, after all. It was Andy. She moved forward with a quickened pace. And Andy did this too.

'Are you Toby's sister?' Andy asked, coming to a halt squarely in the middle of the drive.

'Yes, I am.' Ianthe had been asked the right question, and her pleasure showed it. 'And I don't need to ask if you're his brother.'

'Aye, I'm Andy.' As he said this Andy's gaze was very steady —and not at all of the up and down order. 'But there's a difference.'

'Between the two of you? I just don't see it!' This came from Ianthe lightly, and she managed to shake hands in a conventional way. But she had spoken what was for the moment at least the literal truth: that it was precisely as if it were Toby who was standing before her. Andy's accent, indeed, was like the bit of ribbon one ties round one twin's ankle at birth as a sole immediate means of preserving his identity when the second twin has arrived.

'Aye, that too. But I was meaning there's a difference between the way you're like Toby's sister and I'm his brother. There's a kind of confusion in it.'

'I suppose there is.' Ianthe reflected on this—and also on the fact that, although the accent was there, Andy's Doric could be more sparing than she had been led to believe. 'And I'm the odd one out,' she added.

'I dinna' think you odd,' Andy said—with a sudden impulsive effect but with no hint of impudence. 'And it's Toby and me are odd men out thegither, wi' a' you Feltons gathered round us.'

'Yes, in a way.' Ianthe found herself acknowledging this reluctantly, although the defensibility of such a new view of the situation was instantly apparent to her. 'But you speak as if the Feltons were visiting a zoo, and you and Toby were a couple of giant pandas.' This sounded silly to Ianthe as she said it, but at least it was well received by Toby's brother.

'You don't hae me a' thegither behind bars yet,' he said. 'Although times I can a'most hear them clinking into place.'

Ianthe had been expecting Andy to be rather slow-witted. She believed that identical twins must enter the world with very little, if any, disparity in intellectual potential. But she had been assuming (which wasn't itself too intelligent, she realized) that Toby's education, his exposure since childhood to reasonably informed and alert conversation and so on, must result in his being rather cleverer than Andy. But now within minutes she was abandoning any such notion. Andy might be slower than Toby—at least in getting something by the tail in the field of verbal communication —but slower-witted he was not. Nor—almost certainly—quicker either. She had read somewhere of the possible coming of 'clonal man'. That of course was something quite different from identical twins, and she was entirely vague about it. But when clonal man arrived in large numbers he would bring with him problems at least adumbrated in Tobias Felton and Andrew Auld.

'My aunt and I have just driven home from Didcot.' Ianthe said this because slightly at a loss about how to proceed with Andy. 'You can guess we talked about you—or rather that I asked questions and Aunt Grace answered them. You won't mind my being terribly curious about you, Andy? Toby's finding a brother has been quite something. We've been pretty well brother and sister, you see, Toby and I. It couldn't be otherwise, brought up together as we have been.'

'Aye, mebby.' Andy paused on this, perhaps as noticing that Ianthe appeared to find the form of his concurrence odd. 'I'll be hoping,' he went on, 'that Mrs Warlow spak' no ill o' me?'

'Of course not.' Ianthe thought Andy's question had come with a sudden ingenuous anxiety which she mustn't be amused by. 'My aunt goes in for speaking the truth as she sees it—or turning the conversation, if truth won't at all do.' It was a sign that Ianthe was attending closely to Toby's brother that she allowed a moment for his getting hold of this phrase. She was also recalling an odd thing that Aunt Grace had said about having made a conquest of this youth from the 'hyperborean unknown'. 'She said some things they won't carve on your tombstone, Andy, but she certainly likes you. So I hope you like her.'

'I never knew sic' a one afore,' Andy said with energy. 'She has it twa ways at once. She's auld enough to be my mither an' gie me my bairn's orders still. But at the same time I could—' Andy checked himself as if conscious of having been about to utter something indecorous. 'She's that well-preserv't!' he went on wonderingly. 'My ain mither was no older, but when she died she might hae been my grandmither. It's like that, Ianthe, wi' working men's wives. They hae plenty o' will still, but a' o' something else drain't awa' frae them wi' the toil o't.' Andy's accent had broadened momentarily. 'But Mrs Warlow—' Once more Andy didn't know how to proceed.

'. . . is a complete Cleopatra,' Ianthe said—and at once knew that this was outside the rules when conversing with Andy Auld. Andy would have heard of Cleopatra—but not that, historically regarded, the charms known to Mark Antony must have been of

114

a mature order. Perhaps, speaking to another man, Andy would have said 'quite a dish'—or something even more broadly spoken of the same sort. Ianthe saw that there was a good deal of propriety in Andy. He would be trustworthy in all sorts of minor ways. Probably he had been strictly brought up. She made a mental note to find out a lot about the upbringing of Toby's brother, and even about the aunt with a sweet-shop.

This was a very sensible resolution, and of a piece with most of what had been said so far. But now something happened that oddly changed the temperature—it would have had to be called that—of the encounter. It was simply that Andy, who had still been standing before Ianthe on, as it were, an even keel, and with his fingers tucked lightly within the two little pockets at the front of his jeans, now tilted his hips so as to impose his weight much more on one foot than the other. This slight change of posture had the air of something habitual with him, and of having been made, at least on the present occasion, wholly without demonstrative intent. But its effect was to render Ianthe suddenly and vividly aware of Andrew Auld as a physical presence. Indeed, it was rather more than that. She had just made the amusing discovery that in some artless fashion Andy saw in her aunt what in another society might be thought of as the ideal of the maternal mistress. Now she was glimpsing Andy himself as conceivable in another prescriptive sexual role, that of the plebeian lover. There was nothing wholly out of the way about this. Like most chaste girls, Ianthe enjoyed the occasional experience of being fleetingly and secretly attracted by casually encountered—or merely observed —young men. She was aware of an additional charm or tug inhering in that element of the unknown carried by a personable male from an alien social context. It was entertaining sometimes to imagine how she would make do if she decided to marry the milkman, or one of Farmer Purbrick's labourers of particularly masculine appeal. This being so, there was no reason why she should feel perturbed at momentarily viewing Hawkstone's late assistant in terms of that kind of innocent fantasy.

But in fact Ianthe felt very perturbed indeed. For a moment

she even had a strong impulse to brush past Andy and bolt up the drive—much as Toby had done not far from this spot in a not too distant past. Yet she hadn't fallen into any total confusion, since there remained in her mind one vital area of complete clarity. When, not yet having glimpsed Andy, she had thought up that image of Toby dressed as an under-gardener in the rented room of the Misses Kinch, she had been fabricating a composite of a highly undesirable order. To muddle up Toby and Andy wouldn't at all do. She would be in trouble if she did anything of the kind. And perhaps her father would be, too, were he to do so.

This was a clear but limited perception. Ianthe was striving to enlarge it—and becoming aware of indefinable impediments to doing so—when she recalled that she was still in colloquy with Toby's brother, and that Toby's brother was regarding her curiously through a brief but apparently awkward silence. He could be felt, indeed, as casting round for some conversational resource.

'I've been awa' up in they hills,' he said, 'to the great stanes some ancestor of yours set in a circle there. Your faither came on me gauping at it a', and I made a foo' o' mysel', speering if they were Stonehenge.' Andy glanced at Ianthe bright-eyed, aware that she had been somehow troubled, anxious to make her laugh —which, to her own relief, she did.

'Why not?' she said. 'It's the same general idea. You could call it a kind of mini Stonehenge, anyway—but a very late model.'

'We had a bit o' talk, Mr Felton and me. He's a kind man, and it's hard to say him no.'

'What did he want you to say yes to, Andy?'

'To moving into the big hoose. As his guest, he ca'd it.'

'And what did you reply?'

'That it's to think on.'

'So it is. But Toby won't be pleased if you don't agree.'

'Toby an' me—we're a' richt, Ianthe.'

This had been almost a snub—which was why, Ianthe realized, Andy had for the first time used her Christian name. He was very

'I can see the sort of decision it is, Andy. But please don't go on thinking about it for too long. From the moment Toby discovered who you are, there was bound to be something rather artificial and awkward about your being down there in the lodge.'

'There'll be that wherever I bide.'

'No—absolutely not!' Ianthe said this with a passion that surprised her. 'Not if we're any good at all—any of us.'

'Weel, at least I'll be up to tea. They've got that far wi' me.' Andy's smile came with this, and made him look particularly like his brother. 'But now I must gang my gate, Ianthe.'

'Are you sure you don't use a good many of those Scotch words just to tease and puzzle us, Andy? They sometimes sound rather like that.'

'I must be on my way.' Hearing himself say this made Andy laugh as if he had achieved a considerable stroke of wit, and Ianthe laughed too. Her aunt had said that Andy was 'easy' just as Toby was 'easy'—meaning good-natured in a companionable fashion. Whether he consented to move into Felton House or not, it should not be hard—Ianthe now thought—to build up a brotherly and sisterly relationship between them. It seemed a good moment on which to part with Andy for a time.

'See you don't get run over by my aunt,' she said. 'She'll be coming back from the village at any minute.'

Even as Ianthe said this, there came the sound of something giving notice of its approach on the drive. It wasn't a car, however, but a bicycle—ridden by Elma Loftus, who was gaily ringing its bell with one hand, and waving to them with the other.

'It's that Elma,' Andy said.

IX

'I've MANAGED TO SHAKE OFF MY BORING BROTHER this time,'
Elma said when they had exchanged greetings. 'He said he was
going out shooting pigeons with the vicar. I don't think a clergy-
man ought to shoot anything—do you, Ianthe?—except the
rapids of religious faith and doubt.'

'I'm sure Vivian is the better shot.' Ianthe offered this oblique
response a shade distantly. She disapproved of disparaging remarks about a brother made in his absence: much as one of Miss
Austen's heroines might have done, she judged it to be scarcely
well-bred. She also disapproved of smart things clearly said for
Andy's benefit which Andy would merely be puzzled by.

'But Vivian almost put off the slaughter in order to come over
with me. He has formed a tremendous admiration for Toby, it
seems, and has been getting advice from him about a career. I
believe they have been talking about the army. Andy, has Toby
been advising you about a career, too?'

'I canna' say that, Elma. But I've been having a crack aboot
it wi' Mr Felton.' Andy paused, and Ianthe was disconcerted at
seeing him direct upon Elma a considering glance of a sort she
herself certainly hadn't received from him. This was just as well,
since it was not properly a friendly glance and not at all decorous
either. Elma accepted it with an unoffended but neutral smile,
rather as if she'd had it before. 'There's a thocht,' Andy added
surprisingly, 'o' estate-management or the like.'

'Oh, that would be quite splendid!' This excess of enthusiasm
was quite in Elma's line, but it rendered a little odder what she
next said. 'It's a kind of office work, isn't it? You and Toby will
be able to compare notes about the height of your stools.'

They were now all three walking towards the house, with
Elma wheeling her bicycle. Andy seemed unimpressed by Elma's

Ianthe, had she been given to demonstrations of the sort, would have opened her eyes wide at it. It was very much her hope that Elma hadn't yet got Toby to commit himself on a permanent basis. Elma had gone boldly out on a limb in admitting him as a lover. But no doubt she had chosen her man well in this respect as in others. With any luck Toby was going to be a landowner and a person of consequence in the county; at the worst he would be a prosperous business man. But his main advantage, his strongest selling-point, was his decency. Elma was reckoning that, if the chips went down, Toby when called upon would make an honest woman of her.

Ianthe didn't much like the spectacle of her own mind working in this crude way, inwardly articulating such phrases. But they fitted the situation. Elma hadn't improved since her schooldays; on the contrary she had become a predatory female. It was unpleasant to feel this about an old companion, still entitled to one's intimacy. Ianthe wished she hadn't come to dislike Elma so much, and she wasn't even entirely clear why she did so. She wondered whether, if Elma did now ditch Toby, she would at once dislike her less. It was conceivable that she would dislike her even more, as one who had followed up design with treachery. Had something of the sort actually begun to happen? Ianthe recalled her suspicion, active for some little time, that Toby's affair with the doctor's daughter was running into difficulties. Was it even possible to suppose that, just as Elma was becoming a little tired of Toby, Andy had usefully turned up? If Elma was after Andy now she wasn't after somebody blind to her appeal. That single glance of Andy's minutes ago (which Ianthe discovered had annoyed her considerably, although it was no business of hers) had made that plain enough.

But all this was most unlikely, and there was something squalid even in imagining it. Andy probably knew about Toby and Elma, and Ianthe didn't believe he was the sort of person who would steal his brother's girl. Moreover that gibe about office stools had been distributed equally between the brothers, and was

119

a no evidence of Elma's switching interest from one to another. Perhaps Elma's roving thought had moved quite elsewhere. Perhaps she had an eye on some young man who would turn her into Lady This or That. Elma would really think it much nicer to marry into the nobility than into mere landed gentry—especially when that awkward question-mark still hung over Toby's succession to Felton. But this again seemed implausible. Ianthe doubted whether Elma had any great opportunity of frequenting the ultimate heights of upper-class society. And if her ambition was beginning to gratify itself in this way, why had she come cycling up the Felton drive, waving and ting-a-linging like mad?

Ianthe became aware that the bicycle was now being wheeled along by Andy, who appeared to have considered it proper that he should accompany the young women at least on part of their remaining way. She doubted whether his conception of squiring dames would have extended, however, to taking charge of Elma's machine wholly unprompted, and she supposed that there had been some manoeuvring here which had escaped her during all these cogitations. In fact Andy didn't seem altogether pleased with the job, and Ianthe had the odd thought that he perhaps supposed it to have been imposed on him as a consequence of his servile—or late servile—condition. However much he wasn't dull, such misconceptions were bound to be waiting for him from time to time round the corner of his consciousness, and they would always have to be reckoned with as part of the lurking awkwardness of the whole thing. But now Ianthe recalled the tone in which Andy had said 'It's that Elma' when the cyclist had appeared behind them on the drive. So perhaps what he wasn't too pleased with was Elma herself. This, she reflected, would be by no means incompatible with that glance. She understood that most young men (in this surely differing from most young women) were regularly capable of amorous designs upon members of the opposite sex whom they had no disposition to admire in more general terms. Perhaps this was applicable, at least in some degree, even to Toby's pursuit and conquest of Elma. She found herself rather hoping it had been like that.

'And how's the tennis coming on, Andy?' This question from Elma was the first thing to recall Ianthe's attention to the talk of her companions. But its tone told her at once that what she had missed had probably been several sallies of the same teasing sort on Elma's part. Elma might have been asking a small boy about his cricket after his first summer term at a prep school. It occurred to Ianthe, also, that there was something a little surprising about the use of Christian names established between these two. It was true that she had herself very promptly required the same thing of Andy—but as she and Andy were virtually brother and sister (a way of looking at the thing, this, that hadn't come to her before) that had been entirely natural. Elma Loftus was no more than a visitor. She must lately have been around, it seemed to Ianthe, quite a lot.

'Och, the tennis!' As he said this Andy, who was walking between the girls, turned his head towards Elma. 'It doesna', like some knacks, come by nature. But I'd say I'm getting haud o' it, an' yin day I'll wear Toby doon. He's already short-breathit after twa' sets.'

Ianthe believed, rightly or wrongly, that one of the knacks that come by nature had been invoked by a further look, this time not visible to her. She was about to tell herself, conscientiously, that Andrew Auld couldn't be a very nice young man, after all, when she was reduced to complete astonishment by Elma's rejoinder.

'Whether you win or lose, it must be much better, I suppose, than hoeing turnips.'

'I wadna' say that. They're twa' different things, an' it's an idle thocht that yin's better than tither.' Andy said this so calmly that for a moment Ianthe supposed he must have been unaffected by Elma's remark—a remark which the wretched girl had presumably thought of as belonging agreeably with the cut and thrust of what has been called the duel of sex. But it wasn't so. 'Here's your bike, Miss Loftus,' Ianthe heard Andy say—and saw that the machine had been steered firmly under Elma's nose. 'I'll be going back to the lodge to get changed a bit now.' Andy had turned to

121

Ianthe, and she saw that his face was still faintly flushed. 'But I'll be up for my tea, Ianthe lass, at half-four.'

'He's really rather sweet, don't you think?' Elma asked, as the two young women walked on towards the house together. She seemed not to resent Andy's somewhat abrupt departure, and spoke as if her slightly longer acquaintance with him made him more her property than Ianthe's.

'I think I shall like him very much. You oughtn't to have said that about hoeing turnips, Elma. It was downright rude.' Ianthe couldn't recall ever having directly rebuked Elma Loftus before, and she felt better at once for having done so now. But again Elma wasn't offended.

'Oh, that!' she said. 'I'm sure he didn't mean it, but he was turning just a little too oncoming—and not for the first time. You mayn't have noticed it, but there it was. Young men do so easily get ideas in their heads, and it's only kind to set them right as soon as may be. Otherwise a thing tends to run on, and eventually get out of hand. But perhaps it's not something you've experienced, Ianthe.' Elma paused on this, as if calculating whether a little to run on herself. 'I'm rather worried about Toby, as a matter of fact.'

'Why ever should you be worried about Toby?' As she asked this question Ianthe was almost prompted to halt and confront Elma squarely. But she thought better of this. It looked as if Elma were after a little drama, and it ought to be denied her. 'Why,' she amplified, 'should you have Toby particularly in your head?'

'Well, I suppose we all must in a way, with this thing having happened. It must be difficult for him.' Elma herself came to a standstill on this, apparently to satisfy herself of the satisfactory state of her bicycle's front tyre. 'And, of course, particularly difficult for your father. Suddenly, I mean, having two young men on his hands instead of one.'

'It's not like that at all!' Ianthe said this the more firmly and indignantly because aware that there might conceivably be some spark of truth in Elma's last remark. 'And you haven't said what you mean by being worried about Toby.'

'Well, you see, we've been seeing quite a lot of one another lately, and I've come to feel that just *that* may be getting a little out of hand. I'd hate Toby to begin imagining things.'

Ianthe felt like saying, 'For example, that you go to bed with him.' But this would be wildly imprudent. And she realized—almost with a feeling of surprise—that she had in fact no real evidence that Elma was Toby's mistress. It was simply a conviction that she still didn't doubt for a moment. But this was again a position in which it wasn't very nice to find herself. Ianthe, who valued having occasion for reasonable self-approval, felt that just at present she was experiencing bad luck in various ways.

'Do you mean,' she asked circumspectly, 'that Toby may be coming to believe you care for him more than you do?'

'It sounds horrid, Ianthe, baldly put like that. But yes, really. It has happened before—with other young men, that is.'

'Oh, dear! You mean you carry the burden of being a kind of *femme fatale.* I'm so sorry.'

'I shan't be able to think of you as a friend, Ianthe, if you say beastly things like that.'

Ianthe had to acknowledge to herself the justness of this. She was surprised that so acrid a remark had been drawn from her. But her first reaction to what Elma was trying to establish was of indignation unmingled with any other feeling. It would be stupid to quarrel with Elma, all the same.

'I don't suppose that *femmes fatales* can entirely help being that,' she said, a little disingenuously. 'It would be much less friendly if I'd said you must have been leading Toby on.'

'And then jilted him? That's just what I don't want anybody to think, and why I'm telling you this now. Toby has been a bit insistent about some things, as a matter of fact. But of course there's been nothing wrong.'

'Wrong?'

'You know perfectly well what I mean. And it isn't, of course, that I don't like Toby very much. He's your brother—or almost your brother—so I couldn't *not* like him, could I?' It was with the utmost assurance that Elma said this. 'But I do simply know I don't want to marry him—although I'll be terribly upset if it makes him too dreadfully unhappy. You know, these things—or perhaps you don't know yet—are so awfully *physical* in the last resort. And I just feel Toby and I wouldn't be in harmony together that way.'

The effect of all this on Ianthe—and particularly of that final outrage—cannot have been at all what Elma reckoned on. Ianthe was finally convinced that the relationship of Elma and Toby had indeed been as intimate as it could be, and for the moment at least she didn't care a fig about that; it was as unimportant as would have been the discovery that Toby had been involved in some transitory sexual escapade in Paris or Vienna. What she was conscious of was enormous relief; indeed, in an obscure fashion it was of joy. The situation she had been entertaining as a hypothesis no time ago was now verifying itself as fact. Elma *was* ditching Toby. What she was hard at work on now—what, presumably, she had come tagging over to Felton for—was to lend some decent colouring to the thing. Probably she also wanted to ensure that her dismissed lover *wouldn't tell*. And here, Ianthe saw, Elma was batting on a hopeful pitch. Toby, even if he had to accept its becoming public knowledge that he had been turned down by the doctor's daughter, would be as secret as the grave about this having happened only after he had possessed her—for some time and quite a lot. He would tell nobody—except conceivably his brother Andy, who Ianthe had already guessed might be in the secret of the liaison. So Elma could go safely off and fix herself up with that young nobleman. Alternatively, and if the young nobleman hadn't yet been brought quite under starter's orders, she could fill in time with a brisk amour with Andy. Her recent brush with him, including that nasty crack about hoeing turnips, was perhaps a characteristic prelude to such episodes. And in the new state of affairs Andy mightn't feel that he was being particularly disloyal to his brother.

But about much of this Ianthe felt that she just wouldn't know. She was lacking in experience about such things, apart from the experience—almost certainly unreliable—that one gains second-hand from books. (Elma had a considerable knack of bringing this home to her in casual asides.) But she glimpsed the strange possibility of her viewing Elma's hypothetical subjugating of Andy with as much dismay as she was now realizing, with satisfaction, that the Toby and Elma thing was all over—although it would no doubt have a final phase of miserable shuffling. She had come home full of curiosity about Andrew Auld. But she was finding that she had also come home to some unexpected perplexities as well.

This afternoon's tea-time occasion was much like that already described, except that Ianthe was back at Felton and that in place of the graceless Vivian Loftus another and entirely polished neighbour had turned up in the person of Colonel Motley. In speaking to Ianthe Toby was accustomed to refer to Colonel Motley as 'Aunt Grace's beau', and to reiterate—to the effect of a rather tedious joke—a conviction that Colonel Motley wore stays. He had read one or two old-fashioned novels in which satirical play was made with this idea when middle-aged lovers were in question, and he was not put off by Ianthe's either saying that he would not recognize a pair of stays if he saw them or pointing out that the colonel was by nature of so spare a figure that what he stood in need of was a little padding out. It was only metaphorically that one could call him strait-laced.

Colonel Motley was certainly very correct. It was Mrs Warlow who attracted him to Felton, but although he talked to her quite a lot he always talked just a little more to his host, with whom he was supposed to have in common various lively interests as a landowner, a magistrate, and a local grandee in a general way. He was talking to him now—but talking about Andy, whose acquaintance he had just been cultivating in an agreeably low-keyed and leisured manner.

'Nice young chap,' he said to Howard Felton as they strolled the length of the terrace. 'Looks you straight in the eye. Clean-run effect. But what an astonishing thing.'

'Yes, indeed, Motley. It has been quite a bolt from the blue.' Howard paused to examine this expression, and saw that it wasn't entirely right. 'As a momentary shock, that is. But one knew in ten minutes that he was a decent lad. And Toby, in particular, had a sound instinct about him at once.'

'And your sister, too, I gather.' The colonel commonly referred to Grace Warlow in this way. He seemed to feel that he was entitled to go a little beyond 'Mrs Warlow', but that 'Grace' wouldn't do since he and Howard Felton stuck conservatively to surnames. 'The young man spoke of her very pleasantly. So I take it they get on.'

'Excellently, I'm glad to say. Although at first Grace was a little doubtful about it all—as I suspect my brother over there in Oxford still is. But she has come round to feeling that we ought to adopt the boy.' Howard paused for a moment, as if surprised to have heard himself using this expression. 'Purely in a manner of speaking, that is.'

'Quite so, quite so.'

'Grace says that Andy—we call him Andy rather than Andrew, you know—may shake us up a bit. I don't know what she can mean by that.'

'One of her delightful jokes, Felton.' For a moment Colonel Motley had appeared puzzled. Probably the idea of being shaken up had no great appeal for him. Ianthe declared that she had once heard him utter a private 'amen' when the vicar had reached that point in the prayer book in which it is desired that everything be 'ordered and settled' by the high court of parliament as briskly as possible. 'Does the young man have any thought of a career?'

'We have a notion of hitching him on to Tarling. Grace's idea, again.'

'And a capital one, without a doubt.' The colonel was invariably enthusiastic about Mrs Warlow's ideas. 'Just the berth for him—and very handsome of you, my dear Felton, if it's not impertinent to say so. But old chums—eh?'

This was a great advance in intimacy on Colonel Motley's part. 'Old friends' would have been colourless. 'Old chums' made it

unaccountable that they were not Howard and Charles to one
another, after all. (The colonel had probably decided on a decla-
ration to Mrs Warlow on his next visit, although not on this one.)

'It should be very nice for Toby,' Howard said comfortably.
'Having his brother as a companion when he's down here at
Felton. Teach him to take out a gun and flog a stream and so forth.
I was remarking only the other day that Andy seems to be learn-
ing quite a lot from Toby already.'

'Two-way process, perhaps.' Colonel Motley seemed startled
at having arrived at, let alone enunciated, this idea. 'And very
jolly for you having young people around,' he added vaguely.
'Look at them now.'

The two men had turned and paused at the end of the terrace.
At its other end the rest of the company was on view as a compact
group. The brothers were perched side by side on a broad balustrade: Toby idly kicking his heels, and Andy cross-legged with his
feet tucked under him. Sunlight and a faint breeze were at play
in their fair hair. They were identically dressed—not by design,
but in the classless pale bleached blue of their generation—so that
they showed like a single figure freakishly duplicated by some
optical device. Each was flanked by a plate recklessly piled with
sandwiches and cake. Facing them stood the two girls, holding
tea-cups and making casual talk. Mrs Warlow, having despatched
her own tea, was sitting on a deck-chair some yards away with her
embroidery, her scissors glinting in the light as she snipped a
thread.

'Women standing and men sitting down,' Colonel Motley
said, and gave an unexpected laugh. 'All this modern informality
carries a certain charm, wouldn't you say? Kept within bounds,
of course.'

'Yes, indeed, Motley. We were a stuffy crowd—your generation and mine, I mean. Missed a lot.'

'Too late to begin again now—at least as youngsters still.' The
colonel's glance was on Mrs Warlow as he produced this sage
reflection. 'Not that one's ever past it, they say: love, and that sort
of thing.'

127

'I suppose not.' Howard Felton was too well-bred to have betrayed astonishment before his companion's remarkable speech. It didn't seem to him at all the drill. But he suddenly remembered a joke—it was surely a joke—that Ianthe and Toby had once or twice ventured on about Motley's admiration for his sister. Could there be anything in it? It would be a most disturbing thing.

'That girl Elma Loftus,' Colonel Motley said—clearly with the intention of a little changing ground. 'Might she be rather interested in your young man?'

'In Toby? I think I recall Grace entertaining that notion. But there's nothing in it at all. In fact Toby won't go after girls quite in the way I'd wish.' Howard seemed not unconscious that he had said something rather out of turn himself. 'Elma is a most delightful girl, but I fear her interest in Felton is largely in the house. Knows an amazing amount about it—through the centuries, and from an architectural and artistic point of view. We walked through the place together half-an-hour ago. There's this business of redecorating the saloon, you know. It was the first thing she asked about when she arrived, so we went and had a look together. Those soft Italian pinks and blues on the ceiling can be renewed just as they were. But it's a question about the gold-leaf. Expensive, of course, and too much of it isn't in a modern taste. She's on strong ground there, with a great deal of feeling for all that sort of thing.'

'Is that so?' The colonel's tone was respectful—but sounded a hint of misgiving, all the same. 'A wholesome-looking girl, and lively, don't you think? Meet a fellow half-way. Artistic, no doubt —but not one of the wishy-washy aesthetic crowd.' (Just so, a century before, might an honest English gentleman have said something like, 'No question of the lungs being tainted'.) 'Figure with a good broad base to it, too. No trouble when child-bearing comes along.' These remarks—which again Howard Felton would scarcely have expected—appeared to lead Colonel Motley to a train of thought best accomplished in silence. So there was a substantial pause in the conversation before he spoke again. 'By the way, Felton, how are those Camberley Hybrids of yours doing? They look well enough at the trough.'

This transition, if scarcely elegant, was to a subject in which both gentlemen were interested. They talked pigs and pig-breeding for the rest of their walk along the terrace.

X

THE FOUR YOUNG PEOPLE had been talking about nothing very much, and in fact the easy informality of their pose, so agreeable to Colonel Motley's eye, belied a certain constraint alien to their years. The two promenading elders remained unaware of this as they came up, since the colonel immediately shifted his attention from porcine matters to Mrs Warlow, and his host had fallen into the abstraction of a man who has been given food for fresh thought. Mrs Warlow herself, although engaged upon the tip of a rose-leaf with care, had a clearer view of the situation. All four of these children—she told herself—were in one degree or another of a troubled mind. Ianthe was concerned—for some reason distinctly more concerned than she had been only a few hours earlier in the Fiat—about Toby's relations with Elma. Elma herself exhibited a false vivacity, as if improvising an air of light amusement while inwardly calculating just when to do what. Toby was sufficiently aware of this to be uneasy in a way quite foreign to his character; in fact he was being almost sulky and almost aggressive. Andy, who had normally to put in a good deal of time sorting out the mysteries surrounding him, had an enhanced appearance of wary regard and of what he would call 'biding a wee'. Mrs Warlow found herself increasingly interested in Andy, and not merely because he was proving so disposed to sit at her feet. It seemed to her that the business of being identical could be overdone. What is stronger in determining action than the code of conduct to which one has been brought up? There was no reason to suppose that either brother had the advantage over the other here, morally regarded. The Aulds had also been God's creatures. Indeed, the Aulds might be a better lot than the Feltons were. Or *vice versa.* She hadn't the information on which to judge. But it was assured that Aulds and Feltons as they grew up gath-

ered to themselves all sorts of standards and assumptions peculiar
to themselves and their class, and this meant that Toby and Andy
might react quite differently to the same given situation. Mrs
Warlow found this thought encouraging. It would be rather dull
if Andy were to prove to be just Toby over again—more and
more just Toby as the business of spoons and forks and outlandish
Scotticisms faded out.

It followed from this that in the present situation Andy held
a certain measure of advantage over his brother simply on account
of the attractiveness of the lurkingly unpredictable. One knew
what Toby would do: almost in detail one knew it, let alone that
it would be honourable and tolerably decent. About Andy one
knew intriguingly less.

Mrs Warlow, feeling this, wondered whether the feeling was
culpably frivolous. She wondered too, and with a momentary
alarm, whether it might become Ianthe's feeling also. *That,* she
told herself, might be decidedly tricky; tricky for the truth of the
Felton situation as she saw it. Never venture, however, and you'll
never win.

Mrs Warlow was diverted from these speculations—and from
further pursuing that curious theory of a wholesome shake-up in
which Andrew Auld held so prominent a place—by the necessity
of making conversation with Colonel Motley. Colonel Motley
had in fact no place in any plan she could conceivably form, and
she had to debate with herself whether this should in some way
be intimated to him before she found herself listening to a proposal of marriage. On the whole she thought better not—judging
that what her grandmother would have called 'true delicacy'
would be better served by letting the colonel go ahead in his own
good time and explaining herself to him then. But the problem
a little vexed her, and it was her present feeling that she would
be glad when this tea-party broke up and she could retire to her
studio and abandon embroidery in favour of more taxing professional work.

In fact the party, if it was to be called that, did end rather
abruptly with Toby declaring (in an unusually loud voice) that the

pull up to the village was a filthy sweat, and that he was going to chuck Elma's bike in the back of his car and drive her home. As Elma had made no move to leave (nor Colonel Motley either) this might have been regarded as uncivilly premature. But Toby forced home his point by jumping down from the balustrade on which he had been sitting and propelling Elma forward with what was at once an ostentatious and a half-hearted smack on her backside.

Ianthe, although she had no notion that this was a premeditated symbolic gesture designed to declare to the world the entire respectability of Toby's future plans for Elma, guessed enough to realize that—in a comic fashion, indeed—her brother had an unwelcome surprise ahead of him. In fact Elma was at work on this instantly, allowing herself to register restrained maidenly distaste upon the receipt of the mild assault. Everybody had witnessed it—even Ianthe's father, although he was still in a state of some abstraction. But at least Toby carried his proposal; there were farewells; the bicycle was loaded up; in no time the Aston Martin was diminishing down the drive.

You turned right for Felton Canonicorum; left, and then left again round the park, to gain the narrow bumpy road running up to the downs. Toby turned left—which was abundantly what Elma expected him to do. He swung the wheel, flicked the gear-lever as he double-declutched, accelerated, braked, all with an extra touch of precision which told of his feeling in a masterful mood. Soon he might be playing the sexual rôle that went with this: experimenting in what he took to be an outrageous way, shoving her around according to some idiotic book he'd been reading, or following the salacious counsel of an undesirable chance acquaintance. That was how she imagined his more extravagant notions coming to him, for she doubted if he simply thought them up. And more probably he'd be making ordinary quick blundering love, which was what was natural to him; or he'd be doing that first, and then a little later putting conscientious artistry and timing into what he understood she liked best.

When he wasn't showing off with his *machismo* stuff Toby was really terribly nice. It was what made him rather boring. It was also, somehow, what was going to lend extra amusement to the end of things today.

They parked the car and got out. Toby took Elma in his arms and kissed her—with a certain gravity, and with his hands decorously behind her shoulders, rather in the manner of a young man venturing on such an action for the first time. It amused Elma to realize that Toby felt some occasion of unusual seriousness to be before them. If it was going to be what she now guessed she would be very amused indeed. They separated and walked on, innocently hand in hand.

It was Toby who had found what he called their lair. (Elma, with what was intended as a kind of mock-vulgarity, referred to it as the love nest.) It was a hollow in the turf high up on the crest of the down, and not much bigger than a large hammock. Lying in it, you were quite invisible, but you had only to get on your knees to command every inch of ground for a quarter of a mile around. So apt was it for the purposes now on hand that Toby never approached it without fearing that other lovers might recently have discovered it to be so, and have left some displeasing testimony to the fact lying about. But this hadn't happened yet. If there was ever a faint imprint still left on the grass it was their own.

'Oh, what *fun!*' Elma exclaimed (as she commonly did) when they had both tumbled into the lair. '*Darling!*' she whispered, and sank to her knees. '*Darling!*' She stretched out her legs and in a moment was lying on her back. Toby knelt beside her, and felt that he had never known Elma so swiftly roused. She was flushed and her eyes were bright. Her lips were moist and would be hot. It came into his head (and it would be a wonderful thing to say to her later) that her breasts were moving as if somebody was at work on them with a bicycle pump. He put a hand under her skimpy shirt-like upper garment, flicked expertly at a button on her bra, and let his fingers work. '*Darling!*' Elma said.

At this point—and it was no doubt greatly to his credit—Toby remembered that things were not going at all according to plan. He had brought Elma up here not for fornication—or at least not immediately for that—but for the purpose of telling her they were going to be married. He felt full of delicacy about this fulfilling of his recent resolve. He even felt magnanimous about thus presenting himself as it were with a wedding-ring in his hand. His feelings about a proposal of marriage were probably not very remote from Colonel Motley's; he judged it to be a solemn thing, and in at least momentary disjunction from carnal desire. It ought at any rate to be the prelude rather than the sequel to an act of love.

'Elma,' he said, sitting up, 'I've been thinking we ought to have rather a talk.'

'A talk, darling? How funny you are!'

'A serious talk. About what we mean to each other, and ought to do.'

'Yes, of course. But afterwards, darling.' Elma had arched her back, the more readily to wriggle herself out of her tights. Watching her, Toby was suddenly conscious of being himself more urgently excited than he had been for a long time. Disastrous waste was imminent. His hands went to a button of his own, and then to a zip. Within what seemed a single gasping-time they were making love.

'I think we ought to get married at once,' Toby said half-an-hour later. As he spoke he became aware that, although back in his trousers, he hadn't done up that zip again, and this he now did in some confusion. He was aware that his hair was wet, and that he was still faintly panting, and that it would really be quite pleasant to drop off to sleep. Elma, on the other hand, could have stepped straight into a drawing-room. This made him feel, rather absurdly, at a disadvantage as a suitor. He was also conscious of having begun wrong. He had meant to say, 'Elma, darling, will you marry me?' which would have been more gracious than implying that the thing had to happen sooner or later, anyway. He didn't suppose that Elma would be particular. For some reason he

had never uttered the words 'marry' or 'married' or 'marriage' to
her before—or for that matter 'wife' or 'husband' or anything of
the sort—and it must obviously make quite pleasant hearing now.

'*Married*, darling?' Elma, who was sitting on the flailed and
flattened grass close to Toby's head, glanced down at him with
every appearance of utter astonishment. 'Why, you funny boy!'
Very gently, she lifted a lock of Toby's sweaty hair and twisted
it round a finger before letting it go again. 'I think that was the
last time,' she said. 'So it's nice that it was rather nice.'

'What do you mean—the last time?' Toby had sat bolt upright
and was staring at Elma in stupefaction.

'It has been a boy and girl affair, Toby—nothing more.' Elma
had contrived to assume a kind of aunt-like tone, wholly inappro-
priate from a girl to a boy. 'And now we must both be more
serious. I'm sure you will marry, and perhaps I shall. But we must
both marry suitably, you know.'

'Suitably? For Christ's sake—'

'Now, don't, Toby, get all excited. You must marry somebody with property, for a start. It's quite likely, you know, that
Felton may go to that horrid Oxford don—your Uncle Hugh.'

'You're mad.' Toby was now looking at Elma with horror.
'I'm going to be absolutely independent, whatever happens to
Felton.'

'And as for me, darling, I can only marry a man I love.'

'Go on,' Toby said. He had turned very white.

'Some women are like that—and I've discovered myself to be
one of them. I must have a husband I love, and who loves me.'
Elma delivered herself of this with downcast eyes and a charming
simplicity. 'And it hasn't been like that with us—has it, darling?
It has been oh, *such* fun! It's wonderful that one is *allowed* such
fun nowadays. Just think of our stuffy parents and grandparents,
Toby. But fun is one thing and marriage is another. *Love* is another thing, my poor darling. So we must stop, and just be ever
such friends.'

Toby was now on his feet, with Elma still sitting composedly
on the grass. He blundered around looking for his shoes, which

he'd had to take off in order to take off his trousers. The image of himself scrambling out of his clothes in order to fall naked upon Elma Loftus rose up and revolted him. He knew this was extravagant and silly. But his vanity was outraged. His pride was deeply wounded. He thought of having to tell Andy about this débâcle and of what a fool he'd feel. But at the same time he was conscious of an almost more shocking sense of relief like a small spark deep inside him. Elma had been tumbling out stuff that he knew to be quite insincere, but at the heart of that too there had been an answering spark of truth. He had been infatuated with Elma: the very smell of her, and all that. But love was something different—and something he didn't know about. He wondered whether he had ever loved anybody. He rather thought that, in an odd sexless way, he was beginning to love Andy. He couldn't think of anybody else.

'And now there are just one or two things to make sure of,' Elma was saying. She paused, as if for a moment's intense calculation. 'For one thing, we must neither of us ever tell. Don't you think?'

'What do you mean—tell?' As Toby asked this question, he judged it a very stupid one.

'We must never tell *anybody* that we have been lovers. Or play-fellows, really.' Here came the charming simplicity again. 'Do you agree? Will you promise?'

'I don't know. I can't say.' Toby was still white, and now grim as well. 'If I did get married, I might have to tell my wife in order to feel honest with her. So I can't promise.'

'But apart from that you can? I can.'

'Yes, of course—apart from that. What the hell do you take me for?'

'It's a binding promise—on your honour as a gentleman?'

'Jesus Christ, Elma, don't talk such muck.' Toby was suddenly furious. 'Ask your question another way. Say "Will you keep your bloody mouth shut?"'

'I think that's horrid, Toby.' Elma was now pale too. 'But very well. Will you keep your bloody mouth shut?'

'Yes—and I repeat I can't imagine what you think of me. I suppose it's that I'll boast about you in a club or a pub. It's likely, isn't it?' Toby pulled himself up short, for the contempt in these last words had horrified him. 'I beg your pardon,' he said. 'That was filthy, and I apologize. But I ought to tell you there is one other exception already. Andy knows about us.'

'Andy knows?' This clearly came as a shock to Elma. But in a moment she rallied. 'Oh, Andy,' she said strangely, 'I can manage him.'

Toby got home in good time to change into decent clothes for dinner. Nevertheless he had been absent for much longer than his professed mission required. To anybody curious about this he could of course say that he'd got talking to Elma's parents and stayed to drinks. But he didn't like lying at any time, and he certainly wasn't going to like any more lying about Elma. Fortunately there was nobody around as he put his car away. Or rather —he suddenly saw—there was nobody in the stable yard except Andy. Andy, cross-legged as before, was sitting on top of a platform of baled hay, and looked rather like an inquisitorial heathen divinity. He had obviously been waiting for Toby's arrival.

'Was that a' richt?' Andy called down from his perch. 'Did it go fine?' Andy had clearly taken a good guess at what had been the occasion of his brother's absence. His tone was cheerful, but to Toby's irritated sense it held also a distinctly satirical note.

'Shut up,' Toby said.

'Dear sake! Was the wee mannie no' in form? Ye canna' aye be having sex, ye ken, without ups an' doons as weel as ins and outs.'

'Get to hell!' With this exclamation Toby turned away, being in no disposition for coarse pleasantries. 'I've had enough of your stite, Andrew Auld.' In their occasional altercations—which did happen—Toby had been finding it useful to exhibit a command of his brother's own barbaric vocabulary. But this time Andy didn't respond except with swift action. He took a good seven-foot jump from his perch and planted himself in Toby's path.

'Tell me what,' he said soberly.

'All right.' Toby realized that he wanted to confide in Andy
—and also that there was something upon which he must treat
with him. 'But I'm going to have a bath. Come inside.'

So they went up to Toby's quarters—much as they had done
on the occasion of their first meeting—and Toby had his bath.
Andy, who seemed to accept these ablutions as being in some
degree of a solemn ritual character, leant against the bathroom
wall and for a time watched him in silence but with a fleeting grin.

'Was it a row?' he then asked.

'It was a bust-up. *Schluss!*'

'What's that? Can ye no' talk English?'

'Finish.' Toby had smiled dimly through the steam at this
echoing of a frequent demand of his own. 'She talked about
. . . well, she talked about love.'

'*Love?* Guid sakes! What should she haver aboot that for?'

'She said one oughtn't to get married without it.'

'You mean you've been getting atween that lassie's legs and
then proposing to her?'

'I don't like your language.' Toby got to his feet and grabbed
his towel. Andy's gross conjecture had been so near the literal
truth that it infuriated him. But he at once thought better of this
attitude. 'Sorry,' he said. 'I *do* like your language. It fits the whole
beastly thing. But I did tell you that Elma and I were likely to get
married. I told you after that stupid business in the pub.'

'An' it's that she now says it's no' on?'

'Yes, it's that.'

'Then you're a lucky bugger, Tobias Felton.'

Toby's reply to this was inarticulate, and he strode back into
his bedroom with his feet still making wet patches as he walked.
When Andy followed him his head was already emerging from
a clean shirt.

'It would be shabby,' he said, 'if I were to feel that.'

'Och, Toby, dinna' talk your fine folk's ba's. You're a lucky
wean, I say. An' do you think she's been on wi' anither afore she's
been off wi' the auld?'

138

'I don't care a damn.'

'Or at least she may hae cast an e'e somewhere?'

'She may have cast it at you, perhaps.' Toby, pulling on a sock, became rigid on one foot, staring at his brother. 'I meant that as a silly crack. But perhaps it's true.'

'Mebby. I wadna' ken.' Andy said this very coolly. 'Wha's to tell how a lass is thinking o' him?' Andy paused, and appeared to take note of the consternation on his brother's face. 'Don't be daft, Toby. It's no' a likely thing ava. Yon lass is for the main chance. An' I'm no' that, God save us.'

'It might be just for kicks. The very fact that we're as like as—'

'Twa peas in a pod? Stop blethering, Toby. It's a' nonsense, that. But if it were true, you'd be best being grateful to me for playing yeldrick to you.'

'I don't know what you're talking about. You might sometimes be a bloody Hottentot.'

'The yeldrick's what you ca' the yellowhammer. An' it limps awa' as a decoy to save its wee nest. I might think o' you as my wee nest, Toby.'

'I think you're talking nonsense.'

'It's no' unlikely. I'm just for saying I'd no' be frichted o' Elma mysel. I'd no' be talking kirk-bells tae her. I could manage her fine.'

This last phrase startled Toby. He had heard something like it not very long before. It also reminded him of something it was now important to say.

'Listen, Andy. I've told you about this balls-up today because you knew about Elma and me already. Nobody else knows.'

'Perhaps there are some that think it.'

'Oh, I'm sure not. We've been frightfully careful. But the point is that nobody else is to know *now*. I promised Elma that. So you will keep the secret, won't you?'

'I'm no' likely, Toby, to gang aboot telling it to the corbies and the winds. Or even to lang-lost brithers after a bit o' fliting and fighting in a public.'

139

'Then that's all right.' Toby slipped on a jacket and was ready for dinner. But then he saw that it wasn't entirely all right, after all. 'You do promise, don't you, Andy? Never to tell anybody about Elma and me?'

'No.'

'But you've just—'

'No, I do not. I don't make promises of that kind.' There were occasions upon which, without conjuration, Andrew Auld 'talked English' in a rather devastating way. 'I might have good reason to tell somebody about Elma and you—bloody daft and trivial as it all seems to be. You have to trust me, Toby; not tie me up or give me orders.'

'Yes, of course. I'm sorry.' Toby found himself much abashed. 'As a matter of fact, there's nobody except Ianthe I'd trust as much as I trust you.'

'But Ianthe's no' to hae word aboot it either?' Andy was relaxed again.

'No—because of what I've promised. But it's not a thing one takes to a girl like Ianthe anyway.'

Andy was silent for a moment. The code underlying this was perhaps not sympathetic to him.

'I must awa' to my tea,' he then said. 'I'll be unco late for it. They Miss Kinches will be fair fashed wi' me.'

'Damn your tea, and damn the Kinches.' They were now outside Toby's bedroom, and in the broad corridor. Toby crossed it and flung open a door. 'This is to be your room,' he said, 'and the one at the end too. When the hell are you moving in?'

'Morie-morning, Toby.'

'Really?' For the first time for some hours, Toby felt that something cheerful had happened. 'Tomorrow?'

'I've had my orders frae your auntie. So that's it.'

'But you said you wouldn't be made a monkey of.' Toby was much rejoiced that he could thus poke fun at his brother.

'I was a wee bit to seek then, Toby. But I like your folk. I dinna care if I'm a monkey on a stick.'

'I'll liberate a bottle of champagne from the cellar in the

morning. And we'll drink it at midnight.'

'An' make wee cuts in our hauns, an' mingle bluid, an' be brithers twice over.' Andy was presumably producing this fancy from juvenile reading of a popular character, conceivably connected with Red Indian braves. His next words, however, were soberly offered. 'I'll be in here the morrow, then, and drinking your faither's champagne if you have a mind to it. But there's yin promise I can make to you, Toby laddie. I'll be out again if the day comes on which there's a ca' for it.'

'Which will probably be when you marry the principal heiress in the county.' Toby was so satisfied with this definitive stroke in acquiring a brother that he was prepared to talk any nonsense.

'It's yoursel' had better be thinking o' that, perhaps.'

Toby was again struck as by an echo of something he had already heard. But the impression was momentary. He had glanced at his watch and seen that he had time to accompany his brother for a little way down the drive. This happened for the most part in companionable silence. He found himself wondering what was meant by 'tea' at such an hour. It was a 'high tea' or a 'hot tea', he supposed, according to the region in which it was purveyed; and it meant sausages or kippers or even 'baked beans' on toast. His aunt's cook, he felt comfortably, would do better for Andy than that.

But the trials of the day proved not quite over. Dinner at the big house, although remote from the humble repasts of the folk, was on this occasion a slightly uncomfortable affair. Satisfaction was expressed at Andy's decision, but Toby wondered whether his father, at least, was quite easy about it. He had acted generously and impulsively—which was something he had done once before. He had decided that Andy must be regarded as in the same boat as his adopted son, which was fair enough since they had been quite literally that when a few weeks old. But if Andy was in the same boat as him the corresponding proposition was equally true: he was in the same boat as Andy. In fact Howard Felton's original acquisition had perplexingly doubled itself. If—

141

Toby thought—it was firmly decided that no line was to be drawn between Andy and himself, then that Gordian knot was in a sense cut. But society had already drawn a line by directing the two of them along divergent paths from infancy. And sentiment and long association had drawn another. It would be very odd if either Howard Felton or his daughter or even his sister straightway fell to feeling about Andy as they had for long felt about him. But it might happen. In an unconscious and intermittent way something of the sort might have happened already.

Toby wondered whether such thoughts were going through the heads of the three people with whom he was at table. He didn't like the notion of being part of a conundrum. Aunt Grace was being rather quiet, just as her brother was. But Aunt Grace had a lot to think about in a simple practical way. On her would fall the main burden—it might be put—of teaching Andy how to eat asparagus, or how to get up and open a door without fuss. It would have been Toby's own impulse to take rather an airy view of such matters, and then—he acknowledged to himself—become cross and impatient when difficulties arose. Ianthe wasn't saying much either. He realized—with mixed feelings—that he was much in Ianthe's good books. Her steady gaze when she looked up at him across the table was somehow signalling approval and support. This must be because, having decided to like Andy, she liked his own fair success in coping with Andy so far. His mixed feelings arose from the fact that her attitude showed she didn't even faintly suspect what had been going on between him and Elma. He was quite sure that of that Ianthe would take a very poor view. He was coming, with what he recognized as a rather shameful rapidity, to take a poor view of it himself. It had been the most awful humbug on his part to tell Andy that to the sort of girl that Ianthe was one didn't speak of a thing like that. The truth was that if the circumstances had been such that he had been obliged to tell her he would simply have been unbearably ashamed. This was so even although in the past he had told her almost everything that had ever happened to him. There had been happenings (he believed in a slightly self-dramatizing way) that he'd simply never have got through without her. Aunt Grace, a late arrival he'd never much bothered his head about, although he acknowledged her to be a formidable woman. He had a proper affection for Howard Felton, but often felt subtly distanced from him: more rather than less aware, as the years passed, that currents undersea had picked his true father's bones in whispers. But Ianthe was at the centre of things, as the truest of sisters might be.

Toby found that he had himself neglected to open a door. Mrs Warlow and her niece were leaving the dining-room, its owner having apparently indicated that this was to be so. Just occasionally Howard took it into his head that even on purely domestic evenings this antique convention was to be observed. The two males of the household (father and son) were to be tête à tête for a short space over their wine. So Howard now passed the port to Toby.

Toby disliked port, and never drank it. Edgy after the day's disaster, he felt this forgetfulness on his father's part to be a matter less of mere vagueness than of disregard. He supposed he ought to pour himself port, all the same. But there was also claret on the table—this, too, decanted—and it was what he had been drinking during the meal. He decided to stay with the claret, and made a long arm for the jug. Howard showed no awareness of the asserting of this small difference between them. When he spoke, it was about what obviously preoccupied him for the moment.

'Yes,' he said, 'I'm very pleased about your brother. About his moving in, I mean. He will be much more comfortable here than with those old women. And it's the proper thing, too, as your aunt insists.'

'As I insist as well.'

'Exactly, my dear boy.' Howard seemed to find this quite in order. 'And it's particularly satisfactory that it should be tomorrow.'

This puzzled Toby for a moment, and he wondered whether his father believed that Tuesday was a lucky day in the week. Then he remembered what was going to happen on Friday. His aunt had told him that Mercia Felton had rung up that morning and arranged that Hugh and she, together with a couple of young guests, would come over and lunch at Felton on that day. Toby had also picked up the fact that this visit, although it had for some reason been much delayed, had its origin in the notion that Andy was in some sense to be inspected and passed upon by the Oxford Feltons. Toby had taken a dark view of this notion, and he now saw that his father really did so too. Howard Felton lived to some extent in awe of Hugh, and was known always to consult him on family matters. At the same time he was fidgety under this reliance upon the judgement of a younger brother, and concerned to assert his independence from time to time. This was what he was after now. When the Hugh Feltons did arrive, a big step in determining Andy's standing with the family would already have been taken. This train of thought led of course to the conclusion that the Warden had already shown himself to be—at least tentatively—anti-Andy. But Toby had expected that, and wasn't much perturbed by it. And he did have an intuitive sense that he might find Hugh Felton to be his own friend one day.

'At least we have plenty of room,' Howard went on amiably. 'Although I have told Andy that he will have to share a bathroom with you.'

'We've done that already.' Toby had a momentary memory of his brother—comfortingly calm, bracingly sardonic—leaning against the tiles and grinning at him in his tub. 'And Aunt Grace is fixing him up with a den of his own at the end of the wing. We shan't be breathing down one another's neck.'

'Exactly. It will do splendidly for a time. But have you ever thought about the Mill House?'

'Sir?'

It was very rarely indeed that Toby addressed his foster-father in this highly archaic fashion. But Howard himself, who had no doubt said 'Sir' to his own father several times in the day, was unaware that he had alerted his adoptive son in an uncommon degree.

'It has just occurred to me that—later on, you know—it might

144

suit the two of you very well. Again, of course, just for a time. Marriage, and so forth, would alter things a lot. Do finish the port.'

Toby finished the claret—and rather at a gulp. It was quite clear to him that the owner of Felton House (and of the Mill House too) was unconscious of having said anything very much. But then that was how Howard's mind regularly worked. It was the mind of a man who quite frequently didn't at all know where he was going. It had been like that, perhaps, when it reacted as it did to the *Cornucopia* disaster long ago.

'Marriage?' Toby said.

'It might come very soon, I suppose. Men do seem to marry much earlier nowadays—which means it has to be with girls not much younger than themselves. It has its disadvantages, of course. What's behind all those divorces one reads of is marrying in haste, likely enough. But I'm in favour of it, on the whole.' Howard Felton was fond of declaring himself to be in favour of things. 'So if you and Andy fixed yourselves up next week I'd be entirely delighted. Still, as it's not likely to happen quite like that, the Mill House is worth giving a thought to. Perhaps we'd better get back to the drawing-room.'

Toby got to his feet with very odd feelings—some of which he recognized as not much to his credit. In a sense which he found it difficult to identify, Andy *was* breathing down his neck. But at least it was something that Andy didn't intend to do. Andy would never consent in the slightest degree to stepping into his shoes. But then nobody had a thought that way. Perhaps the situation would best be expressed by saying that Howard Felton's mind was drifting towards the assumption that the brothers had one pair of shoes between them. And that it was a borrowed pair, at that.

Howard had paused with his hand on the knob of the dining-room door, and the air of a man into whose recollection some point of minor interest has come.

'Talking of marriage,' he said, 'do you know that your aunt has had rather an odd idea in her head? It's about Elma Loftus.'

145

'About Elma?' As he repeated the name, Toby saw how much it was going to be a danger signal for some time.

'About Elma and yourself being interested in one another. Nothing in it, I suppose?'

'I don't think anything is going to happen between Elma and me.' Toby saw, too, that as often as Elma was mentioned in the future it would be quite probable that he should have to choose an equivocal form of words in anything he said about her. When he had made her that promise of secrecy he had been thinking crudely in terms of a boastful communicativeness: something he could be quite sure he'd never be prompted to. But what about direct questions? What his father had just asked might well have been so phrased as to require a blank lie as answer. The thought of this made Toby very uncomfortable indeed.

'Quite, quite—and I can't think what has brought it back into my head again.' Howard considered for a moment. 'But—by Jove!—yes. This afternoon at tea. Do you remember that you gave her a pat on the rump? I thought it a little odd—I mean if there was no understanding between you. I'm sure she's not the kind of girl for horseplay of any kind.'

'I'm sorry. No doubt it was stupid—just bad manners.' As Toby was obliged to say this about what, in the simplicity of his heart, he had regarded as preliminary to an announcement in *The Times*, he felt almost equally annoyed with his father and with himself.

'It quite struck me at the time,' Howard Felton said. As he spoke—and rather oddly—he took his hand off the knob, which he then twice patted before opening the door.

In the drawing-room Aunt Grace was working at her embroidery in her accustomed window-seat, and Ianthe was reading a fat book about the Minoans and scribbling notes. It might have been called a cultivated scene, and Toby wondered what his brother was going to make of it. It wasn't this, however, that remained chiefly in his mind for the rest of the evening.

XI

'And your niece?' Mercia Felton asked. 'Does Ianthe welcome the autodidact at the breakfast-table?'

It was Friday, and the Oxford Feltons, with two French girls duly in tow, had arrived and were awaiting luncheon. Mercia (who said clever things, as the wife of a clever Felton should do) was able to ask her question because Ianthe had taken Sophie and Arlette—who appeared to be sisters—on a tour of the house. Ianthe had decided at a glance that Sophie and Arlette were accustomed to houses quite as grand as Felton, and that now as on previous occasions Hugh and Mercia were putting their best foot forward in the display of territorial connections. In France professors were highly regarded—at least (as elsewhere) by others of their kind. But in Oxford these two young persons had probably been unimpressed by their hosts' murkily commodious habitation in a corner of a large semi-conventual building abutting on a busy commercial thoroughfare, and at Felton were expressing the polite gratification of wanderers returned to some norm of human existence. Ianthe, who talked French very well, talked French; and this circumstance Sophie and Arlette clearly found agreeable. Heartened that there was only a quarter of an hour to fill in, Ianthe explained something of the ancientry of the Feltons in considerably less detail than Elma Loftus would have done.

'Yes, indeed,' Mrs Warlow said to Mercia. 'I believe Ianthe likes Andrew Auld, as we are all coming to do. But he may not, I fear, be called an autodidact. What he knows has been taught him, I suspect, in a schoolroom, and since then there has been little burning of the midnight oil. After a day's digging and delving, one presumably simply wants to go to sleep.'

'So he must be described as quite uneducated?'

'Oh, absolutely so. Of course there is what is called the school of life. I judge Andy not wholly uninstructed there.'

'That may or may not be advantageous. Are his morals likely to be good? Agricultural labourers in Scotland would appear to be a mixed lot. Think of Burns.'

Mrs Warlow was silent, although not with the air of one who thinks of Burns. Her glance was upon Andy, who was undergoing *viva voce* examination by Hugh Felton in another corner of the Dutch garden. Mercia looked that way too.

'Certainly,' she said, 'the young man is personable—and precisely as Toby is. The physique, that is to say, is good, and likely to be attractive to any young woman. The features are another matter. There is something peculiar about them, is there not? One wonders from what corner of central Europe they have sprung.'

'It would not occur to me to describe them as central European.' Mrs Warlow permitted herself an accent of some severity. She very much disliked Mercia's dislike of Toby, which proceeded from her feeling that it was to Hugh that Felton ought to come. Perhaps, Mrs Warlow thought, it ought. But the question was an academic one—academic in the special sense that Hugh himself was so academic that he wouldn't at all care to be landed with a large estate, and still less to undergo the disgrace of promptly selling such an ancestral property. On this family issue Hugh appeared to bear a wholly disinterested mind. Perhaps it came of his being a philosopher.

'The resemblance is quite fantastic,' Mercia said. 'It must be most confusing.'

'Not in the least. One quickly comes to distinguish between them—except, perhaps, from a far or middle distance.'

'That must be your professional eye, Grace. But I was thinking of confusion at a different level. I feel, for instance, that there is a sense in which poor Howard might muddle them up.'

'Shall we go inside, Mercia? There should be time for a glass of sherry before Marian summons us.' Mrs Warlow much disapproved of this intruder among the Feltons referring to her brother as 'poor Howard', nor did she wish at the moment to listen to any anatomy of that brother's state of mind. And her suggestion was saved from appearing too abrupt by the fact that there was now a general movement indoors. It was not before Andy, however, had passed a fairly good examination with the Warden.

Andy, for a start, did not resent being catechized. (He didn't even resent it being done with that superfluity of tact which Mrs Warlow had charged against her younger brother.) He had no air of having made himself a dependant of the Feltons and being uneasy about it. Indeed he reminded the Warden, curiously enough, of those among his former pupils who carried round with them a certain consciousness of privilege and security in the simplest economic sense, and whose general easiness of bearing was, although with a decent modesty, enhanced as a result. As Andy's speech was so demotic or at least provincial, and as his mind was virgin of all science and all art, and in particular since he had turned up as the severe Hawkstone's lowliest assistant, this was an impression hard to account for. Indeed nine men out of ten— Hugh, who had a good opinion of his own acumen, told himself —would have been totally unaware of it.

But although he was prepared to approve of Andy as a person, he was some way from approving of him in his particular place in the world at this moment. Here his opinion hadn't changed much since he first heard of the whole business. Howard was a most injudicious fellow, prone to jump into awkward situations; and prone, later on, to find them untenable or unacceptable, with discomforting results for himself and sometimes for other people. There was, it seemed to Hugh, something viewy and unsound in the decision to treat Andrew Auld precisely as if he, like Toby, had been brought pretty well straight to Felton House from the Atlantic Ocean. It ignored too many factors, and was likely to bear hard upon Andrew Auld himself one day. The Warden was not unaware that he might be all wrong in this; indeed he told himself that he quite probably was. Nevertheless if his advice were asked again (only it clearly was not to be) he would still recommend that course of judicious patronage from a distance.

This line of thought, needless to say, caused Hugh Felton to be perfectly charming to Andy. And he hoped that Grace wouldn't be fool enough to put the boy next to Mercia at luncheon. Mercia had acquired a good deal of skill with uncouth youths, since a fair number of such passed through the college. But Mercia wasn't too fond of Toby—this for reasons which perhaps you had to be a philosopher to be immune from. And she might be a little tart with a second and proletarian Toby who had bobbed up at Felton.

This particular error in *placement* didn't happen. Mrs Warlow, with an impossible four men and five women on her hands, had indulged herself in the amusement of seating Andy between the two French visitors. Andy betrayed no consciousness of seeing this as a bad joke; on the contrary, he seemed rather pleased. Ianthe having talked to them in the only language proper in civilization, the two girls were disappointed that this odd member of the Felton family didn't follow suit. He was more tiresomely obstinate even than *monsieur le professeur* at his own table in Oxford, who did at least condescend to be occasionally comprehensible. Their bewilderment grew when the young man appeared scarcely to talk English either. Perhaps he was a Dutch or Swedish cousin of these people? The girls (they were about seventeen, and therefore really women; and they were extremely good-looking as well) glanced at one another in mingled amusement and dismay across Andy's long nose. But this didn't last; it lasted hardly any time at all. By means not very easy to discover, Andy established *rapport* with them almost at once. They were soon hanging on his words—whether these were intelligible or not. They may have been telling themselves that he was like one of *papa's* enchanting foresters or huntsmen.

Mercia Felton, watching this performance from her place next to Howard, may again have thought darkly of Robert Burns. Her sister-in-law was inclined to glance at Toby. For some days Toby had been in a bad temper, and Mrs Warlow thought she knew why. Now he was positively scowling at his brother. The spectacle of Andy getting away with these doubtless vapid but undeniably delectable little Frogs didn't please him at all.

it was very comical. But it did at the same time afford occasion for thought. And Hugh, as might have been expected, found something to say about it. This happened when, over coffee in the open air again, the three senior Feltons proper distanced themselves for the purpose of short conference.

'I'm glad everybody likes those girls,' Hugh said. 'They're of good family and so forth, and quite oppressively educated, as all wretched French kids are. Oppressively good-mannered too, when elders are around. But probably the very devil when only intimates of their own age-group are in question. Even under our ancient noses your new-found Andrew got on swimmingly with them. And did you notice Toby? Well, well!'

Howard hadn't noticed Toby, and it had to be explained to him by his sister that Andy's success with the French girls had made his brother rather cross.

'Oh, I doubt that,' Howard said easily. 'But I rather wish you were right. There's no reason why Toby shouldn't be beginning to think of a wife—particularly with things going well in that acceptance place, as they seem to be doing. Indeed, I've been telling him so. But he's a bit slow off the mark, if you ask me. Not really too interested in girls at all. It's almost rather worrying.'

Mrs Warlow, who had heard this absurd persuasion advanced by her elder brother several times lately, said nothing—confining herself to slightly raised eyebrows directed in her younger brother's direction.

'What about Andrew, Howard?' Hugh asked, plainly in a spirit of experiment.

'I think Andrew may be different in some ways. You remember, Hugh, telling me how identical twins are bound to be the same pretty well all through. Of course there's a lot in it, but it seems to be rather an old-fashioned view, if taken too far. I've been looking into it, you know. No longer ago than yesterday, as a matter of fact. Statistics, and so on. The weight of the genetic factors has to be considered. And it's more an open question than you appear to have thought.' Howard paused on this, perhaps a little daunted by thus openly challenging his brother's superior mental competence. 'So those two boys may, you see, differ in some quite important ways.'

Hugh, like his sister, was now silent for some moments. Howard, although not intellectually very well endowed, seldom fell into quite this degree of incoherence, which was without the slightest significance except conceivably as hinting the movement of his inner mind.

'I hardly know what we're talking about,' Hugh said. 'And I doubt whether Grace does, either. Are you saying that your young Glasgow visitor is more likely than Toby is to go courting and get married and have children and all the rest of it?'

'Well, yes—more or less.' Howard's confidence faltered. 'Wouldn't you agree?'

'On the contrary, I'm bound to say I think you're talking nonsense, Howard. If these two young men didn't have decent principles—as I presume they have—you'd find that in no time at all they were rivals for the favour of half the village girls on the horizon. They've had a row already, I gather—and I wouldn't mind betting a girl was at the bottom of it.'

If this impatient speech didn't offend Howard—who wasn't easily offended—it did discompose him, and he suddenly remembered that he had not yet been sufficiently attentive to his French guests. So the Warden and his sister were left together.

'It *is* nonsense, isn't it?' Hugh demanded.

'Complete nonsense. As a matter of fact, precisely what Toby has been doing lately is carrying on an affair with a village girl. Or a kind of village girl. The doctor's daughter, Elma Loftus.'

'Good Lord! You mean actually—'

'Yes, of course. And guilelessly believing that it has been a deep secret from Ianthe and myself, when it was as obvious as if they'd been making love in the middle of the tennis court.'

'My dear Grace!' It seemed to be his sister's manner of expressing the thing that shocked Hugh at this point.

'But now it has run into some sort of snag—whether permanently or only for a time, I don't yet know.'

152

'Perhaps Andrew has cut in.'

'I think not. He might, by agreement, take her over later. I'd say she's that sort of girl. Only I doubt, come to think of it, whether Andy's that sort of boy. He'd probably rather be off on his own.'

'I must say I don't much care for all this.' Hugh was really perturbed. 'I've got used enough, heaven knows, to the near-promiscuity of the young nowadays. But in a semi-professional way, you know, since they've been all around me for years. But when one meets it in a domestic situation—'

'You exaggerate, Hugh. There's nothing that could fairly be called promiscuity in sight. We have our problems at Felton. That's all.'

'Well, the turning up of this young man seems decidedly to have exacerbated them. I can't understand why you've been on the side of his domestication at Felton. Has it occurred to you that it might even put Ianthe at risk?' Hugh paused, and realized that this was too sinister a phrase. 'Mightn't he fall in love with her? It would be an awkward thing, to say the least.' Again Hugh paused. 'Or—confound it!—she might fall in love with him.'

'That would at least shift things a little.'

'I don't see any necessary virtue in that. Giving Felton a shake-up, and so forth, is something you rather harp on, as a matter of fact. It bobs up whenever we meet.'

'Possibly so.' Mrs Warlow didn't greatly care for being thus taxed with a species of senile repetitiveness. 'But at least we don't meet very often.'

'I'll grant you that things are pretty static here. I'd get impatient with it myself. What's at the bottom of it is Howard's inactive and dilatory temperament. He has never really *done* anything all his life.'

'He did adopt a war orphan, long ago. And now he may be said to be half-adopting another.'

'Just at this moment, he looks as if he'd be very willing to adopt Mercia's parlour-boarders as well.'

At this unexpected speech Mrs Warlow turned round, and

immediately became aware of its occasion. Ianthe having already shown Sophie and Arlette over the house, Howard had apparently determined to accord them an equal courtesy in the gardens. They were now quite far off, but distinctly visible, in a small unwalled orchard of considerable antiquity. Against one large tree was perched a ladder, and on this ladder was perched Arlette. It was almost certainly too early in the season for apple picking, so mere amusement must be the occasion of this ascent. Even as Mrs Warlow looked, it proved hazardous. The ladder swayed; Arlette tumbled; she was saved from falling flat only by Howard's ready hands. It had of course been very sudden, and Howard had not been able to effect his interposition with quite the delicacy he might have wished. But it was all matter for amusement. Howard put an arm for a moment round Arlette's shoulder, as if concerned in a fatherly way to make sure she wasn't hurt. Then all three moved on, apparently laughing, and disappeared among the trees.

'Perhaps you'd call that a shake-up?' Hugh asked.

'It looked more like a shake down.' Mrs Warlow seemed unimpressed by the incident thus curiously observed from afar. 'Howard is fond of the society of young people. And naturally we don't get much of it now, except when Ianthe and Toby are at home.'

'I don't get much of it myself, except for all those confounded young men. But—whether in males or females—give me a little maturity of mind, every time. Howard ought to be looking for a woman five or ten years younger than himself, not thirty or forty.'

'That, of course, depends.' For a moment Mrs Warlow appeared disposed to enlarge upon this, but then thought better of it. 'I have an idea,' she said, 'that Mercia would now like to collect your little flock and get back to Oxford.'

'How did you like those Grens?' Ianthe asked. ('Grens' was apparently short for *grenouilles*.)

'I suppose they were all right.' Toby didn't sound enthusiastic.

'Rather more posh, I thought, than Hugh's usual crowd. They
had a feeling they'd come among the peasantry—by which I don't
mean just Andy.' Andy had hurried back to what he had taken to
calling the 'office', meaning Mr Tarling's house beyond the home
farm, so Toby and Ianthe were alone. 'I felt they were positively
looking for the hay-seeds in my hair. And wondering how we'd
all come honestly even by this modest shack.'

It wasn't very possible to be amused by this travesty, but
Ianthe did her best. She was aware of Toby as having a bad time,
and aware that it wasn't too easy to help, since he was remaining
firmly mum about his catastrophe. She knew that young men react
in various ways to being ditched. One of them consists of falling
into an abyss of self-pity, or into the first cousin of that, when all
control of the matter is taken out of your hands and your doctor
feeds you pills, telling you that they sometimes slightly shorten
the duration of a depressive illness. Ianthe had been instructed on
this sort of thing by a Cambridge friend, who had an aunt devoted
to preventing people committing suicide; and now she had a
momentary vision of Toby constrained to take a condition of this
kind to Dr Loftus. Fortunately this macabre idea hadn't much
probability attached to it. Toby's reaction to the débâcle over
Elma, however that had precisely come about, was more a matter
of humiliation than despair. Wounded vanity, although for a long
time it might assail him in the middle of the night, would stop
crippling his daylight hours quite soon. Moreover there must
already be a rational corner in his head in which a radical reassess-
ment of his late passion was beginning to form itself. Or so Ianthe
hoped.

They had remained out of doors, and were now on the terrace
again, sitting on Toby's favourite balustrade. The stone was warm
from the late-summer sunshine. But Toby, unbidden, had gone
into the little Gothic pavilion and fetched a cushion for her
greater ease. Ianthe was pleased, unusually pleased, by this, and
rather surprised to find it reminding her of that proprietory smack
on Elma's bottom. But as soon as the deplorable episode had thus
recurred to her she divined its significance. It hadn't been a

spontaneous act on Toby's part, and it hadn't been meant to pass undetected. It had been a bizarre way of intimating an engagement—an engagement either already contracted or that Toby believed to be on the verge of being so. So that was it; and she could see too what had happened later that afternoon. Toby—the callow brat—had been grandly announcing or re-announcing that it was going to be his pleasure to make Elma an honest woman, and she had responded to this expected event with a kind of saved-up and malicious rejection. It wasn't a pretty picture, since it showed Elma as a bitch and Toby in a light which, at best, could be called ludicrous. But this last thought, and the phrase 'callow brat' lingering in her mind, only prompted in Ianthe a sudden flow of tenderness for her foster-brother of a sort not startling only because it had been known to her intermittently from nursery days. And now another thought came to her, which explained to her why Toby was dumb about his disaster. The wretched girl had exacted from him a promise of silence.

This almost clairvoyant faculty where Toby was concerned was not always comfortable to Ianthe. Fortunately—she thought —it had its limits. She had no notion, and no wish to have a notion, how the entanglement had begun. Toby's sexual nature was, somehow, an aspect of him she had never let her mind dwell on; nor had she, for that matter, much considered it in other men. Perhaps Toby had put on a turn as—or perhaps he was actually capable of being—a ruthless seducer. If he had gone about 'having' Elma in that way there might be some excuse for Elma to husband an instinct for revenge. Ianthe just didn't know. But she did know (she suddenly saw) that she would always love Toby, whatever flaw the chances of life turned up in him. A family (she told herself) had to be like that.

'When do you go back to London, Toby?' Because of the embargo on Elma and Elma's perfidy (as she continued to judge it) Ianthe had difficulty in finding anything to talk about with the rejected lover. It didn't matter very much, since in a way almost the most satisfactory moments between Toby and herself were silences. But this was a practical question of a neutral sort.

'Oh, in a couple of days, worse luck.'

'Is it frightfully boring?'

'Well, not really. At least I expect it can become interesting in time. But it is just all about money, you know: other people's and your own. I chose the job, and I'm not going to complain about it.'

'I'd say you are, rather.' Ianthe laughed softly, for she enjoyed her own candour. 'And at least you're never away for long.'

'A bloody week-ender, that's me.' Toby grinned wryly, and was himself silent for some moments. 'Ianthe,' he then said suddenly, 'I do frightfully rely on you about Andy. You do like him, don't you?'

'I like him very much.'

'As much as you like me? It looks, you know, as if equal shares is going to be the thing.'

'No. I like you better, although I don't suppose you are any worthier in the regard of heaven. But why do you rely on me?'

'Well, I know I don't just sparkle. But then neither does he. So we get on quite well together.'

'When you don't go pub-crawling.'

'Oh, that! Well, yes. But what I mean is that—Felton all being a bit strange to him still—he may miss me at first during the week. Of course he obviously gets along well with Howard'—it was thus that Toby sometimes referred to his foster-father when speaking to Ianthe—'and he has quite a thing about Aunt Grace in an odd and awed sort of way. But you must be nice to him, too.'

'You are a great oaf, Toby! Am I likely to be anything else? Turn on the haughty high-born lady, or something like that?'

'I doubt whether you're a high-born lady, my child.' Toby occasionally addressed Ianthe in this patronizing way. 'Very well-born indeed. But for high-born your pop has to be a belted earl or something. Shakespeare and that crowd thought of the Feltons as persons of worship, not persons of honour. What was I saying?'

'That I am to be nice to Andy. Well, I quite promise.'

'Then that's fine.' Toby swung his legs idly for some moments —and for some further moments fell to biting a thumb. 'By the way,' he finally said, 'I've something to tell you. I've been ditched.'

Ianthe was about to say, 'Yes, I know—or at least I've guessed —about Elma.' But something, again at an intuitive level, restrained her.

'Tell me about it,' she said quietly—and only then ventured to add, 'Is it something about a girl?'

'No, no.' Toby seemed scarcely to have gathered the sense of the question. 'It's about Felton. I know now. It's not coming to me. And I'm just glad it's definite.'

'*Definite!*' All Ianthe's dismay went into the word. 'You mean that Daddy has actually said—'

'No. In fact, of course not. He never does say, does he? It's not the way his mind works. In a sense, perhaps, he doesn't yet even know.' Toby produced these brief sentences quite calmly. 'It's just that he's planning an existence as a couple of dear old bachelors for Andy and myself in the Mill House.'

'I can't believe it.'

'I believed it at once. It's the coming of Andy, you see, that has flicked the switch.'

'Toby, that's horrible. I don't believe it either.'

'Nothing horrible about it. Andy has shown him what he's been hiding from himself for the sake of a quiet life full of benevolent feeling. Andy's me and I'm Andy, to all intents and purposes; and we just don't belong. We're very nice, but we just don't belong. It has to be a Felton at Felton, and one sees the point.'

'But you *are* a Felton. Legally—'

'Legally is all rot. This is a matter of feeling. But there's one good thing: Hugh has no sons, and now he won't have. So you and Hugh start level. And later on somebody from a female line, or whatever it's called, will have to change his name by deed poll and assume the lordship of the manors and the lord knows what. It has its comic side.'

'It has nothing of the sort.' Ianthe had sprung to her feet. She

158

was pale with passion. 'Oh God, Toby—what a fool I was to say what I did!'

'What do you mean?'

'Quite a long time ago, Daddy talked to me about all this. It was in that indecisive and vacillating way he has—but what he said was that he thought it fair the place should come to me. I was furious. I felt about as unfilial as Goneril and Regan rolled into one. I told him that if Felton ever came to me I'd start conveying it to you—or whatever the word is—without fail on the following day. I ought to have held my tongue.'

'I can't see what good that would have done.'

'We could have cheated him—as he would have deserved.'

'Please, please, Ianthe, don't be so upset. I had to tell you. But I don't want the place all that, anyway.'

'Yes, you do. Don't be silly.'

'I'll become an opulent City gent, and buy a couple of Feltons off the hook.' Toby grinned rather wanly. He was making a very big effort indeed. 'But the important thing is Andy. You do see that?'

'I don't see what Andy has to do with it.'

'It's just that he must never, never know that his turning up had anything to do with things coming unstuck. It would be a dreadful thing between us. He's rather a decent sort of brother, you know. He'd never forgive himself for coming south of the Border. Promise to keep it secret, Ianthe.' Toby frowned, as if some irrelevant memory had brushed his consciousness. 'Fortunately, of course, he knows nothing about all that sort of thing. Inheriting estates, and so on.'

'I think he'll wonder why there he is, sitting on one side of the kitchen fire in the Mill House—and gowking, as he'd say, at his long-lost brother on the other.' Ianthe had put out her hand as she managed this joke, and seized Toby's. 'I'll come and cook for you.'

'You can come and just be a lady. We'll have in the Misses Kinch, crutches and all, to do the rough and everything else.

159

They're rather fond of Andy already.'

'Toby, you should get one thing clear. Of course it's true that Andy isn't all clued up on inheritances, and whose expectations should be what, and so on. But he's very alert and sensitive. I think he may already have picked up a good deal more than you imagine.'

'He hasn't been told about this Mill House idea yet.'

'Even if you are right about what that means—and I think you probably are—it has a quite harmless sound in itself: the two of you being lodged independently half-a-mile away. Andy mightn't do all that wondering, after all. He might judge it quite a good idea.'

'Not when he got hold of what it was really in aid of. And he'd do that in no time, if he's as alert as you say. He'd ask questions and have to be told lies. I'm fed up with lies. It was pretty well lying like mad just not to—'

Toby broke off abruptly and in confusion. It was natural to him to think of Ianthe as invariably in his confidence. He had been forgetting, she saw, the recent disaster-area in which this didn't hold.

'Toby, I don't think we need assume that there's a real crisis dead ahead. You know how wandering Daddy's mind is. After all, Andy has been here no time at all, and any unsettlement of the sort you think you've detected may simply fade out. So we'd better do no more than keep our eyes open.'

'I suppose that's right.' Toby didn't sound altogether convinced. 'It's odd about Felton, isn't it?' he asked, after a moment and on what was almost a wistful note. 'You don't want it, and I don't believe Hugh wants it—although I'm pretty sure Mercia would gobble it up if she could.'

'Mercia doesn't run Hugh, although you might think she does.'

'Yes, I know. So I expect the estate will be sold to an insurance company and the house will become a home for delinquent girls. And those hippogriffs at the bottom of the drive will be replaced with white elephants.'

160

Having said this, Toby cheered up a little. It always pleased him to have achieved anything he considered to be a stroke of wit. And Ianthe, as they walked back to the house together, was quite prepared to laugh. If Toby were really to lose Felton and to be relegated to a kind of week-ending dowager's condition in the Mill House she wouldn't easily cease to be enraged about it. Yet it wouldn't be wise to start feeling sorry for Toby. His limitations and vulnerabilities called forth from her feelings she was not very well able to define. But it would never do to begin commiserating with him on the score of misfortunes, whether real or imagined. He was, she told herself, a very largely privileged young man, and—short of social cataclysm—he would always remain so. His job in the City might be boring, but it would eventually bring him as many Aston Martins as he could desire. From Elma Loftus he had, so to speak, come down with a bump, but not before he must be presumed to have enjoyed a great deal of what she was qualified to give. There might have been times when Andrew Auld was uncertain about his next day's dinner, and most of the dinners he'd ever eaten he'd had to do a hard day's work for in a garden or on a cabbage patch. Not so with lucky Tobias Felton.

The small spectacle of herself falling into this moralizing vein entertained Ianthe, and some sign of her amusement was detected by Toby as they went together through Robert Mylne's dining-room.

'What's funny?' Toby asked, perhaps a little reproachfully.

'I found myself being very wise about it all. Uncle Hugh's chronic condition, don't you think?'

'Well, yes—but I do think Hugh's all right, in a fashion. I even think he mightn't approve of the way your father's mind's moving.'

'That's probably true.' Ianthe was startled. She couldn't remember when Toby had last said 'your father', just like that. When he sometimes said 'Howard' there was perhaps the germ of the same distancing idea. But more commonly he said 'Daddy' as spontaneously as she did. If he was going to be disinherited (for it came to that) he was going to lose more than spacious rooms and numerous acres. Under this perception Ianthe's mood abruptly changed again. She saw that the moralizing to which she had lightly admitted was facile and to be condemned. Her father had perhaps never given his word to Toby that Felton was going to come to him. Nevertheless the fulfilling of any other plan now would be deeply wrong. She had to face the fact that one day—even quite soon—she might have to speak up to that effect. And now she came to a halt in the middle of the room.

'I'll have to talk to Daddy,' she said. 'And I think you ought to talk to Andy.'

'Talk to him? How do you mean?'

'You do tell him things, don't you—even things you mightn't tell to me?'

'Well, yes—I suppose so.' Toby had been thrown into a consternation which was almost comical again by this last question. It shook his conviction that Ianthe couldn't conceivably have an inkling of the Elma affair. In a way, he was now inclined to wish that she had; indeed, that she had somehow tumbled to it in all its horrid detail. For in that case his stupid promise of secrecy would become inoperative, and he could be as honest about it as he wanted to be. 'I don't see,' he said, 'how Andy can really help.'

'I just have an odd feeling that he may be the key to something.' Ianthe frowned as she said this, as if conscious of an indefiniteness she didn't much go in for. 'In any case, I think he's entitled to have the whole situation as you see it explained to him.'

'Even that notion of mine that it's his turning up that has flicked the switch—brought about the grand discovery that I'm not, any more than he himself is, descended from a chap who lined the family pocket from the revenues of Aquitaine?' Toby became conscious of this question as bobbing up from a level of his mind that he didn't greatly approve of. 'Sorry! I didn't mean to talk rot.'

'It's not exactly rot. And did I ever tell you, Toby? I've a theory that you're descended—so Andy too, of course—from Charlemagne. You're terribly like some of his portraits. And he

162

was descended from King David, who was a kind of honorary ancestor of Jesus Christ. So you see—'

'Do shut up, Ianthe.'

'All right. Go back to Andy. If he happens to have—or has already had—much talk with Daddy he may arrive at something like that notion of yours off his own bat. But I'm not sure that he would be as upset by it as you imagine. I don't really know him yet. He may conceivably feel that to be turfed out of Felton would be good for your soul.'

'I suppose he might.' Toby tried to hide his sense that any such feeling would be outrageous beyond belief.

'Anyway, I think you should give him the lie of the land. He seems to me to be rather a loyal sort of person, and he ought to have the information that would give him the best chance of weighing in on your side.'

'I think the idea of sides is pretty grim, Ianthe. But perhaps you're right. I'll think about it.'

'That's what Andy would say, in that lingo of his. I've forgotten the expression.'

'Bide a wee.'

'That's it.'

'At least we know where we are. We can't be booked for surprises.'

'I suppose not,' Ianthe said.

PART THREE

Andy

XII

AUTUMN CAME SUDDENLY TO FELTON. From the house its mists were more evident than its mellow fruitfulness. For days on end little was to be seen through the high windows except Andrew Auld's successor, shrouded in vapour as he swept fallen leaves from lawns and paths while further leaves kept falling round him. He was a mere school-leaver, and disappointingly subject to discouragement as he thus struggled against nature's plan. Hawkstone had little hope of the boy.

Andy, on the other hand, was doing well in the higher sphere to which chance had promoted him. Mr Tarling, a tactful man, reported him to Howard Felton as being 'just as capable as one would expect Toby's brother to be'. Complete candour, indeed, would have constrained Mr Tarling to go a little further than that. Like most of the people who had any concern in the matter at all, he was disposed to be critical of Howard's indecisive stance over the succession to the estate. Had it been made quite clear at the proper time that Toby was to be fully Howard's heir, Toby would have got just that grip on the whole concern which his brother was showing himself very well equipped to do now. As it was, Toby had rather drifted away, and had in effect closed for a grand car and an office stool. Mr Tarling, although very much Toby's man, and disposed to view the situation as produced by a large measure of weakness on his employer's part, felt that there must have been a certain contributory weakness on Toby's own part too. It was thoroughly unsatisfactory—and the more so because of the astonishing fact that (so far as Mr Tarling could see) there was nobody except Toby himself who particularly wanted Felton at all. The anomaly didn't much affect Mr Tarling's own position, since he was pretty well due to retire. But it irked him to see this capable Scottish lad being introduced into the picture in what he

167

conceived as a thoroughly inept fashion. If things went on as they were, Howard Felton might drop dead at any time; the entire concern could simply come under the hammer; and as a consequence Toby's meritorious new-found brother would probably find himself back on square one.

Andy was still inclined to insist on what might be termed his intimate relationship with the soil. When he ought to be studying accounts he was apt to be out on the home farm with a fork-lift, stacking bales of belated hay. He had something of a head for accounts, all the same. On one occasion, when Mr Tarling had judged a word of commendation to be due in this regard, Andy had responded with a somewhat mysterious reference to an auntie who had been proving rather apt at that sort of thing. Of course Andy couldn't thus be claiming that commercial acumen was in his blood. Perhaps he had simply learnt from this old person's example.

Toby had returned to his own account-books in Lombard Street, and to his normal week-ending rhythm. Formerly this had seemed to suit him very well, but Ianthe had become aware that now he wasn't liking it at all. Perhaps its satisfactoriness had consisted in his enjoyment of a kind of portable mistress, accessible in town and country alike. But that was over. Elma, indeed, had for some reason given up her job in Harley Street, and was simply living at home. She continued to turn up at Felton now and then—but it was sparingly, and never at week-ends. There seemed—Ianthe thought—to be a spark of decency in this. She was glad to think that Elma had thus departed into the wings. She had been slow to get out of her head the uncomfortable idea that Andy might prove to be Toby's successor in the enjoyment of Elma's favours. The idea was more than uncomfortable; it was rather horrid as well. She had probably been imagining things in a depraved (and doubtless inexpert) fashion when she had thought to detect something disconcertingly naked in glances passing fleetingly between these two. She had a dim sense that there was some masculine code in terms of which Andy would now be entitled to regard Elma as fair game. It was worrying that

sions upon which Elma did come over to Felton, with or without her rather graceless brother, and the four young people played some desultory tennis, Ianthe found herself quite unable to get this sort of thing out of her system. She was sure that Andy had a lot of what must be called sexual instinct. Even his marked and sober regard for Aunt Grace incongruously betrayed an element of something of the kind. He certainly had no sober regard for Elma Loftus. He didn't even seem to be particularly aware of her. Yet in some mysterious way he compelled her (and it was a deliberate thing) to be distinctly aware of him.

Fortunately—Ianthe thought—Andy seemed not inclined to anything of the sort with *her*. He was even rather more respectful, positively rather more wary, than their relationship (which was as good as a brotherly-and-sisterly one) at all called for. And this, too, she found herself disposed to worry over. With Toby away five nights out of seven Andy was now her natural companion, and their intimacy must increase during the several weeks that still remained of the Cambridge long vacation. It would be right and proper, she was sure, that they should become open allies in Toby's cause, and that they should somehow help him out of the disconsolate and let-down condition which the fiasco with Elma had detectably left behind it. She was sure that Andy knew about this; ought she to confide to him that she did too? But this wasn't possible—or not if she was in the least right about there now being some current of feeling between Elma and Andy. So she didn't talk about Toby at all.

During Andy's office hours—or what would have been office hours if he hadn't been out in the fields showing sceptical labourers how hedging is done in Galloway—Ianthe worked hard at her vacation reading. But if she thus was a learner during most of the day she turned teacher as soon as Andy got back. For here, she discovered, was something she could do—and that Andy let her do. He would let Aunt Grace do it too. But although it was certainly Aunt Grace who dealt with what Ianthe thought of as the knives and forks (or—as Toby liked to put it—with how to perform an introduction or enter a box at the Opera) Aunt Grace appeared to feel that education as more largely conceived ought to be injected into Andrew Auld only in small doses if at all. Ianthe discovered that her aunt's thinking here was quite wrong. It was a literary idea. Book-learning had made Thomas Hardy's obscure Jude Fawley a terrible bore, and Virginia Woolf had cast what might be just aspersions upon self-taught working men. But Andy had a lively mind which grew perceptibly livelier whenever you tipped something new into its vacancies. And the tipping didn't even have to be done with the tact which Uncle Hugh (if constrained to the job) would have brought to it. Andy, so decidedly manly in an exterior regard (particularly when he fell into that unconscious *déhanchement*), and also emotionally so mature when compared with his brother, had at the same time a child's pleasure in acquiring knowledge. Not that he was a respectful pupil. In fact he made a great deal of fun of her. Or he did so until, quite suddenly, that mood of wariness, of prudent distancing, would come on him.

Here was something over which Ianthe puzzled for some considerable time. Quite frequently she thought about it last thing before going to sleep at night. Then one morning, hard upon waking up, she hit upon what must be the explanation. *Andy didn't want to fall in love with her.*

This perception (as she was convinced it was) suddenly pitched Ianthe into an area of feeling in which for a time she seemed to wander bewildered and lost. She believed herself to remember that she had positively felt cheated when Andy had preferred the wretched Elma to herself as the recipient of brief and (as it were) routinely libidinous glances. How perfectly horrid! And why *should* Andy shy away from her—if that was what it came to? The answer was so silly that it was humiliating. From his brother's Felton world he was determined to take away nothing for nothing. If he ate Felton's porridge he was going to thatch Felton's ricks. And he certainly wasn't going to make passes at his benefactor's only child. Ianthe told herself that although this was indeed silly it was also a rather honourable kind of resolution as

too. Andy was very clear that the class you belong to doesn't change simply because somebody nearly runs you over when you are clipping a hedge. Raids across that obstinate barrier are perhaps all right in a frivolous way. The butcher's boy could have a quick 'affair' with an Elma and no great harm need be done. But a marriage between them would prove a shambles more likely than not.

Ianthe had scarcely got out of bed before she realized that nothing of all this would be swimming around in her conscious mind if her unconscious mind hadn't been behaving in a dangerous way. Novels were full—or used to be full—of maidenly females suddenly confronted by the fact that they had for long been madly in love with a gentleman without a glimmer of this exciting state of affairs having crossed their waking mind. It was useful story-telling stuff—but could it actually be in some correspondence with things as they are? The discovery was commonly represented as pleasurable, but if she was herself now up against anything of the kind there was certainly no pleasure involved with it. Was *she* perhaps in love with Andrew Auld? The mere question was inexplicably frightening. Surely one didn't nowadays behave like a girl brought up in some unspeakably morbid Victorian home in which the mere thought of a sexual relationship was held sinful and a just cause of dread? Ianthe had quite often imagined herself in the most scandalous situations with young men—even with butcher's boys, if it came to that. So something uncommonly unwholesome was assailing her now. What was to be done about it? Ianthe answered this question in what might be described, if grandiloquently, as the spirit of her generation. She was in a muddle about Andy. She'd get hold of Andy and have it out with him.

'Maidenly' was of course a term of fun with Ianthe Felton. Yet maidenly she was, and so perhaps better able to initiate her project than to press it very faithfully home.

'I'm going to walk over to Mr Tarling's with you,' she said to

171

Andy at breakfast. 'If that's all right by you, I mean.'

There was perhaps something slightly menacing in this form of words. But Andy, who was at a sideboard helping himself to bacon and kidneys with the air of one long habituated to the usages of country-house life, seemed unperturbed.

'Of course it is,' he said—turning round at leisure. 'It's on the misty side still. But there's no harm in that.' Andy, although still careful not to make what might be described as English noises, was now liable—perhaps through absence of mind—to saying things rather as those around him might have said them. 'I canna' think why you havna' got a dug,' he added, recollecting himself. 'A young gentlewoman roaming the countryside should aye be walking a dug. But I dinna' mind standing in for yin. Woof, woof, Ianthe!'

'Oh, shut up, Andy, and get yourself coffee.' Ianthe realized that every now and then something quite ordinary in Andy—a piece of mere nonsense, say, like this—afforded her a sudden sharp delight. Perhaps it was because he was never more like Toby than in these moments of fun, and that he had just Toby's unassuming standards in the field of wit. But Andy wasn't her brother as Toby virtually was. With Andy the relationship was, after all, only a pleasant fiction—a pleasant fiction that had recently bobbed up, it might be said, over a prunus hedge. Ianthe wasn't very sure that her feelings really went with this. Her feelings, indeed, were much too troubled and confused to afford much certainty about anything. But she could at least see one objective fact about Andy, and it could be roughly expressed by simply saying that he wasn't Toby. He was by many years and many miles not Toby. With Andy she had no past associations worth speaking of. Only a few weeks ago she had been unaware of his existence. But perhaps all this meant that when she found Andy fun she was glimpsing an unknown road conceivably ahead of her: a road not conceivable in Toby's case. These, she knew, were quite sensible thoughts. It was annoying, it was absurd, that they should suggest themselves as owning a hinterland of fear.

Her father had already breakfasted, and was out on his cus-

toast in her own quarters. It was one of her small rituals designed to suggest that she was very much an independent person, helping out in her brother's household for a while. So Ianthe and Andy were alone in a domestic fashion. An elderly parlour-maid (all the surviving indoor servants at Felton House were elderly) came and went. She treated Andy—that inexplicable innovation on the Felton scene—precisely as she treated Toby: with the affection and respectful authority of one who has attended upon a child at table from his earliest promoted years. Andy had come to like this attitude. When it manifested itself in some small concrete fashion (the removal, perhaps, of the spoon that he had scandalously left in his coffee-cup) he would offer Ianthe a quick conspiratorial glance not at all of the kind she could still rather crossly remember his directing on Elma. One of the nice things about Andy was that he had a sense of the comedy of his situation. It went, somehow, along with his self-respect and his self-confidence. Of the latter quality at least—Ianthe saw—he commanded a good deal more than Toby now did.

They finished breakfast and at once set out through the mist —which was quite thick enough to be called a fog. Sometimes they could hardly see the beech leaves their feet scuffed up as they walked. Their pace had to be brisk, since Andy was far from feeling that his position of privilege in the big house discharged him from the duty of strict punctuality at work. Ianthe didn't feel out of breath, but the sense of business affairs directly ahead of Andy had the effect of making it seem difficult to communicate with him as she wished. She had certainly proposed this walk as if it were for something definite of the kind. But now she didn't know how to begin. She had imagined herself saying something like, 'Why do you turn awkward and cagey with me at times, Andy, seeing that we've become such good friends?' But now it was clear to her that this would be impossible. A girl who talked in that way was pretty well advancing a proposal of marriage! As frequently happened, Ianthe was appalled by the vastness of her own inexperience.

173

'Would it be about the house and the estate and all that that you'd be thinking of, Ianthe lass?' Fortunately as it seemed, Andy had formed his own notion of what this walk was in aid of.

'I do think of that.'

'If it's not to be your ain it should all be Toby's. Nothing's clearer than that.'

'I don't know what are the rights of an adopted child at law, Andy. But it's not really in question.' Ianthe was relieved that it was this subject that had turned up. 'They certainly don't extend to an estate and a house that aren't entailed in any way.'

'I think you're right about that. But he promised me. I've been meaning to tell you lang syne. And Toby too.'

'Tell me what? Who promised?' Ianthe was so startled that she came to a halt. But Andy disapproved of this, and she had to pick up her pace again. 'Do you mean my father?'

'Aye. It was when he first talked about my going with Mr Tarling. I kent nothing about this Mr Tarling, and I said I wanted to know it would be for your father I'd be working still. And he said yes. And then I said so that one day it would be Toby's man I'd be. And he said yes it would be that. It was a load frae my mind, Ianthe.'

'Oh, Andy!' Fleetingly, Ianthe felt that she loved Andy precisely as she loved Toby. 'And you think it was a firm promise?'

'It was the thocht I had then. But I'm not so sure, Ianthe. I didn't ken your father that well then that I do now. He's a good man and kind—but not one of those whose own mind is long clear to them. So I'm wondering.'

'Wondering just what, Andy?'

'It's me that's not a' that clear there.' Andy said this humorously—which was somehow not to Ianthe's satisfaction. She felt that he was holding something back from her.

'Have you thought of something I haven't?' she asked. 'If so, please tell me.'

'All in good time, lass.'

'What do you mean—in good time?'

'Mebby there will be what needs a wee bit o' taking in haund

174

later on. But I'd be a richt gomerii ii i didna hae what's needed. So dinna' fash yoursel'.'

'Don't treat me like a child, Andrew Auld.' The dismissive character of Andy's last speech had annoyed Ianthe, and its return to the Doric seemed to convey a shift of attitude in him which she disliked very much. It was as if he had slipped back into some earlier milieu of his own, in which men were superior beings and their own judges of what it was fit their womenfolk should hear. In fact here was a very sharp instance of the trickiness of the whole Andy situation. And what on earth could he have in his mind— could he have in his mind about her family situation—that he thought it proper to reserve as for the counsels of princes? Ianthe, thus compounding the class thing with the related theme of the subjugation of women, was about to add something very tart indeed when she glanced at Andy and saw that he was looking at her with intense anxiety. The dominant male—if indeed he had really been briefly there—had vanished. The result was that Ianthe now spoke not at all as she had intended to. 'Andy,' she said, 'you know how both Toby and I feel about you. We mustn't get across each other about anything at all. Isn't that right?'

'Aye, it is.' Andy seemed surprised and perhaps a little alarmed. 'And you mean you're putting up with me, the twa of you? I can go round saying you like me fine?'

'Yes, *yes!* You know that perfectly well.' This time Ianthe wanted to stop for the purpose of stamping her foot in a childish way on the sodden leaves. Challenged on this behaviour, she would have had to say that she was still cross but now didn't know why. She had been quite mysteriously vehement, and she was no doubt looking at Toby's brother in a fashion more bright-eyed than she knew. A detached observer might have concluded that the young man ought to be gratified, but in fact the young man was looking a little more alarmed even than before.

'I've been havering,' he said quickly. 'And I'd never keep from you—or from Toby either—anything that's certain-sure with me. But a man monna always speak out what's no more than notions flitting through his head.'

175

And with this Ianthe had to be content. They had reached the estate office, and Andy disappeared into it without ceremony for what he no doubt very properly considered to be the serious labour of the day. She herself walked slowly home. The fog, although still dense, was now being shoved about by a rising breeze, so that confusing little vapour trails seemed to be eddying around her. It occurred to her that they matched her inner mind. She repeated to herself the thought that had come to her on waking up. *Andy didn't want to fall in love with her.* She tried a kind of inside-out operation on this. *Andy didn't want her to fall in love with him.* For no reason at all that wasn't intuitive she felt this version to be nearer the mark—if indeed there was a mark at all and she wasn't making things up like a green girl. But she didn't like it a bit. It suggested an Andrew Auld a good deal pestered by silly girls, whether green or not, and who had grown bored with all that and quick to squash it. The whole thing was extremely tiresome, and it was undeniable that she had fallen into the bad habit of thinking about Andy a great deal. She had better get back to thinking about the Minoans. They had the advantage, so far as she could see, of being unattractive every way on.

XIII

I T WAS TRUE THAT DURING THESE WEEKS Toby was taking an
increasingly poor view of Lombard Street. He blamed this on
Elma. He blamed it, just as crudely as he could, on his not having
Elma to hop into bed with when he felt disposed. At the same
time he knew himself to be enormously relieved that he wasn't
going to find himself married to Elma. That idea had been an
awful muddle. And it belonged inside a whole area of muddle.
He had dreams in which he found himself mysteriously in the
wrong street (although it didn't seem to be Lombard Street), and
got himself in such a panic over his inability to find the right one
that he woke up in the middle of a singularly useless sexual
exercise. He was ashamed of this regressive condition, and he was
also ashamed of his new feelings about his job. He disliked the
people he worked beside—particularly the middling-senior ones,
with their satisfied air of knowing how to 'handle' clients in brisk,
confident, spuriously cordial telephone conversations. It was
quite shocking (he told himself in a weirdly archaic way) that
chaps with the air of gentlemen should have taken to scooping a
living out of this money-grubbing jungle. He wished he'd gone
into the army, even if it meant rubbing shoulders with brainless
ticks like Elma's brother. It was something that lots of Feltons had
done for generations; that his own true ancestors—quite conceivably and whoever they were—had done too. There wouldn't
have been much of a living in it, but he knew very well that
Howard—although he was revealing himself as of so inconstant
a mind—wouldn't dream of leaving him without a good many
useful pennies in his pocket. For that matter, Howard had tipped
a hefty dollop of them into Lombard Street. And it was this that
now made his own regrets too late and in vain. He hadn't a clue
as to whether all or any of that money would be recoverable if

he feebly chickened out of the dreary hole. In fact he was bloody well trapped.

Things sometimes weren't much better when he went home. What he was liable to collide with now was not Andy on top of a ladder but Andy in a Land Rover going about some sensible task. He believed himself to have come to hate the Aston Martin; to feel himself a proper Charley in it. Quite often in the City nowadays he found himself having a drink with a contemporary to whom an aunt had given something like a Rolls as a twenty-firster. All that sort of affluence was quite disgusting, Toby thought.

He took to envying Andy, to asking himself why the hell he hadn't himself got into that Land Rover first. But equally he took to largely admiring Andy. There was something almost comical about it. Whether he was older or younger than Andy nobody would ever know. Twins were not, as he'd once dimly imagined, born simultaneously; at school he'd known a boy who was going to be an earl because he'd come into the world a few minutes before somebody else out of the same womb. But what he found himself occasionally feeling now was that he was Andy's younger brother in a quite definite way. He didn't resent this. In fact it was perfectly clear to him that he was more bound to Andy than he'd ever been or would ever be to any other male person.

But this in turn didn't prevent his being jealous of Andy as well. This was a very obscure feeling, but he did know that Ianthe was near the centre of it—and even that it would abate when Ianthe was back at Cambridge with her Mycenaeans or whoever they were. Toby, who was not devoid of a seriously inquiring mind, tried to think this out. He supposed that such jealousies generate themselves among siblings too frequently to be re-garded as morbid or censurable. And Ianthe was unique. She was, that was to say, the one woman in the world who could occasion that sort of jealousy and no other between Andy and himself, since she was Andy's sister precisely in the sense and degree that he was. Of course he had himself been longer in the rôle. But this didn't alter the basic fact.

Toby's thought tended to break off here in what was not perhaps a particularly impressive fashion intellectually regarded. Nor did it clarify itself further when he was actually at home. Although there was now this indefinable awkwardness at Felton, its week-ends held various agreeable distractions as well. Andy, far from hogging Ianthe, appeared a good deal disposed to masculine society and masculine rural pursuits. Surprisingly, it turned out that he could sit a horse, and he and Toby went riding on the downs. Then it proved that he could sit a horse rather better than Toby, and when cubbing started they pursued this mystery together on three successive Saturdays. To have a brother to go fox-hunting with seemed to Toby a very great happiness indeed, and at dinner he was inclined to make boring conversation about drawing this covert and that. Howard had never hunted, neither had Ianthe, and Mrs Warlow held absurd views about kindness to animals. Andy, who was coming to find amusement in polite behaviour, had to take on the job of introducing topics of more interest to the ladies. Howard Felton was rather silent during these weeks, whether at table or elsewhere; he went for his long tramps as usual, but seldom had anything much to report on returning from them. He had never said another word to anybody about the Mill House. But Andy reported Mr Tarling as having received instructions to effect various repairs there. It seemed that something called 'Africanization' was bringing a brother of Colonel Motley's home from an outpost of empire, and that there was a possibility he might like to rent the place.

Toby knew that Colonel Motley did have a brother in the Colonial Service, which during these years was certainly in process of packing up. But he found himself quite unable to believe that the chap was booking into Felton as suggested. His own scepticism here hurt Toby very much, and he became convinced that his first bizarre suspicion had been well in the target area. Things really had come unstuck at Felton as a result of Andy's arrival. Despite the fact that Howard liked Andy—and there could be no doubt about that—he had been bumped into feeling that Felton ought not to be a Foundling Hospital. It was Feltons

179

who ought to be at Felton; and that, in present circumstances, meant just his sister Grace and nobody else. Andy would be treated handsomely. Toby himself would be treated handsomely. But that was it.

This thought took Toby Felton so far down a devastating path that it was perhaps uncommonly odd it didn't take him further. He was in a state of considerable gloom about it all when his uncle's invitation arrived. It was an annual invitation, although it varied a little in date and character from year to year. The first occasion had been the worst. It had come during Toby's earliest days in the sixth form of his public school, and before he had ever been inside an Oxford or Cambridge college even for an entrance examination. But the Warden's summons had to be obeyed. Toby had been obliged to get into his dinner jacket, take a bus to Oxford, and dine at a high table among about twenty dons, nearly all of whom felt they must have a word with Hugh's nephew in the course of the evening. It had been the occasion upon which Toby had taken his dislike to port.

Later he had of course come rather to enjoy this annual solemnity, which had now recurred half-a-dozen times. But this new invitation varied from the others in two regards. It was for some out-of-term affair to which former members of the college were bidden in a big way, so that it was likely to have the character of a regular jamboree. And Andy was invited as well. They were both bidden to stay the night in the Warden's Lodging.

Toby, although not given to fussing about such matters, consulted Mrs Warlow before seeking out Andy himself.

'What do you think?' he asked. 'Is this Hugh's celebrated tact —or is it non-tact? I wouldn't know.'

'I see nothing remarkable about it.'

'It's not, I mean, exactly Andy's thing.'

'That, if true, can't be helped. Now that Andy is with us, it would be invidious for your uncle to invite you without him. And he may judge that Andy will be a resource to you amid a great many middle-aged and boring people. By no means all of them will even hunt.'

'Sarky, aren't you, Aunt Grace?'

'Or he may feel that your brother will keep you from drinking too much.'

As drinking too much was no more Toby's thing than formal academic refection was Andy's, this was a harmless pleasantry. Mrs Warlow put something tart into it, all the same. Her inclination that way had increased of late, as if the general slight jumpiness at Felton were infecting her.

'It says "white or black tie". So I could put on my tails and Andy could have my dinner jacket. Only I'd try to persuade him to do it the other way round. Do you know that I'm over an inch more round the tummy than he is? I'll bet you'd regularly swoon, Aunt Grace, if you saw Andy in a white waistcoat.'

'As the feast will be a depressingly all-male one, I fear your brother's charms may be little regarded. Or yours either. But, since you ask my advice, it is that you take it for granted that Andy will accept. If he doesn't want to go, he won't be slow to say so.'

'That's true enough. And of course it wouldn't come even into my thick head to sound doubtful about it. Andy's worth a whole wagon-load of bloody dons.'

'Say at least a barrowful. But, Toby, I think there is another point. You could quite easily drive home from Oxford after this dinner. Hugh's asking you both to spend the night in college may mean that he wants to talk things over with you.'

'Things?'

'Precisely,' Mrs Warlow said. 'Things.'

'Aunt Grace, have you been talking to Hugh?'

'Not lately. Or not *talking* to him lately. We do correspond from time to time. I cannot pretend that I have the family trick of treating your uncle as an oracle. But I have a sense that he is your friend. And now, Toby, go away and stop fishing. Or fish, if it is a proper time of year for it. It will be a change from galloping round in the middle of all those blundering hounds.'

'I never gallop around in the middle—' Toby, momentarily

outraged, checked himself and grinned. 'OK, OK,' he said. 'And as for Hugh's blessed dinner, no problem.'

It turned out more or less like that. Andy's response to the proposal was quite casual; he said he supposed it was all part of taking a look around—a judgement he might have appropriately passed on a suggestion that he and Toby should pay a visit to the Tower of London or the Zoo. Toby wasn't sure that this attitude was entirely genuine. Andy had never been in Oxford, and it was probable that the existence of the place had scarcely ever entered his head. But Toby had once or twice treated him to accounts (no doubt satirically slanted) of Cambridge life, and as Andy did genuinely like looking around it might be supposed that on the present occasion he'd feel a lively curiosity about an unknown mode of life. Toby had become aware that his brother possessed much less in the way of social prejudices and assumptions than he himself did. Andy was definitely an uncommitted sort of chap. At times you could feel that he was this almost alarmingly. Reviewing what he vaguely thought of as the whole thing, Toby felt clear that Andy did very strongly approve of having a brother. Perhaps, too, other Felton loyalties were gathering around him: there was, for instance, the odd way he appeared struck on Aunt Grace. But you had to feel, all the same, that it was his instinct to keep his options open. And he had so miraged up out of nowhere that Toby was never quite free of the feeling that he might similarly vanish. It was why Toby particularly liked driving Andy round in the Aston Martin: this despite the unfortunate issue of their first considerable trip in it. There, for a time at least, Andy safely was. He couldn't even jump for it. It was like that as they drove into Oxford.

But there had been one near-hitch. The Felton men never now 'changed for dinner' in the full and old-fashioned way unless the giving of a dinner-party required it. Nothing of the sort had happened since Andy's arrival. He had been buying some clothes, and wearing others of Toby's, without any appearance of much bothering. But here suddenly was a sticking-point—rather like

that which had presented itself over the business of his moving
into Toby's part of the house. He got himself into his brother's
dinner-jacket, and didn't like himself in it at all. He said it made
him look and feel like a bloody waiter, and that if he went into
this college place in it he couldn't promise that he wouldn't jump
up and begin moving plates. Although this was a joke, Toby
found himself almost frightened by it, and he hurried off and
fetched Ianthe. Ianthe contrived to turn the situation to laughter.
She got them both half-undressed again. She got Andy into
Toby's tails, just as Toby himself had proposed, but not without
positively tugging at him here and there in the course of the
operation. She performed for him the very difficult feat of tying
another person's bow tie. And then she combed his hair. Then,
because Toby was professing himself exhausted, she started in on
him too. These performances left her excited and triumphant, but
decidedly confused. But the important thing was that Andy had
been vanquished. He studied himself in that long pier-glass before which he and his new-found brother had once stood side by
side—and this time it was in a kind of boyish awe.

'I'm jest richt for the ba'!' he said. 'Ianthe, my dear, I'm
dressed for the ball. So let the band strike up.' Demonstrating
himself as an advanced bilingual person had become a regular
piece of fun with Andy. But it made things a little more confusing
still. The brothers were nowhere more identical than in their
simple view of the nature of wit.

'How many students does your uncle have in this place we're
going to?' Andy asked as they drove.
'About three hundred and fifty, I think. I'm not sure.'
'It's a handfu', that. How does he keep order amang them?
They mon be fair tackets, some o' them.'
'Just go easy on that lingo again this evening, Andrew Auld.
Otherwise you'll frighten them.'
'Message understood. Does he leather them?'
'They're supposed to be too old for that.' It was clear that
Andy had only an inexact notion of the difference between a

public school and an Oxford or Cambridge college. 'I expect he sometimes wishes he could.'

'I've been thinking about your uncle.'

'I wish you wouldn't go on saying "your uncle". I don't really think of him that way. I call Grace Warlow "Aunt Grace" because somehow it seems polite. But I no more imagine she's really my aunt than I imagine the Queen is.'

'Then what about Mr Felton?'

'Well, yes—Howard's my father. I mean I've always felt that he is, in a quite natural way.' Toby hesitated for a moment. 'Perhaps he's more my father than—as it's turning out—I'm his son.'

'Mebby.'

'But I think that, when you've simply been adopted like me, the sense of kinship doesn't spread around. It's hard to explain. But I know that I think of Hugh Felton just as that old chap in Oxford.'

'Do you feel that Ianthe's just that young girl at Felton?'

'No, I don't. Of course not.' Toby hesitated again. 'That's absolutely different,' he went on, rather brusquely. 'We've been brought up together. Neither of us has a single memory that antedates our being kids in the same nursery. So in a kind of a way she's even more my sister than you're my brother.'

'I'd ca' that an unco queer kind o' way.'

'Oh, shut up, Andy. Your uncos are as tiresome as your uncles.' Toby scowled over his steering-wheel, feeling this to have been a singularly silly quip. 'But what do you mean, anyway, that you've been thinking about Hugh Felton?'

'I've been wondering how it would be if this was long ago. Would there have been a time when, if your father had only an adopted son, this Hugh Felton would have to be the heir to things? I'm asking because your father seems to me to have a regard more than's sensible to ancient ways of doing yin thing or another.'

'I suppose he has. But about what you're asking I haven't a clue. I do know that if there were a title in the family—and there

184

was, but it got lost in the wash — it would have to go to Hugh. If
you're a duke or something, you can't just look round and adopt
a brat and say he's going to be a duke after you. But it has usually
been different, I think, with a dozen farms and so on. I call this
a stupid conversation. But we're nearly there.'

'What's that building awa' ahead? Is it the gas works?'

'No. It's something called the Radcliffe Camera.'

'It must be a daft-like place that ca's a thing like yon a camera.'

'For pity's sake, you great oaf!' For some minutes Toby drove
up the Abingdon road in silence. 'I only hope,' he then said
gloomily, 'we get some approach to a decent meal.'

The dinner in fact proved not remarkable in any way. Andy,
although the scene was as strange to him as would have been a
cannibal feast in the jungle, enjoyed it very much. If he wasn't
exactly the riproarious success he had been with Sophie and Arlette, he did rather better than get by—and the more easily, no
doubt, because the idea of getting by wasn't urgent with him.
Perhaps, dutifully respecting his brother's injunction, he made
only sparing use of his more mysterious vocabulary. There was a
general feeling that he was a scientist. Some of the guests who
conversed with him might have been observed quickly to assume
the expression of slightly awed deference which is felt to be
becoming in the presence of a young man understood to be
brilliantly ahead in the field of atomic physics. But when directly
questioned about his activities he promptly replied that he was an
agronomist. Toby had found this word for him in a dictionary,
and they had agreed that thus to describe a retired under-gardener was very funny indeed.

They got back to the Lodging ahead of the Warden, who had
to remain in common room until the end of the affair. This landed
them with the task of a certain amount of polite conversation with
Mercia Felton, who was exhibiting the slight grimness habitual in
Oxford ladies whose husbands have been feasting while they
themselves dine on a poached egg. Rather to Andy's disappoint-
ment, no French parlour-boarders were in evidence. ('Just when
we felt like yin apiece,' he muttered libidinously to his brother

when this became apparent.) But the young men had drunk enough to cope with Mercia in an easy-going way, and Andy even scandalously amused himself by briefly according her his up-and-down-and-roundabout glance. After this she sent them to bed.

'It was sweet of you both to come,' she said as she dismissed them. 'Hugh is particularly pleased. Of course he has been terribly busy tonight. But he is looking forward to a talk with you—with both of you—in the morning.'

They shared a bedroom. Andy had got out of his tails—or out of Toby's tails—before he spoke.

'What would it mean,' he asked, 'about a talking to frae him you wonna hae for an uncle?'

'Back with your double Dutch, aren't you? I haven't a clue.'

'I dinna ken about you, Toby. But I can tell what he's after wi' me. He's for offering me yin o' the Fellowships they were claivering aboot. I feel it in my baines.'

'It wouldn't surprise me a bit,' Toby said handsomely—and added at once, 'Plenty of moronic dons.'

'Let's hae a pillow-fight, Toby, like in the stories about your daft sort of school.'

'It's a bit old hat, that. But why not?'

So for a minute or two they engaged in this ritual absurdity, banging one another on the head. Then they tumbled into their beds and went to sleep at once.

They were awakened at what seemed an unearthly hour by the sound of briskly raised blinds and a rattle of crockery. There was a manservant in the room, equally concerned to pour tea and to announce that the Warden hoped the gentlemen would join him for breakfast at eight o'clock. Andy perhaps found this not out of the way. But Toby judged it an outrage, and insisted to his brother that at Cambridge such barbarous hours were unknown. But there was nothing for it but obedience, and they turned up downstairs as the clock struck.

The Warden was already at table, and alone. Perhaps Mercia

breakfasted in bed. The Hugh Felton daughters were away from
home, presumably in France. The meal was an entirely help-
yourself affair. If Hugh had something to propound, he could go
straight ahead and do so. He began, needless to say, with polite
enquiries: the young men's enjoyment of the previous evening
and the soundness of their slumbers thereafter.

'But do you know,' he asked, primarily of Toby, 'that it has
occurred to me it might be useful to have a talk? On the family
situation, I mean.'

'Wouldn't it be better,' Andy suggested, 'to wait, sir, until I'm
taking a dander round the town?'

'I scarcely think so. It's my sense of the matter that you and
Toby are entirely in one another's confidence. Toby, is that
right?'

'Yes, of course.'

'And I think, Andrew, that you have in a sense a fresh eye for
things, having come among us so lately.'

'I don't spend all that time peering,' Andy said—a shade
belligerently.

'Of course not. But now, Toby, I want to ask you something.
Has it occurred to you that your father'—Hugh had paused on
this, which he had clearly decided to prefer to 'my brother'—'may
marry again?'

'Marry again!' Toby seemed not merely astonished at this
suggestion but scandalized as well.

'Dr Johnson spoke of second marriage—or perhaps it was of
a specific second marriage—as the triumph of hope over experience. In your father's case, it would be the triumph of certain
natural propensities over a somewhat dilatory and wavering temperament. He has been a widower for a long time. I can only say
that, just lately, my observations have tended to my bringing the
matter forward in my mind. Andrew, have you had any sense of
this?'

'Mebby.'

'When we lunched with you at Felton lately, I was struck by

187

the strong appeal which those French girls of ours appeared to exercise over him.'

'I think that's all rot,' Toby said—and didn't at all mind that this was not a courteous expression. 'And if he did marry again it would be his own business, and it wouldn't be fair to put it all down to weakness of character and being slow off the mark and all that.'

'In part I agree with you. At least among his motives—and it might even be the most powerful of them—would be one which many people might judge entirely laudable. The desire for a son.'

Not surprisingly, this produced a moment's complete silence.

'And why not?' Toby said. He had gone very pale.

'There's a bloody big why not!' Andy came out with this very robustly indeed.

'I am in agreement with Andrew,' Hugh said calmly. 'I'd be far from happy to butt in. I hope I'm not butting in now. But I must record that I should wholly disapprove of my brother's so belatedly altering the shape of things at Felton. It *would* be weakness of character, Toby. Howard might well be dead while his child and heir was still a boy, or an unformed lad. I see nothing to commend it except an unphilosophical—indeed, a fond and foolish—notion of lineage and so forth. I'd try to prevent it.'

'I don't think you should say that, sir,' Toby said. 'And I expect Andy thinks it wrong too.'

'Mebby.'

Toby had been badly shaken, and he was shaken still more by his brother's obvious disposition to accept the Warden's point of view. The business of the Mill House had disturbed him, but he had somehow stopped short of seeing in it the particular portent which Hugh Felton believed to have been otherwise vouchsafed to him.

'I shall be quite open with my brother,' Hugh said, a shade coldly. 'Just as I am now being quite open with both of you. It comes simply to this, Toby. The thing would be a mere vagary —and a discredit to my family, if one is minded to see things that

188

'A' credit to you,' Andy said with unabated vigour. 'But *can* you help it? You're no your brother's keeper, Mr Felton—no more than I'm mine.'

'In my view, Toby himself can help it. He can get married.'

This was certainly a surprising remark, but Toby received it as if it were a thunderbolt, perhaps because 'marriage' still meant for him nothing except what he had recently escaped from (or been denied) in the person of Elma. Andy, however, to whom it had been addressed, reacted in a judicial manner.

'Mebby so,' he said. 'It should be thocht on.'

'My brother has this strong instinct for continuities. And he sees his household, his family, coming to a stop. Or that's how I view the matter. And, I believe, how my sister does too.'

'Mrs Warlow?' Andy asked quickly.

'Yes, indeed. I believe that my brother has been a little disappointed—although he is scarcely, perhaps, conscious of the fact —that Toby, although still, if I may say so, so young, has had no thought of marriage as yet. Indeed—to look a little further—if another generation showed signs of coming along, he might shed all that superstition about lineage and ancestry and so forth with no great effort.' The Warden paused warily—as a man is apt to do when feeling that he is being tactful in no common degree. 'And of course in Toby's case there is one specific possibility which it would be foolish to ignore.'

'What do you mean—a specific possibility?' Toby demanded. Toby was looking bewildered and rather scared—which was perhaps what brought Andy to his feet.

'Mebby that it's leap-year,' he said, 'and that some lass may be louping at Toby ower a hedge.' As he produced this piece of nonsense Andy was looking at the Warden very hard indeed. 'It's a' to be thocht o', nae doot, but we monna be previous. And noo we must awa'. Toby, you'd better bring roond your car.'

The astonishing commandingness of this, let alone its full return to the accents of northern Britain, seemed momentarily to

189

nonplus the Warden. As for Toby, he obeyed his brother to the extent of bolting from the room.

'Sir,' Andy said, 'ye dinna ken how kittle this thing is. We know what we want—you and me and Mrs Warlow, although we've never talked about it thegither. But it canna be rushed. There's a barrier to be got awa'.'

'I suppose you're right, young man.' The Warden had stood up, and was looking at Toby's brother with considerable respect. 'There's no legal barrier: I've made absolutely sure of that. The barrier to be broken down is what the anthropologists call the primitive fear of incest.'

'I wouldn't know to put any such words to it. I'd say it's just how they've seen one another for a long time.' Perhaps with the idea of clarity in what could be only a brief colloquy, Andy had abruptly come south of the Border. 'Your sister has had the thought that I might help. At least that's the way I see her thinking. That me being at Felton might help. The shoogle of it.'

'The *what?*'

'I'm sorry. The shake-up in it. Here's me, suddenly. A kind of other Toby—but without all those brother-and-sister'—Andy paused, having to search for a word—'associations.'

'Grace has really been thinking this way?'

'She hasn't ever said it, but I'm sure it's in her mind. If Ianthe came to see me as just possibly a sweetheart, she might be jumped —it's something like that, this idea—into seeing Toby as that too.'

'And what is Toby going to see?'

'He'll see what he's told.' Andy said this with some appearance of humorous intent, but was clearly quite serious. 'There's but a thin curtain, you might say, between him and his knowing what Ianthe should be to him. But it's all that kittle! I can't get the English of that.'

'Difficult. Delicately balanced.'

'That's it! I mustn't be having Ianthe really fall in love with me.'

'And you mustn't fall in love with her?'

'I hae to risk that, Mr Felton.'

'I have an idea that you can trust yourself.' The Warden said this with the deft briskness of one long accustomed to coping with young men. He was silent for a moment, and the sound of the Aston Martin's engine made itself heard in the quad. 'One other question, Andy. It's about my notion of my brother's thoughts on himself marrying. Have you anything more to say—in confidence between us—on that?'

'Only that it might be delicate too.' Andy paused on this. 'Or perhaps'—he then added obscurely—'it might no' be delicate at all. But there's Toby waiting. And I enjoyed my grand dinner very much.'

XIV

TOBY SAID LITTLE DURING the drive back to Felton, and nothing at all on the family situation as viewed from the Warden's Lodging. If he felt that Hugh had been sympathetic and concerned to help he also felt that some of his ideas had been distinctly odd. But there was something odd, too, in the way that Andy had rather quickly shut him up. Toby was conscious of not quite having got hold of that final turn in the talk. It was as if his mind had gone abruptly inattentive in an unusual way. Perhaps Hugh, with marriage buzzing like a bee in his bonnet, remembered something he'd been told or guessed about the Elma thing, and Andy had had the good sense to head him off. But then those two had been left together, and it was Andy who had contrived this by sending him to fetch round the car. So possibly Hugh knew nothing about Elma, and Andy had judged for some reason that he should be told. Toby remembered how Andy had refused to promise that in no circumstances would he betray the secret of the Elma affair. But what would be the point of telling Hugh about it? Andy couldn't believe that, if Elma would only change her mind, her marrying him would restore him to Howard's favour. This seemed nonsense, and Toby was very puzzled. But pride kept him from questioning Andy about those final exchanges with the Warden. In fact it was to Ianthe, later that day and only in reply to questioning, that he first said a word about the Oxford trip.

'How did it go?' Ianthe asked. 'Did Hugh have designs on you?'

'I suppose he did, in a way. Benevolent designs. He was very decent to both of us. I think he's coming to like Andy. I don't expect Mercia does.'

'Bother Mercia! What were the designs?'

'Well, the first point is that he does take rather a gloomy view. About Felton and me, I mean. And I didn't tell him about the Mill House ploy, so he wasn't basing himself on that. Do you know? He has got the queerest idea in his head. He thinks your father is likely to marry again. That's pretty absurd, isn't it?'

'I don't know that it can be called that.' If Ianthe was surprised, it was by the fact that this possibility had apparently never entered Toby's head.

'And he has an odder idea still. He thinks it would help matters if I got married myself. That it would make Howard feel there was a kind of carrying-on effort in train at Felton. Carrying on seems not a bad word for it.' Toby actually paused as if for appreciation of this entirely tasteless quip. 'He stopped short of naming me a bride. Who on earth *am* I to marry? Perhaps the elder of the Misses Kinch would have me.'

'Or you might marry Aunt Grace.'

'The vicar wouldn't do the job. A man can't marry his aunt.'

'She's not your aunt. She's absolutely unrelated to you. Ring up the Archbishop of Canterbury, and he'll tell you that at once. But I suppose Hugh's idea is that there should be little pattering feet in Felton once more. And Aunt Grace is probably beyond that. She'd better be left to Colonel Motley. So what about Elma Loftus?'

Ianthe's lips hadn't closed on this name before she saw that Toby had blushed scarlet. It was a thing she couldn't remember ever happening before. She was horrified at having come out so unaccountably with so brutal a question—and the more so because nothing could immediately be done about it. She couldn't even say she was sorry without transforming the blunder into a fuss, and without betraying a knowledge she was supposed never to have guessed at. All she could do was to pretend that her remark had been quite silly and pointless, and hurry on to something else.

As for Toby, when the blush faded it was replaced by the expression of perplexity which had been becoming intermittently evident in him. He had got to feeling that he never wanted to

193

hear the name of Elma Loftus again. (On balance, this must be held rather ungrateful in Toby—Elma, even if a bitch, having initiated him into an important and pleasurable area of human activity.) He couldn't decide whether Ianthe's having mentioned her in this way now had been serious, or in fun, or in need of an explanation not adequately covered by either of these ideas. All along he'd had a bad conscience that he was letting Ianthe down in the Elma affair; that it had been a kind of lowering of his sights below her expectations of him. In this sense Elma had really come between Ianthe and himself, even although the affair had remained totally unknown to her. And now he couldn't bear the thought of Ianthe thinking ill of him, still less the thought of in any degree losing her. This last feeling even prompted him for a moment to seize her in his arms and hold tight. But he refrained from such an unexampled act.

'What did Andy think of Hugh's ideas?' Ianthe asked. This was the first fresh conversational resource that came into her head.

'I haven't asked him. Perhaps it should be Andy that marries Elma.'

Toby had now said something quite as strange and seemingly unprompted as Ianthe had achieved, and he was extremely disconcerted. Why on earth should he offer such a stupid and hostile remark about Andy, whom he had come to be very fond of, to Ianthe, whom he was very fond of too? The implication had almost been that the doctor's daughter was good enough for the gardener's boy. At best, Toby realized, it was about the feeblest joke he'd ever made—and that was saying a lot. The truth was that he was becoming envious of Andy.

This perception, although it was decidedly a foggy one, was of powerful effect as well. He told himself that the bloody acceptance house was to blame. There he was all week, hard at work turning useless things called bills into equally useless things called prime bills, while Ianthe and Andy were in the enjoyment of a proper sort of life, Felton life, together. It was true that Ianthe was a Cambridge undergraduate. But that need keep her from home

194

for less than half the year, whereas the Lombard Street bastards
judged that three weeks out of fifty-two was a good enough holiday for him.

'Andy isn't at all the sort of person who should marry Elma.' Ianthe made this rejoinder with considerable fire. 'Or even take her on.'

'What do you mean—take her on?' For the first time, Toby felt that Ianthe must really *know*.

'Nothing much. And this is rather a silly conversation.'

'So it is,' Toby agreed quickly, and took Ianthe by the elbow —which was a perfectly customary thing. 'Let's have a knock-up. Just one set.'

So they played tennis for a time—on a court no longer in very good condition, and upon which Andy's successor had swept up only in his deplorably half-hearted fashion. Toby played very badly. Whether silly or not, this conversation had left him both disturbed and puzzled. Why should there be something ungrateful to him in the thought of Ianthe and his brother enjoying one another's company? The feeling was almost like jealousy. (Or at least so he supposed—for it was a novel sort of feeling, or one of which he couldn't remember experiencing more than fleeting twinges, and those probably in his nursery.) Had he really become so fond of Andy that he resented sharing him with anyone? This seemed a shocking idea; it was Narcissus again, resenting a second face peering into that pool. Toby was walking back to the house, companionably enough with Ianthe, when this confused image a little clarified or at least modified itself. And this came about through another image, itself purely and sharply visual. He *saw* Ianthe and himself walking together. But although the one figure was certainly Ianthe, he was by no means certainly the other. For it was a kind of second self, after all, that he left behind him at Felton every Monday morning when, after an early breakfast, he climbed into the Aston Martin and set off for the City of London.

It will thus be apparent that Mrs Warlow's theory of the shake-up (adopted by Andrew Auld as the theory of the shoogle) was by no means the figment of an over-ingenious mind. At least in its obscure workings it did accelerate things. And what would have happened at Felton had the young man from Glesgy never found employment there nobody is in a position to say.

XV

IANTHE WENT BACK TO CAMBRIDGE, and life at Felton House settled down for the winter. Andy, in addition to appearing punctually for meals, spent a good deal of time with Mrs Warlow. She had felt it incumbent upon her to take on Ianthe's rôle as the discreet purveyor of a liberal education. Andy now knew all about eating asparagus, and if he wasn't yet quite sound on entering a box at the Opera this seemed unlikely to be of importance in any immediate future. Having thus modified her ideas about educating Toby's brother, Mrs Warlow gave the subject a good deal of thought, eventually hitting upon the expedient of drawing lessons. Andy proved rather good at this, but not so absorbed in the activity as to fail of attention at the same time to his teacher's fairly wide-ranging conversation. Mrs Warlow, who was not immune to the satisfactoriness of Andy's so plainly regarding her as 'well-preservit', came to rely on his society a good deal. She could envisage developments at Felton which might well deprive her of this, or even result in Andrew Auld and herself going their several ways. And she had to acknowledge that she would miss him rather a lot. But their confidence in one another had grown marked, and she felt at least that Andy would spring no surprises on her.

Howard Felton in these late-autumn days was more peripatetic than ever, and at the same time given to considerable absence of mind. But as well as matters on the remoter parts of the estate the affairs of Felton House itself were now of much concern to him, and particularly the tiresome business of redecorating the saloon. His sister regarded this as tiresome partly because it was going to cost much more money than he seemed to be aware of, and partly because it brought Elma Loftus into the Felton picture again. Elma had thrown up her job in Harley Street, it seemed, because she had spotted a possible 'opening' with a fashionable firm of interior decorators. It looked as if landing them a commission at Felton was the test they were imposing on her, and she turned up at the house on several occasions with a director of the concern. He annoyed Mrs Warlow on the peculiar score that he was possessed of the manners of a gentleman. There was no reason why a house-decorator should not be graced in this way, but Mrs Warlow didn't like it. Still less did she like a lavishness of aesthetic feeling in him which was only equalled by the lavishness of his proposed application of gold-leaf to what even in its present faded state was rather an ornate spectacle.

On these occasions Elma had, moreover, brought her brother Vivian along with her. It appeared that Vivian had overestimated the eagerness of the older universities to accept him into their society, and he was now being coached by the vicar with no very discernible goal in view. Vivian was sulky, but this was no doubt because he was unhappy, and Mrs Warlow judged it much to Andy's credit that from time to time he gave Vivian a certain amount of his company. Whether he saw anything of Vivian's sister other than on those occasions upon which she turned up with the man intent upon bedizening Felton House wasn't clear. He seldom said anything about Elma, and for some time Mrs Warlow didn't question him. She occasionally felt that, despite their absence of reserve towards one another, there was at least some aspect of Andy's present feeling that was obscure to her. Being professionally expert in the field of human physiognomy, she once or twice thought to detect something rather grim lurking behind his generally cheerful air. And eventually she decided that cautious exploration was desirable.

'Andy,' she asked him one day when they were walking together in the garden, 'did you have any sort of private conversation with my brother Hugh when you were in Oxford?'

'Aye, did I. But it wouldn't have been that private if I hadna' hurried Toby frae the room. Your brother was for blurting out that Toby should marry Ianthe—and that way produce a kind of

Felton heir for Felton, nae doot. And it's perfectly true. I'm astray
about yoursel if you don't think that.'

'Certainly I do.'

'But you know what that learned man doesn't: that Toby and
Ianthe hae to mak their own way to seeing theirsels as something
other than brother and sister.'

'They do, indeed. And which will see it first? Ianthe, to my
mind.'

'I'd think that too. And then she'll hae to wait, puir lass, for
Toby to see it—or a'most see it—afore we get any further on that
road. But will your brother Hugh never have told his idea to your
brother Howard?'

'Probably not. And I'm decidedly glad you didn't let him
suddenly confront Toby with it.'

'But he did out wi' another fact o' the matter: that his brother
may well marry and hae a son. We've all of us thought of that I
dinna' doot—or all except Toby.'

'Of course we have. And what was my brother's view of it?'

'He was a' agin it. He said he'd stop it if he could.'

'That seems to me distinctly sweeping.' Mrs Warlow looked
seriously at her protégé. (She had come to feel that this was the
proper light in which to regard Andy, if one aspect of his interest
in her was to be prudently played down.) 'I can imagine my
brother Howard making what all reasonable people would regard
as an entirely suitable second marriage. Its consequences might
be hard on Toby—but to some extent that is a separate issue.'

'Mr Felton—the Oxford yin—doesn't see it quite that way.'
An anxious note had come into Andy's voice, and he was looking
almost warily at this admired woman. 'An' he's a philosopher an'
a' that.'

This sudden ingenuousness was endearing—or would have
been so had not Mrs Warlow suspected that Toby's brother was
not without the power of rather subtly contrived effects.

'And what,' she asked, 'does my brother Hugh dredge up
from the depths of his philosophic mind?'

'He's a clear-thinking man, your brother Hugh, and if Mr

Felton was aiming to marry a douce body of his own age he'd judge it fair enough. But it's too late for a bairn in a cradle to be displacing Toby with ony kind o' honesty at all. It's that that your brother Hugh is saying, and I think he's richt. Don't you?'

For a moment Mrs Warlow made no reply. She was aware of Andy as looking at her with an intentness of regard that came rarely to him. She was aware that, for good or ill, Andy saw her as an arbiter. He was a young man of distinctly independent mind, but in that mind he had chosen to invest her with authority. With matters at Felton standing as they did, she was thus landed with a considerable responsibility. And it was no good shirking this.

'Yes,' she said. 'I do. For Howard to marry a woman half his age with the idea of starting a nursery would be unfair to Toby. Unless, of course, he settled this place and its land on Toby first. And he couldn't do that without impoverishing any children subsequently born to him—which would simply be to substitute one unfairness for another.'

'An' wad it add weight to a' this if the young woman your brother took was no' quite what she should be?'

If Mrs Warlow vaguely sensed a certain hovering illumination in this question, she was a good deal startled by it as well.

'In logic,' she said, 'I suppose not. It's a separate issue again. But humanly, I suppose, yes. Anybody would try to save a brother, or sister, from what must be judged some foolish infatuation.'

'I'd be right sorry to affront Mr Felton.' Andy came out with this seeming irrelevance very soberly. 'But it wadna' be on account o' ony selfish thocht o' my ain. The estate-managing, and a' that. In fact there's something I ought to be telling you that I havna' even telt Toby. Perhaps I've thocht he'd laugh at it. It's about my auntie.'

'The one with the sweetie-shop?' Mrs Warlow was entirely at sea.

'It's no yin sweetie-shop noo. It's about half the sweetie-shops ower a guid pairt o' Glesgy.' Andy's accent broadened as Glas-

gow thus swam up in his mind. 'I've tell ye how she was well-left
lang syne. Weel, she's been prospering ever since. Particularly
since she opened the second factory.'

'The second factory!' Absurdly, Mrs Warlow felt almost scandalized. 'Do you mean that your aunt is the sort of person who
could buy up Felton if she wanted to?'

'She wadna'. It wadna' enter her heid.' Andy offered this very
seriously. 'But you mon understand that she has no true kin, but
only me. So I'm tae her a wee bit as Toby is to Mr Felton. An'
I've aye wanted to be independent—which is why I came doon
here an' foond wark as I did. An' now it wad grieve me sair to
leave ye a'. But I could dae't, if need drove.'

'And open the third factory?'

'In time, mebby.'

Briefly, Mrs Warlow found herself disposed to wonder
whether all this was true. Could Andrew Auld be romancing—
or at least exaggerating wildly? He didn't give that impression at
all. She remembered learning that his foster-parents had at some
time a little come down in the world; it was probable enough that
one or other of them had relations in a prospering commercial
way. Perhaps it was the single sweetie-shop of Andy's first report
that had been a bit of an exaggeration, and his auntie had been
the proprietress of a small chain of such establishments from the
start. What there could be no doubt about was the general spirit
of independence by which Andy had been actuated. It was native
to him, and the death of both his adoptive parents had triggered
it into extravagant action. Mrs Warlow tried to imagine circumstances in which Toby would have struck out in some equivalent
way. Perhaps going after a job in Lombard Street might be regarded as filling the bill. But it was less impressive, somehow,
than putting one's pack on one's back and seeking one's fortune
as a gardener's boy.

Meanwhile, this conversation gave Mrs Warlow a good deal
to think about. And she ceased to be very certain that Andy would
never spring a surprise upon her—or, for that matter, upon other
people as well.

The person who did, as it turned out, have the power of surprising Mrs Warlow at this time was Colonel Motley. The fact was surprising in itself. Mrs Warlow knew very well that the colonel had something to say to her, but that the surprise which would ensue must unhappily fall upon her suitor himself. Colonel Motley owned all the proper modesty and diffidence of a soldier and a gentleman. Yet he was generally held agreeable in the quiet county society he frequented; his small estate, backed by various other resources, afforded him an ample competence; his morals were as irreproachable as his manners; he was prepared to listen with a decent attentiveness to conversation on topics even of a literary or artistic nature; he was physically extremely fit, and he belonged to a very good club. There was no reason why he should not be suitably esteemed by a middle-aged lady understood to be of limited means and to have suffered reverses in the matrimonial way.

So what Colonel Motley must at some early time say to Mrs Warlow was predictable, and only a certain amount of mildly reprehensible contrivance on Mrs Warlow's part had prevented it from happening already. Perhaps she hoped that the thing would wear off, and a slightly painful episode be thereby avoided. She had, to put it crudely, been dodging *tête à tête* encounters with her admirer. Unfortunately the general lack of novelty to be expected in the colonel's talk was a well-established fact among the younger people at Felton. Even Andy, although still in a situation sufficiently novel to militate against boredom in general, did find Colonel Motley boring. So when the colonel appeared one evening at Felton at the hour at which neighbours drop in upon one another for a glass of sherry Andy, who had been alone with Mrs Warlow, shamelessly slipped away. Howard too was absent, having gone up to London for the day on some obscure business occasion. So Mrs Warlow and her visitor sat down together with the duty of conjuring up between them half-an-hour of mildly convivial conversation.

'Do I smell the paint-pots already?' Colonel Motley asked with the familiarity of one enjoying the freedom of an old friend. 'Not disagreeable when there's no more than a whiff of it. But I hope they're not going to work on the whole place.'

'Heaven forbid! But it's true they've begun on the saloon. And I haven't a notion how long it's likely to take.'

'Ah, well—it's the show-piece of the whole house, wouldn't you say? Natural that it should have to be got spick-and-span.'

'So Howard appears to feel. He has been talking about it for some years. But I doubt whether he would have got round to actually doing anything without being prompted by Elma Loftus. The doctor's daughter, you know. She has always gone in for great houses and so on. And now her circumstances have changed and she has a more direct interest in paint-pots and whatever.'

'Exactly, exactly! I quite understand the situation, you know, although I haven't cared to take the initiative in touching on it. Changed plans all round, eh? Your own as well as this lucky young lady's. As a matter of fact it chimes in—that's the way to put it, I think: chimes in—with something I terribly want to say to you. Have done for a long time.'

'Colonel Motley—'

'But first, of course, I ought to say how glad I was to hear of what's in the wind. For your brother's sake, that is. She's a charming girl, I don't doubt. Although, mark you, I'd be just a little uneasy over such a disparity in years. Bring a lively sort of life into the house, of course. All that. But I can't think that such an age-gap is desirable in a general way. What do you think? I hope you agree with me. More companionship, and so forth, between two people more or less of an age, I feel.' Colonel Motley's speech had become spasmodic and agitated. 'So my dear Grace —may I presume so to address you?—I only want to say—'

'First things first, I beg! Do I understand you to say that it is "in the wind", as you express it, that my brother and Elma Loftus are engaged to be married?'

'Well, yes—I suppose so.' Colonel Motley was disconcerted by this unexpected reception of his remarks. 'And it has been under my own eye, you may say, and only yesterday. Your brother and this girl—this charming girl, that is—coming out of a barn together.'

'*Coming out of a barn!*'

'Or round it. Yes, round it, I suppose.' The colonel offered this concession to decorum with nervous haste. 'From the direction, come to think of it, of the Purbrick farm. They'd have been looking at the Blue-faced Leicesters old Purbrick has been going in for. Uncommonly interesting breed. Come a long way—wouldn't you say?—from Barford's Improved Bakewell Leicesters. Yes, that would be it.' For a moment the gallant colonel's confidence had faltered, but now he recovered it again—dimly believing, perhaps, that his own matrimonial chances depended upon the authenticity of the situation he was reporting. 'There they were, you see. Your brother's arm round the girl, and as pretty a picture as you could imagine. Kissed her, as a matter of fact.' Colonel Motley offered this last and definitive communication not without embarrassment—and at the same time made to stand up, as if actually estimating the feasibility of now going to work by storm, and treating Mrs Warlow in the same fashion. The lady, however, was too quick for him, and had stood up too.

'Colonel Motley,' she said, 'I must declare at once that what you say is new to me, and extremely surprising. My brother has said nothing of it, and it would be absurd in me to affect gratification at the prospect of so unsuitable an alliance. I cannot conceive how you could mention it to me except in terms of decent distress. You will forgive me, I am sure, if I feel that I must now be left alone to give thought to it.'

So the colonel took his leave in perplexity and dismay, and Mrs Warlow was left to give as much thought as she pleased to this transformed posture of affairs at Felton House. It didn't take her long to see that Andy had for some little time either known or suspected what was on foot. Perhaps his recent rather unaccountable taking up with Elma's brother had been in the interest of making observations in the matter. But why, then, had Andy not been frank with her about this disgusting threat—which

among other things was going to make Howard an object of
ridicule throughout the county? The probable answer to this
question came to her fairly soon. Andy was far from minded to
be a passive spectator of the fiasco. But what he intended to do
about it he didn't know that she'd approve.

Meanwhile, Mrs Warlow was conscious of the need for one
immediate decision in the matter. Andy, with the boring colonel
safely off the premises, might return to the room at any time, and
her brother would be back from town within an hour. Ought she
to speak up to either or both of them about what she had just
heard? For some minutes she debated this with herself, and then
determined to keep her own counsel until she had slept on the
horror confronting her. Indeed, she might keep it a little longer
than that. She was not without the desperate thought that Colonel
Motley was a shade mad, and had been either inventing or distort-
ing the whole thing.

XVI

A WEEK-END HAD GONE BY during which Toby had not made his customary return to Felton. He hadn't said anything about this in advance; he had merely rung up on the Friday and left a brief message to the effect that he wouldn't be home. It was unusual behaviour, but needn't have been alarming. Young men have their numerous occasions, not all of which need be explained to relatives. But Mrs Warlow, at least, was uneasy, since Toby's absence was so undeniably occurring within a context of family disturbance. Was that visit to Oxford having a delayed effect—Toby being offended with Howard on the basis of Hugh's talk about possible marriage? It had plainly been an eventuality broached only in general terms, Hugh being quite without any notion of Elma's possible place in the picture. But had Toby perhaps got hold of Colonel Motley's discovery (if it was a discovery) from some other source? It would be a very considerable shock to him. And Toby, in fact, was rather easily shocked. In his heart he had probably regarded his affair with Elma as not really terribly nice. And now here was the wretched girl—prompted, this time, by the acquisitive and great-house-hunting rather than the amative side of her nature—actually ensnaring his adoptive father after almost no interval at all. Mrs Warlow found that she was herself capable of viewing this situation as not without an element of comedy, although it was of a disagreeable sort. But poor Toby wouldn't be likely to see it that way.

There was the alternative possibility that Toby and Andy had had a row—that they'd had *another* row, Mrs Warlow told herself, recalling the mysterious affair in the pub. Mrs Warlow felt that you could never be quite sure about young men. A couple of them might, in every major regard, be comporting themselves in a wholly blameless fashion both before the world and to one another, and yet harbour within their conduct some small enclave of the most questionable sort, in which brief animosities could spring up and flourish for a time.

But this was a nebulous notion, and simply didn't square with Andy's obvious concern with furthering his brother's fortunes. By the time Mrs Warlow got this clear in her head another week-end had turned up, and so had Toby. Quite briefly, Toby explained what had occasioned his previous absence. He'd decided to drive over to Cambridge, book in at the Garden House, and look up Ianthe. It had suddenly come to him, he said, that it would be rather jolly to yank her out of her nunnery and treat her to a couple of decent meals.

This wasn't quite Toby's normal talk, and it wasn't at all his normal conduct. He professed as an old Cambridge man to be rather disenchanted with the place, and unprompted by any present pious feeling to return to it; nor had his conception of family duty run to visiting Ianthe there before. Now, apart from the bare fact of the jaunt, he wasn't at all communicative. Although it was becoming chilly even in the bright early-winter sunshine, he spent a good deal of time perched on his favourite balustrade on the terrace, gazing over Felton's gardens and park rather (Mrs Warlow thought) in the manner of stout Cortez similarly engaged with the Pacific Ocean. Mrs Warlow, glancing through a window at this almost with the circumspection of the Misses Kinch behind their curtains, felt that what is called bated breath was required of her. Was the moment coming—or had it actually come—in which she might murmur with Prospero, 'My high charms work' and conclude the chancy mechanism of the shoogle to have justified itself? The thought was so exciting that she quite ceased for a time to worry about the folly in which her elder brother was proposing to engulf himself.

Yet about that folly (on which she was still holding her peace) she now had very little doubt. Successful dissimulation was very little Howard's thing, and it was quite obvious that he was in an unusual state of mind—and one characterized, indeed, by an uncomfortable conflict of feelings. Howard was pleased with himself: there could be no question of that. He was like a small boy who knows he has done—or is about to do—something enormously clever. But equally he was misdoubting, alarmed, and suffering from a guilty conscience. This last state of mind was sufficiently evident even while Toby was absent from Felton, and it became even more obvious in Toby's presence. Toby however seemed unaware of it, and when alone with Mrs Warlow he made no reference to such of the Warden's ideas as had transpired over that Oxford breakfast-table. Toby, quite clearly, was wrapped in other speculations. It was an uncomfortable state of affairs, all the same. Mrs Warlow was relieved when, after luncheon on the Saturday, Toby and his brother announced that they were going for quite a long walk on the downs.

'Wad there be as mony lassies as there are young men at Cambridge?' Andy asked conversationally when they had set out.

'No, not nearly so many. But a lot more than when I was up —and that's no time ago.'

'No more it is. We're young still, you an' me, Toby.' It pleased Andy to give this the air of quite a sage remark. 'Ianthe will hae made some friends among the other girls by now?'

'I suppose so.'

'But ye didna' meet any?' Andy now sounded surprised.

'No.'

'Man, I thocht it wad ha been what you'd gone for. After what that canny man the Warden was clavering over aboot it's being a canty queen you should be thinking of getting bedded wi'.'

'Oh, shut up, Andy. And I simply won't talk to you if you go on piling up that gibberish.'

'Very well. But you really haven't any thought of getting married? It would get that Elma out of your system.'

'I don't want to talk about that just yet. There's something too big and new to get clear in my head. And as for Elma, to hell with her.'

'Tell me, Toby. Was she the first girl you ever had?'

'Yes.' Toby was furious at this questioning, but determined to answer whenever he honestly could. 'Properly, that is.'

'She was the first you really got it up with?'

'I didn't mean that. The first I didn't pay.'

'Oh, that!' For the first time within his brother's recollection, Andy sounded rather shocked. 'Well, well!' he said, 'I was saying we're young still. I've had girls, Toby—three or four, although I've no thought to be a gay Lothario.'

'I suppose not.' Toby wondered who Andy supposed Lothario to have been.

'And yin no' that lang syne. Sorry! One not all that long ago.'

'I think this is stupid. I think it's rather horrid, really, talking about women at that—at that level.'

'It's the only level some of them are there to talk at.'

'Who was the one you had not long ago?'

'Perhaps I'll tell you one day, or perhaps sooner. But it's stupid, as you say. We'll talk about the beauties of nature, Toby, and not of the seraglio.'

'Of the what?'

'The seraglio. Means a knocking-shop.'

In fact for quite some time they talked about nothing at all, walking briskly ahead in silence. But it was a companionable silence, which somehow suggested that these brief exchanges had been satisfactory to both of them. Andy in particular might have been distinguished as bearing a contented mind, rather as if some preliminary investigation had turned out well.

Certainly the afternoon was turning out well. The sun, straight ahead of them, had dropped half-way down a clear sky, moulding the down into gentle ripples buttercup-tinted on their crests. There had been a few early frosts lately but little rain for weeks; the turf was dry but springy still; on one side encroaching plough-land lapped up almost to the ridge they were walking along; on the other undulating pastures faded into distance, with only here and there the dark blottesque of a long wind-break or a close-clumped spinney. It was terrain now almost as familiar to Andy as to Toby, and as Toby seemed disposed to a certain degree of absent brooding as he walked, it was Andy who once or twice chose the path they followed. The late afternoon had seemed quite windless around them, but now suddenly there was a bit of a breeze stirring in their hair and endeavouring, not very successfully, to detach from shoulders or chests shirts damp with sweat. Although not with any particular sense of rivalry, they had been striding out at quite a lick. But now they drew to a halt together, since they had arrived at a spot with a splendid view.

'You can just see they sarsen stones still,' Andy said. 'Stukeley's Folly, but put up by as daft a Felton as there can have been. Torquil Felton Esquire of Felton House, Felton.'

'You'd be bound to be daft yourself if they'd called you Torquil. It's no sort of name at all.'

Toby and Andy had fallen into the habit of sometimes making fun of Feltons of the more antique sort; it was a kind of reminding one another that they were *not* Feltons, but belonged to some other gang altogether: notional ancestors to whom their major loyalty was due. They even invented absurd adventures for Feltons that had never been: a childish amusement at which the better-informed Toby had excelled at first, but at which Andy had rapidly caught him up. But it was something else that happened now.

'I raither fancy yon wee place,' Andy said, pointing a few yards ahead and abandoning received standard English. 'It's a guid hidey-hole.'

'What do you mean—a hidey-hole?' Toby wasn't quite attending.

'Snug room for twa, and a bit o' threshing oot, foreby. An' no chance for a peeping Tom for nigh a mile aroond. Only a cauld wind might tickle your doup a bit, gin your breeks were doon.'

'Andy!' Andy's brother was staring in horror at the utterly recognizable hollow in the turf.

'You might ca' it a love-nest,' Andy said composedly.

'I don't—' But there was no sense in saying 'I don't understand'. Toby did understand. 'She brought *you* here?'

'Aye, did she.'

'Aye, for sure.'

'Elma let you have her—here?'

'Christ, Toby, the puir lass couldna' help hersel. It's how she's like. The same place, and a'most the same man. A'most the same prick, yet yin she'd never had touch o'. She couldna' resist—her nature being a wee bit depravit that way, the puir dunty.' Andy paused for a moment. 'Even,' he added thoughtfully and with obscure satisfaction, 'although it was a richt daft risk to take.'

'It was only here?' Toby asked, pointing at the love-nest (or lair) in his turn. What totally confused him was the deliberation with which Andy had confronted him with it.

'Och, no. Ither places too.'

'And you enjoyed it?'

'Weel, she's no bad. She's no bad at a'.'

'I think it's disgusting.'

'I'll no say there wasna' an element tae it o' poking for poking's sake—which is what you'd ended wi' Elma yoursel, Toby. But I thocht, you see, we'd better get her clear in our heids. And no' being gentry—public hoose, ye ken, and no' public school—I dinna mind kissing and telling. Or telling my ain brither, onyway.'

'I don't know how you could—' Abruptly, Toby fell silent. It had come to him that he was on the brink of quite unforgivable dishonesty. For in his heart (as he had half-confessed to Andy) something had transformed itself, and as one consequence his brother having had his breeks down with Elma Loftus troubled him no more than he'd have minded his absent-mindedly using his tooth-brush. 'We'd better be getting home,' he said. 'And of course I don't care where you misconduct yourself with wenches, randy Andy Auld.'

'Then that's fine.'

So they retraced their path in a manner as companionable as before. But Toby remained puzzled. Andy must know that he was now as safe as houses from Elma, anyway. So why expose her?

The pleasingly equivocal character of this expression caused him, much to Andy's surprise, to give a sudden shout of laughter. And then he asked a serious question.

'Andy, why have you told me this? You must have known already that I'm quite, quite finished with Elma.'

'We should hae no secrets the yin frae the other.' Andy paused on this explanation for a moment. 'Although there may be an exception now and then.'

With this Toby had to be content. It wasn't difficult, since his thoughts were tending to be far away—absorbed in a wholly different matter.

With the two young men out of the way for the afternoon Mrs Warlow had been attempting a cautious exploration of her brother's mind. She found that her concern was less with the direction than with the pace of that mind's moving. There was a good deal of obstinacy in Howard's make-up, although it surfaced only on comparatively rare occasions. She had learnt to read the signs of his being in such a mood. Some of them were trivial and indeed almost ludicrous. He had, for example, acquired over the years a certain number of neck-ties and cravats and scarves so injudiciously chosen as to have attracted the explicit censure of both Ianthe and herself. There was also an ancient tweed jacket, admirably tailored and in a bold checked pattern perfectly proper for a country gentleman to wear, which was yet so mysteriously and absolutely wrong that Ianthe declared it made her father look like a decayed bookie. All these garments, although they had often been sternly denounced as fit only for the annual Church Sale, were cherished by Howard Felton, and donned from time to time as a perhaps unconscious symbol of an intransigent frame of mind. He was wearing one of the ties today.

It annoyed Mrs Warlow to have to take account of so grotesquely small a portent of change. Of the change itself she no longer had any doubt. Howard was proposing to make Elma Loftus mistress of Felton House. He might even yet, of course, change his mind. He was given to changing his mind. Or again,

fashion—and follow this up by putting it off a second time and a third. But to bank on this was to fail to reckon with Elma, and also with Howard's own countervailing sporadic impulse to precipitate action. The most immediate headache was here. Howard might rev up at any moment and shoot past the fatal point of no return. Mrs Warlow (who was in some danger of thinking rather wildly of the whole thing) even imagined a kind of elopement on her brother's part. He would simply prove to have vanished one morning, leaving a note transfixed to a pin-cushion.

Thus confronting the present horror of the time, Mrs Warlow reviewed various desperate expedients. She might tackle Howard herself and tell him he was an old fool. But, however she wrapped up the message, just that was what the message would be, and it was only too likely that the effort would be counter-productive. Even if her brother were not antagonized, he would start telling her (in his best vein of universal benevolence) that Elma was as charming as she was virtuous, terribly well up in the arts and so forth and in Felton history as well, and that her parents were decent and unassuming folk who would in no way make a nuisance of themselves.

The decent and unassuming folk were Mrs Warlow's next thought. She would call on Dr and Mrs Loftus and represent to them the extreme unsuitability and impropriety of the projected match. But this would be to behave like some haughty female patrician in an early-nineteenth century novel, and she doubted whether she could at all convincingly sustain the rôle. It wouldn't be any good, anyway. A more prudent course appeared to be to seek the support of her younger brother. The Warden had revealed himself as very distinctly Toby's man, and would be absolutely opposed to Howard's marrying even a much more eligible bride than Elma; he would frown on the idea even were that bride securely past child-bearing age. Unfortunately Howard was much more given to seeking his clever Oxford brother's advice than to accepting it. She couldn't altogether blame him here, since Hugh had always annoyed her a good deal. Moreover, Mercia would butt in, and that would be intolerable.

Thus hither and thither dividing the swift mind, Grace War-low had seen the afternoon go by in vain. At half-past four she had presided over Howard's cup of tea without making any head-way in her problem. She sought to divine his intentions without prompting him to any explicit statement of them, since any such statement must be one more step on the road to absolute commit-ment. This proving a technical impossibility, she prudently with-drew to her customary window-seat and a particularly boring piece of embroidery dictated to her by a tasteless busybody who was organizing the replacement of church hassocks. Howard, much more contentedly, applied himself to the local weekly paper. This rag, which reported in terms of titanic struggle the current squabbles on the rural district council, and added to this a generous pictorial record of the weddings of plebeian persons, the activities of Boy Scouts, and an occasional extreme dotard waving a telegram from the Queen, Howard invariably read conscientiously from the first page to the last, since he believed that it was among his duties to keep in touch, as he expressed it, 'with all that sort of thing'.

Tiresomely circumstanced in this fashion, Mrs Warlow felt her tendency to irritability grow. She told herself that she was not in her true element at Felton, that Howard should be let do as he pleased, that Divine Providence had no duty to see to it that Tobias Felton became a landowner, that *sub specie aeternitatis* the succession to Felton was precisely as important as the exorbitant water-rates and disputed rights of way upon which Howard was instructing himself at the other end of the room. Then she glanced through the window and saw Toby and Andy returning up the drive. They were coming along at the double, each in turn kicking ahead of them an empty tin which they must have come upon by the roadside. *Regardless of their doom*—Mrs Warlow told herself—*the little victims play!* Only there wasn't any doom—or, if there was, it lay inscrutably in the future, and had nothing to do with the elderly proprietor of Felton House kidding himself that he was discharging a duty to the line of the Feltons by treating

These thoughts didn't at all affect Mrs Warlow's sense that something must be done. She glanced again at the two young men now nearing the house, and considered them in turn as likely allies. Andy was already in a substantial sense her ally. The main crisis of the moment they hadn't specifically discussed, but she now realized that it had been in Andy's thought as well as her own. Something he had said—she couldn't recall quite what—had hinted that the possibility of precisely the present disaster had been in his mind. And Andy Auld was the more effective of the brothers. Mrs Warlow had given up the notion that identical twins must be identical in the weight they pull. Andy, however much he was now on the verges of affluence on the strength of the sweetie-shop auntie, had hoed a harder row than Toby. He *was* harder. One could even imagine him exercising a ruthlessness that Toby would consider it not quite nice to command. But it was true, too, that Andy, despite his acceptance and domestication at Felton, enjoyed or suffered no such standing in the affair as did his brother.

So what about Toby himself? Mrs Warlow saw that Toby couldn't on his honour interpose in the matter. Were he to reveal that he had been where Howard proposed to be, denouncing Elma Loftus as a kind of demi-semi fallen woman, unfit to be Felton's châtelaine, he would thereby be acting directly in his own material interest. Mrs Warlow knew very well that there was simply no road that way. Toby's lips would (as novelists say) be sealed. The outrageous thing would happen and he would keep honourably mum.

'They're back from their walk,' Mrs Warlow called out to her brother across the room.

'Toby and Andy? I expect they've had a very good tramp, and will want their tea.' Howard said this with satisfaction but while scarcely looking up from his newspaper. A moment later however he added (obscurely, it might have been felt), 'Oh, by the way, that reminds me, Grace. I wonder if you'd walk over to the Mill House one day? Tarling seems to think there will be difficulty in fitting in another bathroom. And we must have that—for Motley's brother, you know, if he cares to have the place. He'll want a guest or two from time to time, no doubt. And one can't very well ask guests to share one's bathroom, eh? Not as these things are nowadays.'

'I suppose not.' Howard—Mrs Warlow thought with sudden extreme impatience—was actually thinking to salve his conscience by awarding two brothers in their earliest twenties a bathroom apiece—as one might conceivably feel it incumbent upon one to do for a couple of maiden aunts known not to get on too well together.

XVII

THE FINAL CRISIS PROVED, very blessedly, to be an entirely private affair. This was a matter partly of luck and partly of Andy's sagacity. Andy's thinking was seldom—how could it have been? —of a very sophisticated sort. When he read a book it wasn't one aspiring to the finer subtleties of psychological fiction; it was commonly about James Bond and people of that kind. His imagination therefore tended to frame things for him in terms of broad effects. When he realized, as he had now come to do, that at Felton the ball had been lobbed decidedly into his own court and that if he didn't take a vigorous swipe at it nobody else was likely to do so until time ran out—when Andy realized this it was his natural instinct to envisage a grand confrontation scene as in the last few minutes of a movie. He was even disappointed that Ianthe wasn't at home, so that she could applaud from the front row of the more expensive seats. And he might actually have moved in this disastrous direction if he hadn't—quite by chance and later that Saturday evening—come upon Howard Felton carrying the champagne.

It was a magnum bottle of champagne, an object which had never previously come under Andy's close observation. So Andy stared at the bottle before he looked at its bearer—but when he did thus look this became a matter, if very briefly, of a stare too. It was clear that Howard had simply descended to the wine cellar (which was under the wing of the house in which Andy's quarters lay) and there possessed himself of this inconsiderable if fairly costly portion of his own property. He bore, however, what could only be characterized as a detected appearance—much as might (although Andy didn't think of this) a club servant who has been surprised by the secretary misappropriating what is proper only

217

for the consumption of the members. Could Howard have taken to the vice of secret tippling? The magnitude of the magnum rendered this an improbable explanation of the perplexing spectacle. Moreover Howard in addition to being oddly nervous was curiously excited, which isn't the same thing. Andy had remarked this earlier in the evening. While he and Toby were still having their belated tea Howard had withdrawn to his study, and a little later Andy, passing that way, had chanced just to hear the murmur of a telephone conversation. Since then the proprietor of Felton House had been wandering round in a perceptibly agitated manner. But, if agitated, he was damned pleased with himself as well. Andy was now reflecting—and to some purpose—on this when Howard spoke.

'Oh, Toby,' Howard said, '—Andy, I mean, I beg your pardon—have you seen *The Times*?'

'Och, I dinna' see *The Times.*'

'I don't mean that. Do you know where they've put today's *Times*? I want their telephone number. They give it on the last page.'

'I think your sister will have put it in the library.' *Christ,* Andy said to himself, *he's fixed it up on the telephone with her and now he's for getting it into the newspaper. And he's going to make us drink that bloody stuff at dinner to celebrate.* Aloud, however, Andy asked, 'Shall I fetch it for you?'

'No, no—I'll go along there myself.' Somewhat indecisively, Howard put the magnum down on a side-table in the corridor and hurried off. With no indecision whatever, Andy followed him. And at the library door he said politely, 'May I have a word with you, sir?' and followed Howard into the room.

It now seemed to Andy that matters were, perhaps, falling out rather well. What wasn't wanted, he was coming to see, was too many people coming to know too much. And this would inevitably happen if there was a row—or rather if there was a row extending beyond the walls of this gloomy book-filled room. That he had been rather hankering after such a show-down now struck him as extremely stupid. He had a bomb in his pocket, but an

opportunity for quiet diplomacy seemed to be the first thing. And
here it was.

'Would I be right in thinking'—he asked, still very politely,
and in what he called to Toby his best BBC—'that you and Miss
Loftus have the thought of getting married?'

'Yes, certainly. Certainly.' Howard had swung round and was
staring at Andy in a way that Andy felt to call for analysis. Howard
was startled, for one thing, and rather childishly vexed that his big
moment of surprise, champagne and all, had been short-circuited
in this way. And, for another thing, Howard continued as confident and pleased with himself as Punch. And for a third (and here
Andy saw the point of crisis) he was extremely angry. Although
he wasn't perhaps going to say so, he considered Andy's question
as a monstrous impertinence. Here in fact was what Toby called
the class thing, lashing its tail like mad. It became instantly clear
to Andy that he wasn't for a moment going to be allowed to
reason with Howard Felton. Quiet diplomacy was out.

'An' do ye mind if I speer anither thing?' Andy had abruptly
dropped the BBC. 'Just when wad this graund waddin' be like tae
come aboot?'

There was a moment's silence, during which Andy thought
that he was going to be ordered out of the library. But its owner
controlled himself.

'Quite soon, if you must know. Perhaps in two or three
months' time.'

'That's fine. It wadna' be sae guid if it were the morrow or the
day after, Mr Felton. For then any man-chiel Elma bore tae be
your heir wad be as like to be mine as yours, puir bairn. Mair like,
mebby—your ain years considered, sir. But no' Toby's. Toby's
turn in Elma's bed is lang syne ower.'

Half-an-hour later Toby, coming upstairs to get ready for
dinner, stuck his head into Andy's room.

'I say,' he said, 'I'll tell you a funny thing. There's a bloody
great bottle of champagne on a table near the bottom of our
staircase.'

219

'Och, that was Howard.' Andy had forgotten about the champagne, which was careless of him. But he wasn't at a loss. 'He got muddled, and thocht the-day was his sister's birthday. And then he minded better, but he's forgotten tae pit it back again.'

'I've a good mind to liberate it.' Toby said this without conviction, for he was thinking of something else. And suddenly he sat down on Andy's bed. 'Andy,' he said, 'there's something that I ought to have told you about already. It's something tremendous that Ianthe and I discovered about ourselves when I went to Cambridge. It still almost bewilders me, and I expect it will stagger you, just as it did me. But, you see, it's heavenly too. We're in love and always have been. It's as strange and it's as simple as that. We're going to get married just as soon as we can.'

Andy felt no occasion to be staggered, but he managed to mingle a small measure of surprise with his congratulations. Then, and very judiciously, he went to collect the forgotten magnum of champagne and return it to the cellar.

* * *

The important thing, Mrs Warlow came to see, was what various people didn't know. Poor Elma, when taxed by her disillusioned suitor, must have seen nothing for it but to admit to the moral misconduct that was costing her Felton House, but nobody except Howard and Elma herself knew anything about what must have been a painful scene. Howard didn't know that anybody except Andy had penetrated to the fact of the so-sadly shattered project of marriage. Toby knew people had been saying Howard might marry, but he had no idea that Elma had been his choice, or that Andy had seduced Elma (if it was to be called that) simply for the purpose of manufacturing a block-buster such as no gentleman would have thought of. All these ignorances were conducive to things settling down.

Andrew Auld, however, didn't settle down. He was pretty sure that, although he had saved Howard Felton from making an unco gran' fu' of himself, he wasn't going to be forgiven in a hurry for the manner in which he had been obliged to go about

220

it. So Andy obeyed a summons from his auntie to come and manage certain affairs in Glasgow for an indefinite period. Toby, although other things were on his mind, was very upset, and made various stipulations about correspondence and reunion. Ianthe wondered whether Andy had a further reason for discreetly departing. And Andy, indeed, when he did depart, murmured to her that he'd be back when her bairns were safely around her— this perhaps with a dash of Scottish sentimentality pardonable in the circumstances. As for Howard, he was very subdued for a long time. In fact he didn't fully cheer up until Ianthe presented Toby with a son, and Felton in consequence with a Felton heir, albeit through the female line. Colonel Motley remained single, and Mrs Warlow eventually took over the Mill House.